THE CONSEQUENCE
OF REVENGE

ALSO BY RACHEL VAN DYKEN

The Consequences Series
The Consequence of Loving Colton

The Bet Series
The Bet
The Wager
The Dare

The Ruin Series
Ruin
Toxic
Fearless
Shame

The Elite Series
Elite
Elect
Entice
Elicit
Bang Bang
Enforce
Ember
Elude

The Seaside Series
Tear
Pull
Shatter
Forever

*Fall
Eternal*

Renwick House

*The Ugly Duckling Debutante
The Seduction of Sebastian St. James
The Redemption of Lord Rawlings
An Unlikely Alliance
The Devil Duke Takes a Bride*

London Fairy Tales

*Upon a Midnight Dream
Whispered Music
The Wolf's Pursuit
When Ash Falls*

Seasons of Paleo

Savage Winter

Wallflower Series

*Waltzing with the Wallflower
Beguiling Bridget
Taming Wilde*

Stand Alones

*Every Girl Does It
The Parting Gift
Compromising Kessen
Divine Uprising*

THE CONSEQUENCE OF REVENGE

RACHEL VAN DYKEN

SKYSCAPE

SKYSCAPE

Published by Skyscape, New York

www.apub.com

Amazon, the Amazon logo, and Skyscape are trademarks of Amazon.com, Inc., or its affiliates.

ISBN-13: 9781477830642

ISBN-10: 1477830642

Cover design by Kerrie Robertson

Library of Congress Control Number: 2014960264

Printed in the United States of America

To the Rockin' Reader group!
Without you guys I wouldn't have been able to write
Colt's and Max's stories—thank you so much for your
incredible input and encouragement!

CHAPTER ONE

MAX

Stupid Starbucks.

How hard was it to make a cup of coffee?

I checked my watch again and tapped my foot against the cement floor. When it was finally my turn, my voice caught in my throat.

Well, well, well. New barista. Have I mentioned I have a weakness for a girl in an apron? No? Well. Now you know.

Smiling, I placed my hands onto the cool countertop and leaned forward, "Hey, girl."

The barista's eyebrows shot up and then a scowl I assume she reserved for rapists, terrorists, and people named Max appeared, rendering my balls a little shaky and my confidence a bit stunned. "What can I get for you?"

I allowed myself a few seconds as I slowly took in her form and then finally settled my gaze on her pretty brown eyes and cropped golden-blond hair. "Blonde roast." I smirked. "With a bit of honey."

"Honey's on the side counter," she said through clenched teeth, tapping her fingers against the register. "Is that all?"

My smile fell. "Stand still."

"What?" Her hands froze in midair. "What's wrong?"

"Stand still . . . so I can pick you up." I winked and waited for her response. Yeah. I was a badass.

The girl's arms fell against her sides. "Really?"

I interrupt your regular programming in order to tell you some vital information. I'm not that guy. The one who actually thinks cheesy pickup lines work on girls. They don't, at least not in the way normal guys think they do. But more on that later. Continue.

Was I losing my edge? By this point the girl usually laughed or at least rolled her eyes in amusement. I tried again. "Baby, if you were words on a page, you'd be what they call fine print."

And sealed.

All that was left was her swooning across the bar into my waiting arms.

"Next!" She looked behind me.

"Wait. I didn't even pay!"

"It's fine." She nodded. No amusement flashing across her pretty face, just irritation and a possible right-eye twitch. "Really. Go."

"Aw, our first date." I leaned in and licked my lips as she quickly poured the coffee and handed it to me.

"Sure." She nodded enthusiastically and pointed to the end of the bar. "Now go away."

"Absence makes the heart grow fonder." I blew her a kiss.

"Oh, let's hope not," she said through clenched teeth.

Ah, rejection. Oh, well, it's not like I was really turning it up or anything. For crying out loud, she looked like a clinger anyway. The type of girl who would gorilla me to the bed and then pound her chest and roar when I lied and told her I had to go take care of my sick Chinese grandmother.

Clingers always saw through the lies.

That's why I'd suddenly develop a sickness so horrible that she didn't want to be near me for fear of dying in two weeks.

Swear to all that's holy, last year I had swine flu for a month. It was touch and go—really touch and go.

With a sigh I grabbed my coffee from the counter and made my way toward one of the empty tables. I was meeting Jason, who just so happened to be my best friend Milo's brother. Jason and I had slowly, and I do mean painfully, excruciatingly slowly, started to become friends after Milo married his best friend Colton.

Of course that happened after I spent an entire weekend convincing their entire family that Milo and I were engaged. At various points I was gay, attacked by their horny grandmother, and imprisoned, but that's another story that I'm pretty sure will need to be censored if ever retold in public, feel me?

The point? I might have lost my best friend to marriage, but I'd gained Jason in the process, though his only goal during the last few months, since I'd graduated college, had been to get me off my sorry ass. But let's be honest, I have a really nice ass, why not sit on it? Am I right?

Plus, work bored me.

If being a gentleman of leisure could be an actual occupation, I was all for it. That's what being rich does to people—it makes them lazy. And I was example A.

I had money, so why work?

Apparently getting your hands dirty gave you purpose—but I still wasn't sure how dirty I wanted to get. Don't get me wrong . . . I was all for being dirty with the right girl, in the right situation—take mud wrestling, for example. What sane man says no to that type of dirt? But things like farming? Um, no thanks.

Stupid goats. I shuddered and took a sip of coffee, not that all farmers had goats but still, just thinking about them freaked the shit out of me. They had red eyes. Only animals possessed by Satan had red eyes.

Well, animals and Jayne—bitch be cray cray. The run-in I'd had with that particular ex-girlfriend during Jason's wedding weekend was enough to give me nightmares for life. I don't want to relive it. Ever. Not even by telling you.

All I'll say is that I saved Jason from marrying her. I basically took one for the team, and I'm pretty sure what happened is frowned upon by the law in all fifty states, so maybe he wanted to meet me to hand me a trophy or a medal or something for saving his pathetic life. I mean, the whole purpose of coming down that weekend had been to save Milo's love life, but I also helped keep Jayne away from Jason, whom she'd lied to and told she was pregnant. It was a whole . . . thing. Like something you'd see on TV and say, "That shit doesn't happen in real life." Um, yeah, it does. Jason is exhibit A. He's the prime example of why you don't have sex with crazies. Hell, if God punishes me by giving me nothing but sons when I'm married, I'll use him as a prime example of why you don't have sex *ever*.

I sighed and checked my watch just as Jason walked by the front door like he was waiting for something. He answered his cell, then smirked.

Sketch.

I waved him over once he walked through the doors.

"What the hell, Jason?" I pointed at his face, the one that was still breaking into the biggest damn grin I'd ever seen. "You have the smile. What gives?"

"Can't a guy be happy?" He shrugged and looked around the coffee shop, then checked his phone.

"No." I shook my head, eyes narrowing. "Especially considering said guy hasn't gotten laid in months and still can't secure a date from our mutual friend Jenna. Tell me, have the yoga classes improved your flexibility or are you actually turning into a chick after doing downward dog so many times?"

Jason's stare burned holes through my body. "Thanks, Max, for the reminder."

"Reminder about your soon-to-be female status?" I nodded. "Anytime."

"Nope." He chuckled to himself. "The reminder of why I'm doing this."

"Doing what?" Damn that coffee was good. Imagine what the blond girl would taste like?

She'd give in. Eventually.

They all did.

I truly bat a thousand. No lie. Wait, okay, so actually that's a minor fib considering my best friend Milo didn't fall for my charm. Then again, she thought I was gay when she first met me. I looked down at my Prada shoes. Note to self: rethink footwear.

I rolled my eyes and took a long sip of coffee. The door to the shop opened and a camera crew waltzed in.

Huh, some lucky bastard must have won money or something.

They walked toward our table.

I turned around, so I could get a good view of whoever they were surprising.

"Max Emory." A soft-voiced man said my name. Why was he saying my name? I turned, slowly, and came face-to-face with orange. No, really, just orange. His face was so orange it was like staring at the sun.

"Uh . . . yeah?" The cameras were directly in my business, all my business. My eyes narrowed, then fell on Jason. He was partially covering his face with his hands and smirking—the ass.

"Congratulations!" Oompa Loompa patted me on the shoulder with his orange hand and flashed a white grin at the camera. "You're the new Bachelor on *Love Island*!"

It was then that my eyes fell to the name on the shirts the crew was wearing. "*Love Island*—Sink or Swim, Season 5."

"Jason"—somehow I managed to sound calm when my insides were quivering with fear—"tell me this is a practical joke."

"Oh, I assure you!" For real. If that man hit my shoulder one more time, I was breaking one of his fingers. "This is very, very real! Aren't you excited? You're going to be spending the next three weeks in luxury with twenty-five of the most beautiful women in America. And hopefully, you'll find true love."

"Yes," I hissed. "Because I've been looking so hard for it—love."

"Oh, we know." The man nodded. "After the death of your fiancée I imagine you're just . . . a bit broken inside."

"My dead fiancée," I muttered under my breath. "Yes, well, the death still feels fresh in my mind."

"I'm sure." The man nodded.

"Almost as if it just happened two seconds ago," I continued.

"You poor soul."

Jason coughed.

I kicked him under the table.

He winced, but the bastard was still smiling.

"Let's have a round of applause for our new contestant!" The man clapped his orange hands together like a dancing monkey and slapped my shoulder. Again.

"And cut," another man said. The lights flickered off and the camera was shoved away from my face.

"All right." The announcer guy grabbed a stack of papers from a person behind them and tossed them onto the table. "You'll have to sign a few waivers before we get started and take a drug test as well as a few other examinations just to make sure you're healthy enough to participate."

I scanned the first page.

"Accidental death?" I croaked. "Are you throwing me out of a plane?"

The guy laughed. "Of course not."

I relaxed.

"We did that last year. Poor bastard landed in shark-infested waters. Of course that season had more of a *Survivor* theme."

"Of course," I repeated, then kicked Jason again. "And, um, if I want to back out?"

The smile on the guy's face froze. "Why would you back out? You already signed your consent when you applied."

"When I"—my eyes narrowed in on Jason—"applied."

"Well,"—the man shrugged—"go ahead and fill these out. We'll be in touch after your exams, and do try to cooperate with the doctors. They're only doing their jobs. Here's your appointment sheet. Don't be late! If all goes well, we fly out in two days!"

The camera crew left.

Oompa Loompa followed.

"I should kill you for this," I muttered.

Jason grinned. "You can't. It specifically says in your contract that serving time in federal prison is against their rules."

"Oh, I think I'd like to make an exception," I said, scanning my appointment sheet. I had one for the dentist at noon. Another at the doctor for an STD test, naturally, because what? It was humanly possible to sleep with that many different women and get out alive without getting my nuts twisted off?

And finally.

"You've gotta be shitting me." I slammed the paper down and groaned into my hands.

"What?"

"A prostate exam?"

"Just give a little cough and turn your head—it will all be over."

"Question: How many times have you had to say that to girls in bed?" I asked. "Twice? Three times?"

"You're a jackass." Jason pounded his hands onto the table. "And you deserve everything coming to you."

"How do you figure?" My voice rose.

"Sex isn't an occupation."

I snorted. "I beg to differ."

"Annoying the hell out of me isn't an occupation either. You need a job, you need to get off your lazy ass and make a man out of yourself."

"Don't need to make a man out of myself," I pointed out. "Erica did that for me when I was fourteen, she told me so."

Jason pinched the bridge of his nose. "Look at it this way—at least if you die on your trip . . . you'll be buried right along with your sin."

"My sin?"

"Lust." He grinned. "Hey, you need a ride to the appointments, time's wasting. Wouldn't want to be late for your . . . date with the doctor."

"I hate you so much that if I didn't already feel bad about your own sister giving you two black eyes—I'd punch you in the face."

"Oooh, feisty, the doc will love that."

CHAPTER TWO

MAX

I eyed all the creepy skeleton posters in the doctor's examination room and cringed as the smell of antiseptic burned my nostrils.

"I can't believe I offered to come with you," Jason groaned from his chair in the corner. "I should be sainted or something."

Jerking around to face him, I pointed at his chest. "Friends go with friends to get prostate exams."

"Um, I think you've confused that with the phrase 'Friends don't let friends drive drunk.'"

I gave him a serious nod. "That too."

"I'm not staying in here when he touches you." Jason shuddered.

Wincing, I sent him a glare. "Do you really think I want you to watch me get molested by another male? Seriously? What if you film that shit and it ends up on YouTube?"

Jason's face broke out into a devious grin.

"For real." I seethed. "You do anything like that and I'm gluing your nuts together."

Jason rolled his eyes. "What? Are you going to drug me, strip me naked, and superglue my man parts?"

A coughing interrupted our conversation.

The doctor had made his entrance. He eyed both of us and grinned. "Which one's the lucky fellow?"

Jason pointed.

I looked behind me and prayed God would deliver a fatted calf. Hey, it happened in the Bible! God provides! In desperate times!

Sweating, I gulped and gave a solid nod. I was a man. I could go through with an exam. I mean—

Holy hell.

The doctor's hands were huge.

Side note: I'm well aware that I tend to exaggerate, but either he was having an allergic reaction or he was a giant.

"So." He slapped on his gloves and rubbed them together.

Jason paled and put his fist in his mouth like he was going to throw up.

"You two together?" The doctor pointed between us.

"Yes!" I wailed. "And um, we want to be sure both of us are safe for . . . activities." That's right, bastard. I was going to throw Jason under that exact same bus and watch as the wheels went round and round.

"Oh." The doctor glanced between Jason and me, then gave a firm nod. "All right, then, so I'll just start with you and move on to your friend." Holy shit. Those words made my entire body convulse. Swear I was rethinking having two balls and a bat. For once in my life, I just wanted to strike out. Break my bat, hand over the balls, and rock back and forth in the corner.

"Have you been sexually active in the past six months?" The doctor sniffed and started pulling out supplies, laying them across the table. I watched in horror as visions of getting abducted by aliens danced like sugarplums in my head.

People die from fear.

It could happen.

I read stories where people would just spontaneously combust.

And it was about to happen if the heat in my body and all-around shaking were any indicator.

"I have to—" Jason ran toward the door and slammed it behind him.

"Weak stomach?" The doctor chuckled.

"He's afraid of my nakedness—makes him feel like less of a man."

"O-okay." The doctor laughed again and motioned for me to turn around. "Now, drop your pants to your knees."

Let it be known that no man. NO MAN should ever hear those words from someone who could pass as his great-grandfather.

The cold air bit my ass as I turned and waited.

"Now, bend over."

Shhiiittttt.

I did as he said, cursing Jason and all his future children.

"Now, this may be cold."

Just let it be *small*.

"And a bit painful, it's totally normal to experience some discomfort."

"Ha-ha." I laughed dryly. "Guess we know what it means if it's comfortable, am I right, Doc?"

And silence.

Worst thing to say when you have your pants at your ankles and the doctor's about two seconds away from making you see stars. Where were the drugs?

"Now try not to tense up."

Ha, seriously?

"Here we go."

Oh. God. Did he need to count down?

"Turn your head and—cough."

"Mother of God!" I shouted, hitting my hands against the metal table as the doctor made his intentions perfectly clear.

"Cough!" he shouted.

"Stop yelling at me!"

"I'm not yelling!"

"I want to go home now."

"Almost done!" The doctor laughed uncomfortably.

I choked when he removed his digits from my special place. I had one of those moments, the kind where you feel so used you're not sure whether you should cry or laugh.

"All right! You can put your pants back on."

I felt ashamed. Like I'd just been screwed and not even offered dinner for my gallant efforts in the bedroom. Holy shit, was this what girls felt like after one-night stands?

Where the hell were my flowers?

At least give me a sucker or something . . . maybe a sticker? Saying I got . . . never mind. Those types of stickers were probably illegal.

"Now." The doc took off his gloves and washed his hands.

Right. LIKE I WAS UNCLEAN!

He put on a new pair.

And the torture train just kept tooting.

Ha, tooting, see, it's funny because . . . never mind.

"I'll just need to draw some blood." He pulled out a giant-ass needle and I had one of those moments that I'm sure every five-year-old experiences right before his mom holds him down while he gets a needle in the ass.

Terror.

"This won't hurt a bit." He laughed nervously.

HOLY SHIT, STOP LAUGHING!

I winced as he pricked my arm and started drawing blood. His lips were moving but I wasn't really catching anything.

"All donnne." His voice was low. Why was he talking so slow?

"Youuu cannn gooo noowwww."

I shook my head and tried to go to the door but was met with total blackness before I took two steps.

The last thought in my head?

I was trapped in a room with a man who'd just seen my Mighty Max. I hoped to God he hadn't liked it.

CHAPTER THREE

MAX

So apparently they do still give suckers. But the catch is you have to cry really hard in order to receive one. Either that or you have to pass out. I sucked the lollipop and winced as I slowly walked out the doors and toward the waiting car.

Jason was listening to music and tapping the steering wheel.

My balls were sad.

Really, that was all there was to it. I could sugarcoat it and say I was man enough to survive the exam, but I swear to all that is holy, I would never be the same. I'd probably shriek every time I saw an old man with large hands.

It had taken ONE experience to classically condition me to hate grandparents everywhere.

"So." Jason cleared his throat. "Sorry for running out on you."

"He touched me," I whispered.

"I know, man . . ." Jason coughed. "I just, I panicked. No man should have to . . ."

"He yelled at me."

"Max—"

"I said, I said . . ." I started rocking back and forth. "I said I wanted to go home." My teeth clacked together as I started sweating. "And at night. When I go to sleep. I'll see those hands, Jason. I'll see both of them."

Jason cleared his throat. "I, uh, I sort of got something for you."

"You did?" I blinked away the fear and watched as Jason handed me a paper bag.

Curious, I opened it and smirked. A six-pack of beer and chocolate.

"The, uh . . ." Jason scratched his head. "The chocolate has a flower on it, you know, kind of like . . . special chocolate."

My eyes welled with tears. "You did this for me?"

Jason nodded and patted my back. "He didn't even ask for your middle name before doing—what he did. What type of doctor does that?"

"A monster." I started unwrapping my special chocolate.

"Yeah, well." Jason put the car in drive. "We'll get you drunk enough that you won't remember."

"God, let's hope so." I polished off the chocolate and cracked open a can of beer.

"Dude!" Jason smacked me. "No open containers."

I stared at him. And downed the whole thing. Then opened a second. "You were saying, Officer?"

"You know I can arrest you, right?"

"Do it. I'll just tell everyone you went with me to a prostate exam—and liked it!"

"You wouldn't!"

"You know that bus—the one that keeps running me over? I'd chain myself to you, no hesitation. So you should really think through all your choices, Jason. Revenge is a bitch."

He pulled up to Colt and Milo's house. "Believe me, I know."

"Hey!" I pointed to all the cars parked in the driveway. "Are we having a party?"

"Yup!"

Smiling, I grabbed the rest of my beer and waltzed through the front door.

"Congratulations!" Milo started jumping up and down, then threw her arms around my neck. Panicking, I pushed her away.

Colt pried her arms from me and held her back. "Careful, babe, he's been with the doctor."

"He told you!" I yelled.

Colt smiled. "So, got any STDs?"

"Swear, I'm this close to purposefully infecting myself with herpes so I can pass it along like a true friend. Feel me?"

Milo raised her hand. "You'd be passing it on to both of us."

"Milo!" I gritted my teeth. "Not now!"

"You drunk enough yet?" Colt smirked.

Grumbling, I stepped past him and looked at the banner they'd hung in their hallway.

"To the new Bachelor."

"Tell me—" I downed another can of beer. "Did you know, Milo? Did you help your satanic brother?"

Milo's guilty face was all it took for me to charge toward her, but she hid behind her husband.

"Come out and fight me like a man!" I demanded.

"But I'm a girl!" she said from behind Colt. "And think of it this way, you get to be the Bachelor."

"I am thinking of it that way! It sounds like a free ticket to hell! Those women are crazy! You do realize you're putting me on an island with twenty-five Jaynes? The last episode we watched, a girl said her job was people watching. People watching is not an occupation! And they want me to find love? I'm officially going to be the first Bachelor that tries to get abducted by pirates."

Jason cleared his throat. "They couldn't actually prove that pirates were parading around that island, man."

"Not," I seethed, "the point. How do I get out of this without breaking the contract? Or getting fined for already signing something that I'm pretty sure one of you forged? All I have to do is tell them you screwed me over. Case closed."

Nobody spoke for a few seconds, then Jason piped up. "We kind of sort of had a lawyer help us . . . um, lock you into the contract. Even if you said it was forged, technically your signature is on it, and you can't prove we did anything, especially considering all the e-mails back and forth between you and the casting directors."

"E-mails? You hacked my e-mail?"

Milo rolled her eyes. "You've had the same password all four years of college."

"And now I have to change it!" I yelled, bordering on hysteria. I was completely and utterly screwed.

I pinched the bridge of my nose. "Okay, let me ask a different question. What if I don't find someone I'm fond of?"

"Oh." Milo stepped away from Colt. "No worries, as long as you finish the last episode you're still under contract. We had a lawyer look through everything and—"

Colton smacked his hand over Milo's mouth while Jason groaned behind me.

"Betrayed." I shook my head. "By my best friends. A bunch of Judases!" I roared, running over to the silverware drawer and pulling out knives. "You wanna stab me in the back while you're at it? Huh?"

"Max." Milo rolled her eyes. "Put the knives down."

"No!" I waved the knives in the air, slowly backing up. Unfortunately there was a chair there. I tripped, sending the knives into the air.

The minute my ass met the floor, I saw one knife impale itself in Jason's thigh. What are the odds? Right?

"Son of a bitch!" Jason wailed, slamming backward against the wall, causing the clock to fall on his head. He slumped to the floor, cursing the entire way. With shaking hands he pulled the knife out of his leg. Please . . . there wasn't even any blood. "This is why you need to do the show! You're a danger to me and everyone else around you! The universe is clearly trying to tell you something, man."

"That's right." I pointed at him, ignoring all the universe-being-out-of-whack shit pouring from his mouth. "Karma's coming for you." I made a cutting motion with my hand.

Just as Jason tossed the clock at me, I ducked, causing it to hit Colt in the stomach.

"Guys!" Milo stomped her foot. "Stop it! Max, you're going. The papers are signed; stop being a baby. Plus your face is perfect for TV."

"Flattery won't work." Okay, fine, so my chest puffed up a bit, but still.

"Two of the contestants are models." She held out a DVD.

"What's that?"

"Your women." She grinned. "Wanna see?"

"Damn it." I crossed my arms and stared at the DVD. "Are there any brunettes? You know I love brunettes."

"Ten." Milo winked. "After all, I helped them cast. What kind of friend would I be if I let them pick out all those girls?"

"Aw, Milo." I pulled her in for a hug while Colton glared. "You really do love me. I almost like you again."

"Yeah, well. Jason and Colt helped." She held up her hands as if she wasn't the only one who'd done the dirty work.

I clenched my jaw. "And when you say *help*, they picked all the crazies?"

"Two." Colt coughed. "But to be fair, the producers were adamant about picking a few girls who were . . . untamed."

Smirking, I rocked back on my heels. "Just call me a zookeeper 'cause I'll tame them all day. All day, son!"

"Yeah," Milo croaked. "One hasn't shaved her legs in ten years."

"Son of a hairy bitch." I groaned and pressed my fingers against my temples. "Fine, put on the DVD, but I want whiskey."

CHAPTER FOUR

MAX

"Okay." Colt rubbed his hands together. "Now does everyone have a work sheet and a pencil?"

I lifted my pencil in the air and momentarily imagined shoving it in Colton's leg. Instead I wrote my name at the top of my work sheet—you know, like I was still in third grade—and sat back on the couch.

"Jason?" Colt offered a pencil. "You participating?"

"Hell, yes, I am." His snicker was not giving me warm fuzzies. Then again, I'd probably lost all ability to feel warm fuzzies after my run-in with the doctor that morning. I would have sold my left nut for a bag of frozen peas to sit on. But that would have meant showing weakness.

I needed to get used to hiding all weakness lest any of those women see a chink in my armor and attack me with their razor-sharp nails. I'd watched the entire last season with Milo since I had nothing better to do, and now that I'd moved to the area I had exactly no friends, except for her. Those women had been crazy, straight-up crazy. Maybe it would have been better to stay in the city and be miserable there, but my parents were too close and I knew it would be only a matter of time before they came knocking. I didn't have the strength to say no to my father's face when he offered me the shiny nameplate and job I didn't want. I hated letting people down and letting him down from afar seemed like a better option.

"Attention." Colt cleared his throat. "Each person has a work sheet with twenty-five spaces. Now, as you write down the girls' names, I want you to associate the contestant with something that will help you remember her."

I raised my hand, not really because I had any questions but because I figured it was the fastest way to stop the roller coaster of doom that I was currently sitting on. Maybe if I told them the idea of going on a dating show hurt my self-esteem, they'd buy it? Then again, even if they did buy it—I still had a damn contract I would have to get out of.

Colt eyed everyone. "Any questions?"

I raised my hand higher.

"Anyone?" Colt's eyes passed over me. "Okay, good. Press 'Play,' babe."

Grumbling, I put my hand down and waited. The DVD started, and music that sounded suspiciously like a wedding march floated in the background. "Welcome to *Love Island*," a voice said.

"Holy shit. I saw this movie! They almost died!" I pointed at the TV and cringed. *Island, island*—why did that sound like a trap? Did I have a way to escape? What if I got an allergic reaction and needed a hospital? I was allergic to bees! Did they realize that if I got stung I could die? And what about island fever? It's a real thing! And rashes, and spiders, and ho-oly shit on a stick.

Goats. What the farming hell?

Did islands have goats?

I suddenly had a horrifying vision of a red-eyed monster chasing me toward sharks and pirates. What would be a worse death? Being kicked by a goat or eaten by it?

"Wait!" I raised my hand. "I have a question."

Colton turned up the volume, the bastard.

"Twenty-one days to love!" the voice boomed as the TV showed visions of beaches and couples laughing as they ran like gazelles across the white sand and tackled each other in the water. Swear I saw a shark in the distance.

"Are you ready to meet the contestants?" The music picked up.

"No." I shook my head. "I will never be ready. Ever. Not in a million years will I be happy to be sitting on this couch and watching crazy in the form of twenty-five single and sexually frustrated women try to sell themselves to me."

I blinked and thought about what I had just said. Sexually frustrated . . . hmm . . .

"Meet Flora!"

A girl jumped in front of the camera and giggled.

Those green eyes be crazy.

"Hell. No." I tried to get up from my seat but was pulled back down by Milo.

"She could be really sweet!"

I glared at Milo, then watched the TV as the blond girl frolicked. Yeah, no exaggeration, she freaking frolicked through the park and then picked up a stranger's puppy and let it lick her lips.

I wrote down her name and then wrote "germs" next to it. Bad juju. Hmm, would the word *germs* actually help? I scratched it out and replaced it with *bitch*. You know, because she licked a dog's face.

"I just want to fall in love," she said to the camera. "Is that so wrong? I want a man who can take care of me, who will provide for me, who will go on adventures with me." She sighed and giggled happily. "I know he's out there somewhere."

"He is," I said under my breath. "But his name isn't Max."

Colton fast-forwarded the DVD.

A pretty brunette flashed across the screen. I leaned forward. Her boobs were huge. Okay, not that I was judging by her body—but damn, I could learn to love her, even if—

I shuddered as she started speaking.

Or shrieking. Was that English?

"I want a man who won't cheat on me!" she yelled.

I flinched.

"This bastard better not kiss any other woman or I'm going to murder him!" She grabbed the camera and looked straight into it. "You hear me? You got that? You keep it in your pants!"

Mighty Max and I winced in unison.

"Yeah." Jason chuckled. "Good luck with that one. I put *crazy* next to her name, what'd you put, Max?"

"*Jayne.*" I shrugged and put a star next to it. "It's my red word. My trigger word. Almost like a safe word except it reminds me of extreme danger or caution. I also use *Grandma* as a trigger word though last time I did that Reid pissed his pants, so yeah . . ."

"Clever." Colton nodded.

Another girl appeared on screen. Her smile was . . . pretty. I shifted a bit in my seat, my pencil hovering over the paper. "Hi, I'm Becca."

"She's hot," Jason interjected. "Is that your pick, Milo?"

"Yup!" She crossed her arms. "And she's local!"

There was something familiar about her, but I couldn't quite figure it out. Pretty golden-blond hair, really pretty eyes.

". . . I'm a student so I work at a local Starbucks and . . ."

With a grimace I imagined a green apron on her and nodded slowly. "Yeah, guys, she's a no-go."

"What?" Milo smacked me on the leg. "She's perfect!"

"Agreed." Jason pointed. "She's hot and it's not the scary type of hot that makes men cover their privates."

"Oh, she's hot all right." I chuckled nervously. "I told her so this morning."

Milo's eyes narrowed. "And when you say you told her so, you mean you used one of your really creepy pickup lines and got all up in her business."

"They aren't creepy!" I yelled. "I have a seventy percent success rate!"

"And the other thirty percent?" Colt just HAD to ask.

I shrugged. "I've been slapped a time or two."

"He wore a cup for an entire semester because girls were starting to kick his little friend."

"Not little." I sent a wink to Milo and blew a kiss.

And received a sucker punch to the gut from Colton.

"Thanks," I wheezed.

"So." Milo ignored my inability to breathe. "You used a pickup line and she laughed?"

"Er, sorta." I wrote "prude" next to her name and tried to change the subject. "Let's look at the rest of the girls, yeah?"

"What was the pickup line?" Jason asked. "I'm curious now. What do seventy percent of the women out there fall for?"

Yeah, no way in hell was I getting out of this one. "'Hold still.'" I coughed and blurted out the rest of the line as fast as I could manage. "'So I can pick you up.'"

Jason's face remained blank. "Pick me up? Pick me up where?"

"You know." I rolled my eyes. "Pick. You. Up."

"Dude!" Jason burst out laughing. "You wanted to weigh her?"

"What? Hell, no!"

"She thinks you called her fat." Milo groaned into her hands.

"How does that sound like a fat joke?" I almost snapped my pencil in two and threw it across the room. "I wanted to pick her up, as in pick her up, or like hit on her."

"Question." Colt raised his hand. "Would the pickup line be any better if you said, 'Hold still while I hit on you?'"

"That sounds like a domestic violence case to me." Jason's tone was serious.

"Whatever. You guys just don't understand how to hit on a girl." The room fell silent.

"Colt?" Jason nodded. "You thinking what I'm thinking?"

"Babe." Colt turned to Milo. "Sometimes a man's gotta do what a man's gotta do."

"I'm lost. Anyone else lost?" I looked at my three friends.

"He needs to know the error of his jackassery." Jason nodded. "Come on, let him, Milo."

Grumbling, she folded her hands over her chest. "Fine, but if one bitch cops a feel I'm ripping her hair out."

"Hot." I nodded. And ducked as Colt lunged for me again. "I'm still lost, by the way."

"You're an ass."

"Caught that." I motioned for him to get on with it.

"And you have no idea how to speak to women."

I smirked. "Dude, if you guys are spending all your time speaking, you're clearly doing it wrong."

"Should I slap him?" Colt asked Milo. "Or do you wanna do the honors?"

I stood and moved away from the couch, pencil thrust into the air like a sword.

"I pick the bar." Jason stood and stretched. "Winner takes all."

"What are we doing? What are we taking?"

"Out." Colt puffed out his chest and stood. "May the best pickup line win."

Backed into a corner. Like a damn rat. "You sure you guys want to go up against me? I mean—do you even know my track record?"

"Yeah, you said seventy percent." Jason smacked me on the back. "But I'm feeling lucky . . . one hundred percent lucky."

I scowled. "You don't stand a chance."

"Watch. Me."

CHAPTER FIVE

MAX

I popped my knuckles as we walked into the bar. It was going to be too easy. Poor Jason didn't stand a chance. The guy was a walking accident. If he wasn't holding a bag of peas against his balls by the end of the night, well, I'd eat my hat. Of course, I wasn't wearing a hat, so I'd just have to pretend, but you get what I mean.

Colt on the other hand kept getting glares from Milo, so I knew he wasn't going to bring his best game.

Leaving me . . . the win.

I know it seems ridiculous—how does a guy pick up so many girls using cheesy lines? Listen up, because what I'm about to give you is the equivalent of free gold, your ride into the promised land, your bread, your butter, your freaking passport into heaven where women always engage in pillow fights and take off their tops. Just. Because. They. Can.

It's not about the actual pickup line—hell, no. Do I look stupid? It's in the delivery. Always in the delivery. Girls love a sense of humor; they love a guy confident enough to put his balls against the wall while she holds the only hammer capable of smashing them to tiny bits.

Jason thought it was about the pickup line.

No, my 70 percent success rate had everything to do with how I made the girl feel important.

So basically he was going to look like an ass.

I was so ready for that front-row seat. Hell, where was the popcorn?

"Look, there's one." I pointed to a lonesome girl sitting at the bar. She had that slouched, pouty look about her. Her eyes kept darting from her drink to the bartender, then back to her drink, fingernails tapping against the glass in a smooth cadence. By the looks of it, she'd had a really long day and was feeling slightly insecure, and it was possible she had just been stood up.

"Cake." Jason patted me on the chest twice before walking up to her. I followed him but took a seat a few chairs down. I wanted to actually hear the slap when it happened.

"So." Jason cleared his throat. "In honor of saving water, from here on out, I think you should just shower with me." His smile was huge.

The woman, however, looked like she wanted to stab him.

"Ha-ha." Jason leaned forward. "I'm Jason." He held out his hand.

She stared at it like he was diseased and then glared.

And that's my cue. Without wasting any time, I walked up to the girl, put my arm around her, and said, "Hey baby, is this asshole bothering you?" Jason's eyes went wide as saucers, and he lunged for me, but Colt held him back and led him away.

"Yeah." She relaxed beneath my arm. "Thanks."

Once they were out of earshot, I pulled my arm away and looked at her drink. Scotch, interesting choice. "Hey." I tapped the bar. "Get the woman a double. She just had a drunk guy with limp dick hit on her."

Swearing was heard behind me. I had to fight to keep from laughing out loud.

"Thank you." She exhaled. "I hate creeps."

"Oh." I sat on the stool next to her. "Me too. It seems they're everywhere these days."

"Yeah." She leaned against the countertop, her breasts nearly popping out of her white button-up shirt. "So what's your name?"

"Hmm, right now?" I tucked her hair behind her ear. "Whatever you call me—I think I'll die happy."

"Oh." Her eyelashes fluttered against her cheeks.

"Hey, man," Colt said, coming up next to us. "Sorry to interrupt what I'm sure would have been a freakishly interesting conversation about how beautiful this woman is and how much you understand her. Um, but your wife called and she said if you don't come home in like five minutes she's setting your bike on fire." He cringed and looked at the woman. "He got his car taken away last week on account that we're pretty sure he gave his neighbor herpes."

Stumbling away from us, the lady swore and stomped off.

"Apparently"—I stole her drink and tossed it back—"we need some ground rules, asshole."

"Nope." Colt smirked. "No ground rules, just one-liners. You failed."

"I'll do it." Colt was seriously out of his element if he thought he could land a girl with one pick-up line and not get the crap slapped out of him. "One pick-up line. Where's Jason?"

Colt pointed at a table full of women. "Hunting."

"Too bad his spear is limp, huh?" I crossed my arms over my chest and watched as Jason tried to engage the group of women.

They were smiling like they were into it, but he was losing precious time, and a few of them started looking behind him as if they were waiting for someone to rescue them.

I walked up and slunk my arm around his neck. "There you are, gorgeous!" With a smirk I kissed his cheek and blew in his ear.

"What the hell!" Jason pushed me off.

"He's embarrassed so easily." I laughed with the women and tickled Jason's sides. "Come on, lover, you promised to take me to *Hunger Games*, and daddy's so, so hungry. Rawr!"

"Aw!" The women sighed all over themselves. "How sweet! How long have you two been together?"

"Too long," Jason answered just as I said, "Not long enough."

"Have fun!" One of them winked at me. I winked back. Hell, yeah, if I were gay, she'd make me rethink that decision. I'd be back for her later.

"What the hell, man!" Jason pushed me away when we were back at the bar. "My lines were working!"

Colt came up next to us with Milo. "It was like watching a blind person play Battleship." He shrugged. "You may as well have been shooting blanks."

"I do not SHOOT BLANKS!" Jason yelled.

"Could have fooled me," a female voice said from behind us.

My balls started to tingle. Huh, I knew that voice. I turned around and almost hid behind Milo.

"Jayne!" Jason shrieked.

"Asshole." Her eyes were cold and lifeless. Well, what did you expect from a vampire who fed on the souls of others? A smile?

"What are you doing here?" Milo, precious little Milo, had a sweet tinge to her voice that sounded genuine. If I spoke to Jayne it would come out more like a snarl and then I'd start chucking garlic at her face while chanting Bible verses.

"Oh." Jayne tossed her hair.

Every man near me held his breath along with me—you know, just in case she put poison in her hairspray.

"I'm just getting a drink with friends." Her eyes zeroed in on Jason. Feeling bad for the guy, I stepped closer to him and grabbed his hand.

He actually squeezed it.

Let it be known that when a dude squeezes another dude's hand, he's in a bad place. A place where beer doesn't exist and women want to cuddle after sex and discuss feelings.

"Dude," I whispered. "Say the word and I'll kiss you right on the mouth to deter her affections."

"Thanks, man," Jason whispered back. "But I can handle this."

"That's great." Milo went to stand in front of us. Great, so now we needed protection from Mighty Mouse. What? Was she going to try to kick Jayne in the shin if things got crazy? On second thought, a catfight would be . . .

Oh, sorry. I think I blacked out for a minute. What was going on?

Milo reached into her purse and pulled out a bag of gummy bears. "Sorry, Jayne, I'm just starving! All those drinks and stuff, you want one?"

Jayne shrugged, took five gummy bears, and tossed them back. "Thanks, Milo, and thanks for listening. You're so great."

"What just happened?" I whispered to Jason. "I blacked out."

"Me too." Jason's eyes were glazed over. "But Jayne's had a rough week at work, Milo was comforting her, and Colton was trying not to gag when Milo gave Jayne a hug."

"Ha. Dude better disinfect his wife before playtime." I cringed while Jason gave a little shudder.

"Bye, guys." Jayne walked off.

Milo's grin was wider than I'd ever seen it before. Like she could seriously have wrapped that grin around her own head twice.

"Aw, shit." I pinched my nose. "What did you do?"

"I have no idea what you are referring to." She put the gummy bears back in her purse.

"I thought you were hungry? Why are you putting the bears away?"

She looked down guiltily at her purse. "I promise I wasn't actually going go to go through with it!"

"Huh?"

"Drinks." Jason pushed us all toward the bar. "Go through with what?"

We all sat at the bar and waited for Milo to take a sip of her drink. She winced and then started talking really fast. "Okay, so you have to know I would never, ever have gone through with it. It's just I heard these gummy bears caused, uh, intestinal issues, and, well, last week Max was being really annoying while watching *MasterChef* and wouldn't shut up, so I bought the bears in hopes he'd . . . you know, have to use the bathroom more often than not and leave me in peace!"

"So you thought to poison me!" I yelled.

Milo rolled her eyes. "Please, they're gummy bears. Hardly arsenic. Besides, we don't even know if it works that way!"

In that instant a red-faced Jayne came barreling by us and nearly collided with the door to the bar before opening it and running out into the fresh air.

"Hmm." I scratched my neck. "It's like bitch repellent. Gimme!" I reached for her purse. "I need those for the show!"

"No!" Milo jerked away from me. "That's so mean!"

"The kettle and pot are both black, Milo. Just FYI."

I tried to grab her purse again, but was fought off with her nails. Holy shit, the girl was scrappy.

Finally Colt grabbed her purse and pulled it away from both of us. "It's like watching first graders fight."

"Thanks, man." I tilted my beer toward him.

"So." Milo's shoulders sagged. "Should we head back home or—"

"Hell, no!" I ordered another beer. "Not until we have a winner."

Milo sighed. "Fine, okay. So how about the three of you just use one-liners and whoever gets the best responses in the next, say, fifteen minutes wins? I'll be the judge? Then can we please go home?"

"Fine," we grumbled in unison.

"Ready." Milo held up her hand. "Set. Go!"

I ran full speed like a blind cheetah. Seriously I was that fast. Four women. At a table.

"Hey there, can I have your phone number?" I asked the first cougar.

"Why?" Her penciled brows shot up in disdain.

"Well." I sighed and leaned over so that our faces almost touched. "I'm going to be in the hospital for a few weeks and I could really use a beautiful lady to talk to while I'm down and out."

Her face cracked into a smile. "How about I just punch you in the balls right now, since you're already heading to the hospital?"

I jerked back. "Violent. I could dig that."

"Go away."

"Going." I stepped back and made my way to the next table just as I heard Jason say, "You look like a Smurf. A hot Smurf. All tiny and you're making my balls—"

"Holy shit." I laughed aloud. And then heard the familiar sound of a cheek getting slapped followed by the sick feeling in my stomach at the thought of that same female kicking me in the balls.

The next table I walked up to was filled with college students. I knew that only because they were wearing NYU sweatshirts and looked like they would rather study than get drunk. Hmm. Smart ones. I had to be careful lest I find my face drenched in beer.

"Hey, girls." I waved and shoved my hands in my pockets, then tripped on purpose, nearly landing on the first girl's lap. "S-sorry."

"Aww, do you have a stutter?" She asked. Well, that was bold.

"O-only when I'm n-n-n-ne . . ." I looked away. "N-n-nervous."

"Oh!" She grabbed my hand and pressed it to her chest. Mighty Max did a little happy jump. "You're just the sweetest!"

"Thank you." Well, here went nothing. "By the way, my hands are freezing cold, as you can tell, could you warm them for me?"

The smile froze on her face.

Mighty Max stopped rejoicing and took the protective stance. "Sure."

"What?" I almost choked on my tongue.

"Yup." She leaned forward, sliding my palms downward, and then beer went flying in my face. Ah, there it is.

With a nod and a salute I walked off and returned to the bar, where Colt was taking shots like there was going to be a tequila shortage and Jason was alternating between rubbing his jaw and holding ice against it.

"You all lose." Milo shook her head. "Congrats, you're all losers. Can we please go home now?"

"Never!" I slammed the table with my hand and winced when a peanut lodged itself between my fingers, then went flying into the bartender's face.

Okay, so maybe we'd need to go to a different bar now.

Cold air bit me on the ass as the door opened.

Jason smirked.

Colt laughed.

And Milo sighed happily.

Damn it.

I turned and came face-to-face with my brother.

"What the hell are you doing here?" I asked, eyes narrowing. He'd been visiting a lot recently, which was shocking considering he was still in therapy over Jason's grandmother feeling him up in his special place. Thrice.

"Colt texted me." He licked his lips. "One-liners, huh? Seems you guys have the worst luck in the world. Watch and learn."

"Cheater!" I yelled. "No Reids allowed! It says so in the rules."

Reid rolled his eyes.

"Aw, let him." Milo laughed. "This will be the most entertainment I've had in months."

"No!" I nudged Milo. "You don't understand, women seriously strip in his presence, one time an old lady passed out and he gave her CPR thinking she was dying and she grabbed him by the neck and didn't let go. She did it on purpose. On purpose, Milo!"

Milo rolled her eyes.

"Reid, tell her!"

Reid just shrugged while the guys stared at him like he was some sort of magic sex god.

"It's true." Reid sighed. "Women tend to get . . . feisty when I'm around."

"Please." I rolled my eyes. "Last summer a chick rubbed up against you and said, 'Baby me.' Pretty sure you'd make a killing just getting women pregnant if you ever felt so inclined."

"Something's wrong with you guys." Jason shook his head. "No, seriously. Something is very wrong."

"Whatever." Reid reached behind Milo and popped something in his mouth, then cracked his knuckles and walked up to the first few women he saw.

"Uh-oh." Milo gasped.

"My thoughts exactly." I groaned as both women started playing with Reid's collar and then rubbed up against him.

"No, not that." She held out the bag of gummy bears. "He took a handful. I'd pulled them out of my purse to throw them away."

"Well, shit." I chuckled.

"Ha, oh, believe me." Colt sighed. "He'll be doing plenty of that in a few minutes."

CHAPTER SIX

MAX

I would be a bad brother if I didn't actually stay in that bar and wait for Reid to shit his pants. I mean, I could have left him! Instead, like a freaking saint, I waited by the bar while Reid worked his magic.

"Any minute now." I crossed my arms and chuckled as Reid suddenly froze and did a little headshake as if clearing cobwebs—or perhaps gummy bears. "I wonder how many you have to eat. What's the brand again, Milo?"

She told me.

I searched my phone.

Bingo.

A grin that I'm sure looked a hell of a lot like the Cheshire cat's spread across my face as I read customer reviews, or as I'd like to call them, stories from hell.

"How many he take?" I asked casually.

"Like ten." Milo shrugged.

Laughing, I watched Reid start to back away from the women.

Their faces fell—rejection washed over their features. Reid stumbled back, his face flushed red. And then he made a beeline toward us.

"I have to go!" he all but shouted. "I don't think I can drive, I don't think . . ." He winced and held his stomach.

"You sound like you're giving birth to a goat." I chuckled as another sound a bit like a shriek emerged from Reid's mouth.

"Why me?" he asked aloud. "Why is it always me?"

"Um." Jason raised his hand. "To be fair, it's like we row the same boat, Reid. You deal with emotional attacks from elderly ladies and I get straight-up attacked, only I'm pretty sure I'd rather be physically injured than deal with lusty grandmothers and intestinal gas brought on by sugar-free gummy bears."

"I'm allergic"—Reid's eyes widened—"to anything sugar-free."

"Please." I waved him off. "You had an attack one time."

Reid's eyes narrowed. "I was in the hospital a week."

"On account that you ate the whole bag of sugar-free chocolate. Reid, you're lucky they were able to even pump your stomach." Sugar-free chocolate also made him a bit crazy; he had kicked two nurses in the process of the stomach pumping.

Another gurgle emerged from Reid, though the jury was out as to which end of his body was the one doing the talking.

"Guys, I need to go to the hospital."

Rolling my eyes, I looked at the rest of the group. "We should probably take him to be safe."

"I can't drive." Colton held up his hands. "Tequilasha."

"You met a girl named Tequilasha?" Milo yelled, and smacked him on the back of the head.

"No. He means *tequila*." Jason rolled his eyes. "Geez, Milo, you've been here the whole time."

"Can we discuss"—Reid groaned and held on to me for support—"this in the car? On the way to the hospital? Please?"

"I'll drive." I snatched the keys from Colt as we all walked out to the parking lot and piled into the car.

"Reid, get on top."

"Top?" Sweat started pouring down his face. "On top of what?"

"The car." I pointed. "Hospital's only like two miles away. Just pretend you're a dog and let your tongue hang out."

"Nothing will be hanging out!" Reid shouted. "Why are we even discussing this? I need a doctor!"

"And I need to not smell whatever's cooking inside of that stove of yours. Ten bucks says it's burning and churning."

Reid wiped his face with his hands. "I'm not getting on the car."

"Dude, just pretend you're car surfing."

"Guys!" Milo shivered. "Just get in and stop arguing. You all bicker more than girls."

"Fine." I held up my hands in innocence. "But don't say I didn't warn you guys."

"I can control my body," Reid muttered under his breath as he got in the passenger side and put on his seat belt.

"We all in?" I checked the mirrors, adjusted my seat, and looked at my teeth in the mirror.

"For the love of God, Max! Just drive!" Reid shouted, his voice cracking at the end.

Grinning, I started the car and backed out of the parking lot.

Things were going great. Jason hadn't slammed his hand in the car door or anything, Milo wasn't punching him, Colt wasn't puking, and Reid seemed to be—

"Oh, God." Reid hunched over and then a sound I'd never heard another human being attempt, let alone actually make, erupted from his lips. Watching Reid was like watching something on the Discovery Channel.

"Hey, uh, you okay?" I reached out and patted his back.

"Don't!" Reid started rocking back and forth. "Don't touch me. Makes. It. Worse."

So naturally I kept rubbing his back.

"I can't—" Reid's teeth started chattering as another sound came from him, only it wasn't from his mouth.

"Was that?" Milo leaned forward and then started gagging. "Let me out, let me out!"

Reid shouted, "Guys, I think I have an alien inside of me, I think I'm, I think I'm possessed . . ."

"What's that smell?" Jason sniffed. "It's like . . ."

"Rotten bear," I finished, trying to lean as far away from Reid as possible. Finally I opened my window and sucked in some fresh air. "Almost there, buddy, hold tight."

"I can't. Hold. On." Reid's chest was heaving. "I'm not that strong, man. I've never been the strong one. You, you're the strong one."

"You're not dying!" I shouted. "Not on my watch!"

"Maybe." Reid winced. "Maybe it's better this way." His head slammed back against the seat as he let out a scream that sounded like he was being split in two by Thor's hammer. "Oh, sweet mother of God!" Reid reached for the door handle. "I'm jumping! I'm going to jump!"

"Reid, no!" Colt reached around and held him against the seat. "We're almost to the hospital. Think of something happy, like go to another place."

"But not the bathroom," I interjected. "Don't go there in your mind because we don't want it to somehow translate into reality."

"I see a light." Reid held out his hand. "Guys, I'm combusting from the inside out . . . give my iPhone to Jenna . . ."

"Jenna?" we all yelled in unison.

"Such pretty legs."

"Holy shit!"

"I wish! It's not holy!" Reid wailed. "It's evil! It's so, so evil!"

"You've been seeing Jenna?" Jason pushed his way to the middle console and punched Reid in the arm, which resulted in more toxic gas being released into the atmosphere, making everyone in the car start to gag.

"So?" Reid's teeth were chattering. "If she could only see me now."

"Jason!" Colt yelled. "Put your phone away! You are not sending pictures of Reid to Jenna!"

"Damn it! Jenna's mine! Do you realize how many classes I've been to?

"Reid does a better downward dog!" I yelled above Jason's voice. "Just leave Jenna out of this!"

"I'll downward dog you and we'll see who's better!" Jason fired back.

"Don't," I whispered. "Just stay away!"

"Oh, sweet death!" Reid wailed. "I can see Pop-pop." He reached into the air and fluttered his fingers as we pulled up to the last stoplight before the turn to the hospital. "Pop-pop, why are you so young? He's running, Reid. Pop-pop's running!"

"Damn it! Stay with us!" I hit the accelerator, causing Jason to collide with Reid again.

"It's coming!" Reid's voice shook as he let out another wail and then . . . burped.

"You swallow, you son of a bitch!" I yelled. "You hear me? Swallow!"

Reid shook his head.

"Swallow it!"

Jason slapped me on the shoulder. "Funny, I had this exact conversation with—"

"Mmsdlfksdklfhdsfh!" Reid shook his head and tried to open his door.

"Damn it, Reid!"

"Colt! Restrain him!"

I pulled into the hospital parking lot and gave everyone, myself included, whiplash as I jerked to a halt and ran around to the other side of the car to grab Reid.

"Stay with me, little buddy!" He nodded and then puked onto the ground. I rubbed his back and helped him walk through the hospital doors, followed by everyone else.

"I feel . . ." Reid swayed on his feet. "Hot."

"Keep your insides inside," I instructed. "Okay?"

A really pretty nurse approached us and smiled.

Reid turned, coughed, and puked on my shirt.

Just as I shook her hand.

"Hi, I'm Max. The new Bachelor. And my brother's about to give birth, so if you could get us a chair with those stirrup things—it's going to be a long night."

CHAPTER SEVEN

MAX

There were probably better ways for me to impress the opposite sex—ways that didn't involve flatulence or puke, but hey, I was working with what I had! You can't blame a guy for trying!

Reid coughed. "Hurry."

The nurse gagged. "I'll just go get a wheelchair and free up a room."

"Make sure the room has a bathroom!" I called after her while she scurried off and coughed.

I think I was getting used to the smell of puke. Hmm, probably a bad sign.

"How you holdin' up, man?" I slapped Reid on the back just as he doubled over in pain.

"Who knew?" Colt shrugged, walking up with Jason. "I mean, sugar-free gummy bears?"

"The devil!" Reid coughed. "The very devil possesses those bears!"

"Here we go!" The nurse returned with a wheelchair and a hospital gown. "If you'll just follow me I'll take you to your room."

Jason's mouth dropped open.

He was openly and very awkwardly staring at the nurse. I mean, yeah, she was hot, but come on! Reid was dying!

"Remember how you said you'd take one for the team and kiss me on the mouth?"

"Er . . ." I stepped away. "So not the time to be discussing this."

"Punch me in the face," Jason ordered.

Colt and Milo shoved past us and followed Reid and the nurse while Jason grabbed my shirt and basically he-manned me up against the wall. "Do it!"

"Stop yelling!" I fought against him.

I didn't expect him to take it so far as to slap me. But he did. And when I didn't punch him back, he slapped me harder.

I was officially his bitch, no, really. Swear, it was like we were in a relationship and I'd just pissed him off by not folding the towels just right.

"Stop slapping me!" I lunged for him and then clocked him in the jaw. Jason, of course, went tumbling to the ground.

"Nurse!" he yelled.

The pretty nurse stopped walking and turned around. With a gasp she ran toward us. "What happened?"

Jason pointed at me. Bastard. Glaring, I answered, "I have anger issues."

"He does." Jason sniffed and dabbed his jaw with his hand. "Geez, man, control yourself!"

"Dying!" Reid shouted. "In case anyone cares!"

The nurse stopped in her tracks at the sound of Reid's voice, and then Jason doubled over and clenched his face. "I think something's broken!"

"Giving birth to a small penguin!" Reid shouted over Jason's fake whining.

"Oh, for the love," I grumbled and then slapped Jason on the back as hard as I possibly could. "Suck it up, she can examine you in Reid's room."

"You know how private I am, Max." Jason scowled, holding his jaw.

"Um." The nurse turned bright red. "I'll figure something out, but we really need to put some ice on that." Her gaze met mine. If looks could kill I'd have been descending into hell right about then.

Right. Like I purposefully poisoned my brother and then punched Jason in the face. Why was I always the bad guy? Furthermore, why did I always have to take the fall?

By the time we made it into the room, Jason's whines had turned into some sort of hoarse moaning that made it sound as if he were a mating pig rather than an adult male in pain.

Reid, on the other hand, soiled himself. Twice. And then prayed for God to call him home at least five times, all before the nice nurse gave him some happy drugs and a change of clothes.

"Where are Colt and Milo?" I looked around the empty room. "Did they—"

A flash of color caught my eye.

Curious, I walked out of the room to find Milo and Colt making their way toward the exit.

"You dirty. Little. Whores."

Milo and Colt both stopped in their tracks and slowly turned to face me. That's right—I caught their guilty asses!

"And just where do you think you two are going?"

Milo looked down at the ground. "I'm sick."

Colt coughed on her behalf and then hit her back. "We're both sick."

"With lies," I spit. "With dirty lies!"

"It's not what it looks like!" Colt held up his hands in defense, I slapped them away and scowled.

"The spawn of Satan"—I pointed at Milo—"gave my brother poisoned bears, and thanks to her, if anyone lights a match anywhere near this hospital we're going to have an explosion on our hands. If I, the nonguilty party, have to stay, then you have to stay too. Breathe through your mouth!"

Milo started backing away. "But—"

"No excuses!" I pointed at Colt. "Control your wife, Colt!"

With jerky movements Colt grabbed Milo's purse and started digging, then pulled out a handful of gummy bears and held them next to his mouth.

"I'll do it!" he shouted. "Don't think I won't!"

"Whoa!" I held up my hands. "Whoa there, little buddy, just put the bears down."

"Colt—" Milo's voice wavered. "We can talk about this. Come on, baby, let's just go back inside."

"No!" Colt shouted. "I say no! Why should I have to stay and suffer when it's not even my fault?"

"Dude." I reached out my hand you like how you do when you first meet an aggressive animal and want it to know you mean no harm. "Just give me the bears."

"How do I know you won't make me stay?" Colt's eyes narrowed. "How can I trust you?"

"Look." I was losing patience fast. "Just hand me the bears and I'll let you walk away. Colt, you can still walk away from this. It's not worth it."

"Isn't it?" Colt's voice shook. "How do you know? What if I'd rather suffer than sit in your brother's poisonous gas?"

"Dude." I waved him off. "He's totally healed now. They gave him drugs, he's sleeping like a baby."

Reid's voice carried down the hall. "It's coming!" A shriek erupted from his room. "Ballllsssss!" Was he weeping? "Holy Hannah!" Wow, didn't know he had such a set of pipes. "Hannah Montana!"

Once the screaming stopped, I chanced a look at Colt. He'd dropped the bears onto the ground.

"Good choice." I nodded. "Take my hand. We're going back in there. Reid needs us now more than ever."

"You can't make us." Milo lunged for my hair. Nobody touched the hair. It was held in place by at least seven different products that cost more than the T-shirt she was wearing.

"Back off!" I held up my fists.

"Dude, are you going to punch my wife?"

"He has a thing about people touching his hair, he says it's more sensitive on account of its glossiness," Milo said.

Colt rolled his eyes.

"It's a real thing!" I yelled just as Reid let out another yell that in fact harmonized with mine. See? Talented. Both of us bastards.

"Guys!" Jason poked his head out of the room and took a huge breath of air. "Things just got real in here."

The nurse, the hot one, ran out of the room with tears streaming down her face.

"Lawyer up, gummy bear bitches!" Reid yelled. "I'm coming for you!"

"Yeah," Milo grumbled. "Let's go before Reid has a hernia."

I walked as slowly as humanly possible toward that room, hoping that in the five seconds it took me to get there, a miraculous healing would occur. Either that or Reid would just pass out from the pain.

No such luck.

He looked like he was giving birth as he lay on the bed clutching his stomach. "Dude, the drugs aren't working."

"Here we are!" The nurse stepped around us, holding a giant-ass needle in her hands. If someone approached me with that big a needle I'd start running. I wouldn't even hesitate.

Reid was clearly in too much pain to remember he also had a needle phobia, so when the nurse approached with the relief and he actually turned around and lifted his ass into the air, I thought, hey, big brother's growing up.

She inserted the needle.

Reid jerked to the left.

And something snapped.

I was hoping it was a bone—seriously, nobody wanted a needle stuck in his ass. That shit took surgery.

The nurse stumbled backward. "Don't move!"

"What?" Reid started moving.

Jason ran to Reid's side and held him in place. "Sorry, buddy, the hot nurse says you can't move."

The nurse blushed and ran out of the room.

"Guys." Reid shuddered. "Is my naked ass pointing towards the sky?"

Complete silence blanketed the room as we all tilted our heads in unison. Reid's ass was in fact pointed toward the sky, but he was probably too high to realize it.

I coughed and mumbled, "Course not," while a chorus of praise rang from the group. "Reid, you look great! After all you've been through! Is that a six pack?" I elbowed Milo, who was laying it on a bit thick.

"Whew!" Reid nodded. "Good, because I totally can't feel my legs right now."

"Bad sign?" I mouthed to Colton.

He shrugged as the nurse walked back in with a doctor.

"Well, damn." The doctor examined the spot where the needle had gone into hiding and then slapped Reid's ass.

I coughed to cover my laugh.

But then the doctor slapped Reid's ass again.

And I lost it.

Hey, I got a prostate exam! It's not like it's all been flowers and rainbows for me either!

Jason sent me a seething glare as he fought to hide his smile. Reid moaned. The doctor slapped again.

It was like a really poorly made porno, like one you'd show kids in order to get them not to watch porn. All you'd have to do would be to say, "And this is what happens when you watch naked people . . ."

You puke, get gas, and have a hot nurse watch while an elderly doctor slaps your ass in order to locate the needle that broke under your skin.

"Aw, there it is." The doctor smiled.

"He found your balls, Reid! Yay!" I joked.

Reid showed me the finger.

"Probably a bad time to do that . . ." Jason commented.

"Now, I'm going to squeeze a bit." The doctor's gaze was focused on Reid's whiteness as he pinched.

"Ouch!" Reid wailed. "That hurts!"

"Stop moving!" The doctor swore. "I'm almost there."

"Please don't say those words to me." Reid shook. "Please don't say those words!" He was full-on begging.

"Aghhhhh!" the doctor yelled as he pulled out the needle that had embedded itself in Reid's skin.

At some point Colt had covered Milo's eyes and Jason had covered Reid's, not that Reid could actually see his own ass, but I think it was the principle of the matter.

"Now"—the doctor clapped his hands together—"you'll have to lie on your stomach for a bit while the nice nurse gives you an IV. I'll come back in to check on you later. Are you going to be okay, son?"

"Go." Reid's voice shook. "You've done enough, just go."

The doctor chuckled and walked out of the room while I whispered under my breath, "Was it as good for you as it was for me?"

I received a smack from Colton for that one.

Two hours later, when Reid had finally fallen into a fitful sleep and I was contemplating sneaking out, my e-mail alert went off.

I checked the message and felt the color drain from my face.

"Records clean! Pack your bags, your flight leaves tomorrow."

"Well, hell," I muttered.

"What?" Jason yawned. His jaw was starting to turn yellow from the punch he'd received.

"I don't have herpes. Damn it."

"And you wanted them *because?*"

"Now I have to go on the show!" I swore and almost threw my phone. "Hey, we're at a hospital, so there has to be some sort of curable disease I can catch by tomorrow, right?"

Jason shrugged. "There's always the gummy bears."

"Dun-dun-dun . . ." Reid sang from his bed, lifting his arms into the air like he was directing an orchestra. "I still taste them. It's the red bears that are the worst, they have more bark to their bite than the green ones. Holy shit! Am I going to hate Christmas now? Because of all the red and green?"

"Go to sleep, Reid." I rolled my eyes.

CHAPTER EIGHT

MAX

Reid was out of the hospital, but because of the number those devil bears had done on his digestive tract, the nice doctor—you know, the one who needled him—said he wanted to do a checkup in a few days.

I instructed Reid to wear a cup just in case the doctor got too friendly.

Reid did not laugh. Instead he's been wallowing in his apartment ever since.

At this point I was a bit concerned for Reid's mental health. I mean, when you lose your sense of humor, what do you have left? But Jason assured me that while I was on the Island—ugh, I still shuddered thinking about it—they would keep an eye on Reid.

"Do you have everything you need?" Milo asked for the third time while I pulled my bags out of the car.

"Yes, Mom."

"Toothpaste?" she asked.

"Yes."

"Advil, just in case?"

"Yes."

"Condoms?" Jason coughed.

"There will be no sex!" I yelled, gaining unwanted attention from a nice elderly lady who had a patch over her left eye and a permanent smile on her face. Mighty Max quivered in fear.

"Sure there won't." Jason rolled his eyes. "How about a bet?"

My ears perked up. "What kind of bet?"

"You fall prey to your carnal nature," Jason tapped his chin, "and you suck it up and finally start looking for a job away from your family's dynasty and drop the whole poor-me act you've got going on."

"I have direction!" I seethed. "I just . . . need more time!"

"Sure." Jason chuckled. "But hey, if you can't handle it, then—"

"Fine," I snapped. "And when I win, you have to dye your hair black, get a nose piercing and wear a shirt that says, 'I feel things' for an entire week."

Colton burst out laughing. "Can you imagine the reaction at the police station?"

"So?" I held out my hand. "A gentleman's wager?"

"A gentleman's bargain." Jason took my hand in his and shook.

"Guys are so stupid," Milo muttered as she stepped into my arms and gave me a hug. "Now keep your pecker in your pants or I lose two hundred bucks to Colt." She tugged my ear so hard I saw stars. "Seriously, Max. I don't lose bets. I don't care if you have to tape it down, just don't let it out."

"I'm really—" I swallowed. "Really uncomfortable right now."

"Good." Milo stepped back. "Remember this conversation every time you want to dip your honey into a pot, and we'll be golden."

"You just ruined both honey and drugs for me. I'll never get high again." I sighed.

"Dude." Colt slapped me on the back, then whispered in my ear. "You get yours, you hear?"

They were officially the worst friends in the history of friendship.

"Right." I nodded. "I'll try to, um—"

"Don't try, man. Trying doesn't get you to third base. Trying gets you a walk to first. All right? You want a grand slam, how do you get a grand slam?"

How sad that he was trying to convince me to sex strange women. I had half a mind to feel sorry for Milo for being married to a man that desperate to win a bet.

Then Milo made eye contact with me and crossed her legs, then gave me a thumbs-up.

Never mind. They deserved each other.

Colt pushed me away from the crowd. "Look, if you need, like . . . help getting your bat to . . ." He bit his lip. "Swing?"

"Yeah." I winced. "Wouldn't have gone with that word choice."

"All you have to do," Colt whispered in a low voice, "is just imagine how good winning feels. You want to win the game, don't you, Max?"

"Uh, yes."

"You hesitated."

"I was confused."

"About winning?" Colton smacked my chest. If he kept smacking me I was going to kick him in the nuts. Feel me? "You want to win, Max. Losers don't get prizes."

"Right." I nodded.

"You want a prize." Colt held my face in his hands. "And we don't lose to Milo. Okay?"

"So . . ." I sniffed. "Just to be clear, you want me to play baseball with the girls? And you don't want me to lose?"

"What?" Colt shook his head. "No, it was a metaphor!"

I gave him a dumb look, wondering how far he'd take it.

He shifted uncomfortably on his feet and then held out his hands in front of him. "You know those noodle toys? That people have at their pools?"

I managed to keep a straight face. "You mean those really hard ones that people beat each other with? Those noodles?"

"Yes!" Colt sighed in relief. Damn, teasing him was just too easy. "Imagine that you're the noodle."

"I'm the noodle." I repeated. "Got it."

"And you want your noodle to make contact with the um . . . tube. The floating tube!"

"Why?" I shook my head. "Why do I want the tube?"

"Because she's—it's hot!" Colt all but yelled.

"But I'm already cool because I'm in the pool."

"Someone left you outside the pool and you're very . . . hot, and dry, and needy, you need the tube."

Holy shit. Why wasn't this getting filmed? I crossed my arms. "I see, so I need the tube in order to feel . . . satisfaction?"

"Yes." Colt rubbed his hands together. "So glad we understand each other."

"Hey." Milo walked up to us. "Max is gonna miss his flight if he doesn't leave now. What are you boys whispering about?"

"Oh, it's nothing." I chuckled and put my arm around Colt's neck. "He just thinks the best way for me to find that special girl is to have a pool party. Baller idea."

Colt groaned.

"Seriously." I nodded. "Can't wait to smack my noodle around those tubes, it's going to be . . . so refreshing."

Colt stiffened.

"Well!" I slapped his back. "I'll see you guys on the other side! Remember, I left my will in the safe."

"Bye!" Everyone waved but Jason.

"Look." He pushed me away from everyone and slapped my back. "I know you're pissed we forced you into this, but think of it as an extended vacation where you can really think about what's important in life."

I squinted. "Are you being serious right now?"

"Yes." His jaw flexed as he looked down at his feet. "You can't just sit around all the time. A man needs purpose, and maybe this is what you need to find yours."

"A dating show?" I asked sarcastically, irritated that he was actually making sense.

"Enjoy yourself." He nodded. "You never know, you may find the one, and in my mind that's the easiest way to find direction . . . a woman can motivate a man to do anything."

The man should have taken a long hard look at himself in the mirror—I wasn't the only single bastard, not by a long shot, and how the hell would a woman make my life better? Women always equaled more drama.

"Are you saying I need love in order to find a job?"

"Well, clearly threatening you didn't work."

"You're not my dad."

"It's time to stop arguing when your comebacks are along the lines of 'You can't make me' or 'You're not my dad.' Just saying." Jason held up his hands.

"Max!" Milo huffed from a few feet away, "you need to go!"

With one final look at Jason and the rest of the crew, I nodded my head and turned on my heel.

Suddenly I felt really optimistic about the opportunity.

Optimistic, until I saw a group of twenty-five women. Boarding. The. Exact. Same. Plane.

"Welcome!" The orange guy from before ran in front of me. "We're going to start filming so just . . . act normal."

Someone reached into my pants and added a microphone to my shirt. My mouth dropped open as the heads of the women slowly turned.

Unfortunately I recognized one of them right away.

The barista from Starbucks.

Yeah, here's hoping she doesn't push me out of the plane.

CHAPTER NINE

MAX

"Well, go ahead." Orange man ushered me forward, and I stumbled a bit and tried to think of an excuse as to why I needed to stay back and stare at the ground. Who was I kidding? I wasn't ready for this! I had absolutely zero protection, no backup whatsoever. And was I really stable enough to find love and keep it? Not that I wanted love, but if it presented itself . . . yeah, I was overthinking things. It was a TV show. I needed to get in, get out, and go home. Period.

Safety! I needed safety or a home base or something that I could like sit on that would protect me from the women. Invisible cloaks be damned! Hell, where was the elderly eye patch lady when a guy needed her? She'd have scared even the bravest of women. Swear, I'd kangaroo myself into her fanny pack—and like it.

"Ladies." Orange man clapped his Oompa Loompa hands together. "Welcome to *Love Island*! I'm Rex Harding, and I'll be your host for the next three weeks."

Oh, so were we all choosing porn names? Was that how reality TV worked? If so I would totally call myself Maximus Hightower.

Dibs. For real. I could see my tagline now. "Afraid of heights? Why not climb my tower?"

So my tagline needed work.

"Ladies." Rex pushed me toward the crowd of perfume. My throat started constricting as flowery scents invaded my nostrils and choked the life straight out of me. Must. Get. Oxygen.

I had a sudden vision of a giant flower chasing me through the airport with a woman attached to every petal.

"As you can see"—Rex cleared his throat—"this is the new Bachelor, Max."

Maximus Hightower, but whatever.

A series of sighs and giggles erupted from the swarm, making me shake a little in my tight leather boots.

Must. Not. Make. Eye. Contact. Swear my balls didn't know whether to rejoice or just tremble with fear. On one hand, I had a few beautiful women salivating in my direction—on the other, I had a few beautiful-but-desperate women salivating in my direction, and a desperate woman was not an attractive woman. Feeling lonely was a foreign emotion for me, but over the past ten minutes that's exactly how I'd felt. It sucked, because it made me wonder how much I relied on my friends to keep me happy while I found myself.

One of the girls licked her lips and mouthed a "Hi." Then promptly dipped one of her talons into her mouth and bit.

Tremble with fear. Definitely tremble with fear.

"So." Rex laughed. "Everyone be sure to check your bags. And remember, nothing over fifty pounds."

I snorted.

All eyes went to me.

"Ah." I stuffed my hands in my pockets. "Dare I say a few of you are going to be overweight?"

Some of the girls gasped and covered themselves with their arms.

What? I meant their suitcases! Not them!

Sighing, I scratched my head and grabbed my own suitcase and stood in line.

"You're shorter than I thought you'd be," a tall woman who looked like she could eat me sniffed above my head.

Um, I was six-one. Not short by any means.

Then again, I only came up to her shoulder. Holy shit, her feet were huge! How did she find heels? She was an Amazon and I was the little plaything she wanted to chase through the forest. Shit. Did that make me Little John? Or like . . . Maid Marian? You know, from that one cartoon with the foxes.

Damn, I'd had a thing for Maid Marian when I was little. She was foxy. Ha-ha! Yeah, I was glad I had myself to keep me company while I fought for my life.

I stepped away from Predator and shrugged. "Yeah, well, you're tall."

Good one, Max. Swear brain cells everywhere just rolled over and died with all the juice it took for me to come up with that one.

"I know." She smirked. "But height has its advantages."

Okay, I'm a dude. We have perverted minds and all that. But I had nothing. Nothing. I tried to conjure up images of what the hell height had to do with anything and all I could think of was her picking me up with her bare hands and me wrapping my legs around her chick-style and holding on for dear life lest she drop me on my head and cause me to have a concussion.

Focus on her face, Max. If I focused on her face things looked better. She was pretty, with dark hair and bright-green eyes.

And then she smiled.

And that damn shudder happened again. Why were women suddenly terrifying me?

I backed away and bumped into another chick, causing her cell phone to crash to the floor—and shatter.

"I am so sorry!" I bent over to pick it up and bumped heads with her. She fell on her ass and I stumbled into the Amazon, whose nails dug into my skin. I yelped and fell forward just as the girl started to get up.

She fell. Again.

Only this time I fell on top of her.

"Aw, shit," I said aloud as I realized who it was. Becca. The same Becca from the coffee shop. The pretty one who wanted a front-row seat to my tar-and-feathering.

"Excuse me?" She huffed underneath me.

Huh. Nice body. Nice . . . feeling her wiggle underneath my—

"Get. Off!" she spit.

"Sorry." I stumbled back and offered her my hand.

She did not take it.

I wiped my hand on my jeans. As if it were sweaty, which it wasn't; that just seemed like the right thing to do.

"I'm sorry I made you fall." I cleared my throat. "Twice."

"Yeah, well." She dusted off her pants and sighed as she glanced at the broken cell phone in her hands. "It's not like you did it on purpose."

"Or did I?" I joked, trying to lighten the situation.

Her eyes narrowed into tiny slits.

"So not a jokester, huh?" Kill me now. "I really am sorry . . . about . . ." Hell, I was ready to apologize for world hunger, her look made me feel that guilty. "Your phone and . . . ass."

"My ass?" she hissed.

Her hair was longer than I'd originally thought. Hmm.

"Next!" the lady at the ticket counter called.

"After you." I let her go ahead of me. See, I could be a gentleman. Unfortunately she was still glaring at me and ended up colliding with Amazon. Both tumbled to the floor. Only Amazon covered Becca's entire body with hers.

"Ohhh." I snapped my fingers. That's what she'd meant. She'd smother me to death with her height. Hooray!

Drinks, where were the free drinks? Didn't they have drinks on this show? Damn it! Give me alcohol!

I wish I could say that the rest of the trip was like one of those Lifetime movies where people bicker, then end up falling in love and holding hands as they walk into the sunset with their equally hot bodies and all-around happy dispositions.

False.

Two of the chicks got sick on the plane. One of them threw up a seat behind me, making me gag.

The turbulence was something out of a horror movie and if one more drunk girl shouted, "Snakes on the plane!" or "He can snake my plane anytime!" I was seriously going to parachute out of this thing—without the chute. Feel me?

"So." Rex plopped down in the empty seat next to me. "I take it you've had a while to read through the rules and regulations."

"Yup," I lied.

"Well." His eyes narrowed. "Just to be sure, I brought an extra copy. Scan through it and put your initials at the bottom."

"Right." I took the thin stack of papers and started reading.

Luckily the girls weren't allowed to talk to me, since the show hadn't officially started. They were filming for promo but that was it.

Rex mentioned something about their being under a gag order or something, with their contracts making it impossible for them to talk to me while we were actually flying, without being in breach of their agreements. Something about not wanting to miss all the good stuff by not filming. I hoped they would stay true to that because it looked like the crew was firing up cameras already.

Yay me!

I took a sip of my beer and started reading through the rules.

The Bachelor may not give monetary gifts to the contestants.

Oh, maybe they'd had problems with Bachelors in the past paying contestants to leave. I'd be lying if I said I hadn't thought about it. A vision of Amazon woman came to mind.

The Bachelor may not contact the outside world during his time on the Island.

I rolled my eyes. Right. Even prisoners got a free phone call.

The rules made sense. I continued reading and then got down to the really legal stuff.

Mayhem Media Productions is not liable for any accident occurring during the four-week filming period. Death, even if accidental, could occur. Any hospital bills or mental health issues caused by the show or its affiliates are hereby the sole responsibility of the contestant.

"Death?" I said out loud. "Who's dying?"

Rex chuckled from the seat in front of me. "Just legal jargon."

I started sweating. "Has anyone actually . . . died?"

He grew very quiet.

Too quiet.

It was the type of quiet that made you itch all over and start tugging at your clothes. Because. They. Were. Choking. Me!

"Not to worry," Rex finally said. "He shouldn't have jumped."

"Jumped?" I croaked.

"Right. He had a weak heart." Rex coughed. "Say, how's your ticker? Seemed the doctor did nothing but sing your praises."

That happened when another bro was impressed with Mighty Max. Then again . . .

Was it wrong to pray I never saw that doctor again? I gave an uncomfortable shudder. "Well, I'm glad he was impressed."

"Impressed?" Rex gave me a funny look, then took a sip of his drink. "I wouldn't go as far as to say that—I mean, at first he was a bit confused."

"Confused?" I leaned forward. "Well, that's what every man

wants to hear from the doctor who held his balls in the palm of his hand—literally."

Rex chuckled. "Oh, not that, he just found it curious that you were going on a dating show when you already had a partner."

Well, crap.

"I see."

"That is another rule." Rex pointed to the stack of papers and sniffed. "That boyfriend of yours isn't serious, is he?"

"Oh, hell." Was Jason seriously going to haunt me even when he wasn't with me? "No. It won't be a problem."

Rex turned red and pulled at his shirt. "Yeah, well, the doctor said you two were pretty chummy and you know that's a breach of contract to—"

"We broke up!" Holy shit. What was I doing?

Rex's face fell. "I see, so this must be such . . . great timing." He waved his hand around as a girl teetered her way down the aisle toward us and promptly puked in the seat to my left.

I jumped out of my seat and moved to the window seat while a stewardess walked by and started cleaning up.

"I'm sick," puke girl whined.

I gagged and stuffed my fist in my mouth as I tried to lean far away from the fumes. Rex's face went back to looking an orangey-purple. "Lola, take a minute, then tell me what's wrong."

Lola? What the hell kind of name was Lola?

She nodded and then plopped down onto a seat and put her head between her knees. Her stomach heaved again—this time making it into the nice little paper bag they provided for those types of things.

It needs to be said. I didn't have the strongest stomach. I wasn't the type of guy who could hold your hair while you puked and not be affected. Did that make me the worst possible boyfriend ever?

Maybe. It's entirely possible I'd throw you a towel and run out of the room gagging.

I know it's romantic to women—oh, my gosh, he's so sweet he held my hair while I puked up last night's hot dog and enough rum and Diet Coke to kill Captain Jack Sparrow!

Seriously? What do you women read? How the hell is that romantic? Give me one reason. One. Just one. I don't even need three.

Oh, wow, silence, big shock. You wanna know why? Because it's gross. Because if I had long hair and I were leaning over the toilet, God, you would not, ever, in your right mind waltz into the bathroom, put it in a ponytail, rub my back, wipe my mouth, and think, *Wow, I really love this guy*, oh, look a cracker!

Lola heaved again.

"I, ugh, gotta—" I pointed to the bathroom and ran down the aisle like I was getting chased through the Amazon. Ha, see what I did there?

"Going somewhere?" A tall figure stood in front of me.

Well, speak of the devil and she appears. Note to self: the woman is a mind reader.

"Yeah, I was going to, um, take a piss." I said it crassly, in a way that would make her think I was the most unromantic man ever to be created. Question, if I peed on her, would she run away or find it hot?

Her eyes hooded.

In her mind marking her was probably some sacred mating ritual— I'd find myself tied to a tree on that damn island while she danced around me and pointed at my parts.

"After you." I let her go in first.

Smirking, she leaned down. "Why don't we go in together? Nobody's looking anyways . . ."

"You want to pee with me?" I laughed nervously, trying to step away. Oh, shit, she moved so she was blocking me from running. I was trapped. I was sweating. Damn you, Jason!

Amazon—I'm sure she had a name but I didn't want to know it lest I classically condition myself to pee my pants every time I heard it said aloud—eyed me up and down and licked her lips. "No, I want to play with you."

"Ha-ha," I chuckled. "It's against the rules."

"I don't follow the rules."

"No shit."

She hovered near me and then, no joke, lifted me into the air, my feet dangling, her breath hot on my neck. Where was Rex? The plane wasn't full and the curtains to coach were pulled. In that moment I wondered if this what Frodo felt like when he was fighting orcs. Helpless? Small? Afraid? Did she smell fear?

"Oh, there you are!" Becca threw open the curtains and sighed, directing her attention to Amazon. "Sherry stole your pine nuts."

Amazon dropped me onto my feet, swore under her breath, and started stampeding down the aisle toward her seat. I was half-tempted to chase after her and yell, "Git!" But that would have suggested I had been the one to scare her off, and sadly that had been done by a pint-size barista who looked like she found the idea of serving me rotten coffee . . . invigorating.

Becca rolled her eyes and reached for the bathroom door.

"Uh, thanks," I mumbled. "For white-knighting me like that . . . it was . . ."

"Degrading?" she offered. "Embarrassing?"

"Um." I sniffed and tried to puff up my chest to make myself look like more of a man instead of a toddler. "I was thinking brave?"

She rolled her eyes.

"That's twice now." Why was I still talking? Clearly she would rather see me jump out of the plane than actually talk to me, yet there went my mouth!

"Twice?" She tilted her head, pieces of blond silky hair falling across her bare shoulders. "That I've saved your ass or that you've made an ass out of yourself?"

I laughed. "Aw, my jackassery is interchangeable!"

"Probably not something to celebrate." Becca winked and opened the door to the small bathroom, closing it behind her, leaving me in the hallway with a stupid grin on my face and a slight tingling in my chest.

What the hell?! I coughed.

I hit my chest.

The tingle remained.

Well, damn.

"You okay?" Rex came up behind me and offered me a drink.

"Just fine." I threw back the entire drink in one swig and waited for that annoying little feeling in my chest to go away.

Nothing.

And four minutes later, after I'd found my seat, the feeling returned tenfold when Becca made her way down the aisle back toward her row.

Turn around. Just turn around.

And she did.

But instead of blowing me a kiss, winking, flirting, really doing anything that would establish that I was the catch in this scenario and not her—she turned and smiled. The smile. The patronizing smile known worldwide as the friend smile.

I'd just been zoned.

And that feeling in my chest?

It was there to stay.

Damn crushes.

"Try to get some sleep." Rex walked by me and winked. "We've got a long day ahead of us."

"Sleep," I mumbled. "Right."

"Oh, here you go." He slipped me a pill and nodded. "It will help with the nightmares."

"Um, nightmares?" I examined the pill.

"Not really FDA-approved, but . . ." Rex chuckled. "You'll need the strong stuff to be able to sleep at night."

I gulped. "*Is* the pill a temporary thing or—"

Rex laughed nervously and wiped some sweat from his brow. "Only two of our Bachelors have ever had to see the psychiatrist past the recommended year."

"A YEAR?" I shouted.

Rex nodded. "Twenty-five women." He swallowed. "The way I see it, a year's getting off easy."

"Swell." I popped the pill in my mouth and swallowed.

"Good choice." Rex patted me on the shoulder again, only this time I barely felt it. Holy shit! I was flying, soaring through the air. Superman. I'd just turned into Superman. If Reid could see me now!

I fell into a dream-filled sleep—where I saved damsels in distress and kissed girls named Becca. It was nice.

Until I woke up.

CHAPTER TEN
BECCA

"He looks weak," said Gina, who was sitting to my left.

Um, how about anyone would look weak standing next to her? She looked like she'd just finished competing in the CrossFit Games and had decided to kill her male competition for the extra challenge.

"I think he's hot." To my right, Stormy giggled.

Ugh. On one side I had a man-eater and on the other I had a giggler, someone who when nervous decided the only way to break the awkward tension was to fill the air with the sound of her laughter.

Only I wouldn't call it laughter.

Stormy made me want to never laugh again. Seriously, she was a joy stealer, who almost ruined the experience of being happy for everyone just because she was so terrible at expressing it.

"Whatever." Gina clenched her pine nuts in her hand. "I'm going to win the money regardless."

"So you're here for the money? Not for Max?" Stormy asked. Holy crap! No giggles! My mouth dropped open in shock, and then the giggles came. "*He, he*, I just think, *te, te, te, te*, he's way hotter than the quarter of a million dollars they're throwing our way. Besides, if you find love with Max you both get the money!" More giggling, more blushing. I wrapped my hands around my seat belt so I wouldn't do the same thing to her neck. Wow, two hours on a plane and I was already getting violent.

"I'd crush him with my bare hands." Gina popped another nut into her mouth. No worries, the visual wasn't lost on me. Poor Max wouldn't last a day in her clutches, which was probably why I felt the need to save him.

I was *that* girl.

I rescued dogs.

Slammed on my brakes when ducks crossed the road.

And freaking bawled my eyes out like a baby when I saw *How to Train Your Dragon* in theaters.

My poor nieces went home and announced to my sister that I'd cried so loud in the theater that the manager came and tried to offer us our money back—he thought I was upset.

I'd made up a story about how I'd just broken up with my boyfriend. Lies. All lies. But I didn't want the hot theater manager to know I was actually just really crushed that Toothless had almost died.

Yeah, needless to say, I'm not the first-choice aunt to go to movies with anymore.

"It's a competition." Gina cracked her knuckles; I scooted toward Stormy and winced as Gina continued popping body parts. "And I'm going to win. You girls don't stand a chance."

I swallowed. "Right."

"Some of us are here for the right reasons, Gina." Stormy sniffed and looked away, ending the conversation and making me feel so tense I wanted to jump out of the plane. I'd always hated the middle seat anyway. Where the heck do you put your arms? Both girls were taking up so much space that every time I decided to inhale it was a tossup between sucking in the air that was permeated with the odor of pine nuts or the air that smelled like baby powder.

Gross.

"Ladies!" Rex clapped his hands from the front of the plane. "The competition has officially begun."

Squeals were heard around the plane, followed by laughter and more giggling. If I hadn't needed the money I would have seriously quit right then and there. But two hundred and fifty grand? It was a lot. And even if I only survived the trip and was one of the last four girls? I still took home twenty, which would be more than enough to pay for my last two years of college, plus housing.

That was the agreement between me and my parents. They had paid for two years; I would pay for two years. I'd taken out loans for my junior year and now that I was starting my senior year, reality was starting to hit me in the face. I needed money—fast.

"Your first mission," Rex said, interrupting my thoughts, "is to earn the Bachelor's trust as well as his love. Earn both, and you win half a million dollars. Or, at the end of the game, you can choose to go your separate ways and take your half of the money, leaving the Bachelor at the altar."

Rex paused dramatically. "But our Bachelor this year, well, he's special . . . I'm guessing you won't want to dismiss him too early on. After all, it's not every day you have the opportunity to marry a millionaire."

Gina dropped the pine nuts onto the tray table and swore.

Stormy giggled.

A girl in front of me collapsed and needed to be slapped to be woken up.

A flight attendant started handing out champagne. Right, because that's just what these girls needed. More alcohol. Because that always helped people make sound decisions.

"All of you are here for two reasons." Rex eyed us all suspiciously, his orange face dancing with delight. "Money and love. But this year

66

we've brought you both in the same package. The choice is yours. Now, let's get to know the new Bachelor, shall we?"

I took a glass of champagne and watched in fascination as Max appeared on the screen.

"What's your full name?" a female voice asked.

Max rolled his eyes. "Are you serious right now? What are you filming this for again, Milo?"

The camera shook a bit. "Er, my future children. I want them to have memories of you, Max!"

Max's brow furrowed. "Because I'm going somewhere?"

The girl named Milo laughed. "No."

"Because you're assassinating me?" Max winked. "Seriously, Milo, what gives?"

"Fine." She set the camera down and walked around to join Max on the couch. She was really pretty. Funny, they looked good together. Almost too good. "Grandma asked me to."

"Grandma?" Max eyed her suspiciously and crossed his arms. Muscles bulged beneath his white T-shirt. Suddenly a bit . . . parched, I took a long, soothing sip of champagne. I hadn't noticed he was so fit. "The same grandma that took advantage of my brother, Reid, and made it so he weeps whenever he sees dentures? That grandma?"

"Don't be dramatic." Milo sniffed.

"Milo." Max braced her shoulders. "I'm the one who has to hear him sob into his pillow at night, dude's got it rough."

"Dude's a celebrity playboy." Milo rolled her eyes. "He'll be fine."

Max released her. "Also true."

"She wants us to build memories."

"Funny," Max joked. "Pretty sure the last thing Reid wants is to remember anything to do with your grandma. Swear that woman has the strength of Samson. Did you know she held him down and—"

"No more details." Milo waved him off. "Now, introduce yourself."

"Does she have dementia?" Max asked.

"Er, yes." Milo nodded. "Severe memory problems."

"I'll be sure to pass that information along to my brother. Maybe now he'll stop sleeping with a knife under his pillow."

"Max!" Milo smacked him. "Focus, now, state your name, weight, height, and favorite color."

Max's eyes narrowed before he turned to the camera and shrugged. "Max, and I'm not giving my last name because that's just ridiculous, I mean I'm pretty sure Grandma knows how to use a computer. How do I know she's not going to Google the shit out of me, find my home, seduce my brother, and take over the world?"

"Details." Milo waved him off. "Last name?"

"Emory." He sighed.

"Favorite color?"

"Peach."

"Liar."

"Orange."

"Max . . ."

"Fine, I like green because it reminds me of grass which in turn reminds me of your grass allergy and of that one time we rolled around in the grass for hours and I kissed every single part of your—" Max grinned. "Oh, hey, Colt, didn't see you there."

I heard a male mutter, "Ass" in the background.

"Job?"

"No thanks." Max shrugged.

"No," Milo groaned. "What's your job?"

Max's face paled as his body slumped a bit, then as soon as the action happened, it was like he snapped out of it, pulling a panty-melting smile out of nowhere and flashing it at the camera in such a way that I felt hot and cold all over.

"Aw, sweetie." Max licked his lips. "I think we both know I have a job that I take very, very seriously. After all, what type of man would I be if I didn't give of myself to all those single women? Come on, you've had a taste. You know it's good, so good that—" A pillow came flying at Max's face from behind the camera. "Colt, wow, you just keep popping up places. Weird, I didn't even notice you standing there. But then again you know what they say, small presence, small pe—"

"Max!" Milo shouted. "This is a disaster."

"Hey." Max held up his hands. "You're the one who wanted to film me for Grandma." He shivered. "Wow, just saying that out loud sounds like I sold my soul to pornography for the elderly."

"One more question!" Milo looked at the camera with desperation. It lifted and I figured the guy named Colt was on the other end. The camera zoomed in on Max's perfect face.

Damn, not even a scar.

No mark.

Nothing.

His skin was perfection. Then again, he was probably some metrosexual misfit who got his jollies by buying face cream and hitting the Nordstrom Anniversary Sale every year.

The guy probably couldn't chop down a tree to save his life.

"What are you looking for in a woman?"

"Why the hell does Grandma need to know that?" Max roared.

"Curious minds would like to know," Colt said, zooming the camera in even further on Max's perfect blue eyes. Wow, he was just . . . too pretty up close.

"Perfection," Max answered. "I want perfection." He looked to Milo. "Then again, I already had that and it didn't work out so well." Milo blushed, he winked, Colt cursed. "Fine, fine." Max turned toward the camera. "I'm easy. If I had my choice—I'd choose someone who could be my best friend every single time."

Milo's face fell. "Max—"

"We done?" He got up from the couch, his smile was forced. "I gotta go check on Reid and . . . yeah, see you guys for dinner."

The screen went blank and then another homemade movie popped up in which Max was engaging in a popcorn fight and then playing Ping-Pong like it was World War III.

The last scene was of a shirtless Max on a run, sweat pouring down every plane of his chiseled chest.

"Stats." Rex cleared his throat while the frame froze on Max's six-pack. "He's heir to the Emory Hotel chain. Net worth around twenty million, give or take a few. He graduated from NYU with a degree in poli-sci, which he has yet to put to any use. He plays lacrosse, soccer, and enjoys going for long runs. Your first competition . . ." You could hear a pin drop in that plane. "Get him to kiss you. He kisses you—you stay. No kiss? You're on the next flight out. You have forty-eight hours."

CHAPTER ELEVEN

MAX

Chocolate. Damn, it tasted good. Milo held out the doughnut, but just as I leaned forward she pulled it back and took a bite, sinking her white teeth into the softness of the dough—stealing the breath right out of my body.

"Be the doughnut, Max." She winked.

"How about I just kiss you?" I offered lamely. Because that's what best friends do. It had started as a stupid crush, but there's something about seeing the girl you're crushing on not crushing back, that kind of kills a man's pride. Sure, we would have never worked. But when she'd married Colt, I'd kind of lost a part of myself. The only part I actually liked. She'd made me feel confident, carefree, and selfless . . . so losing Milo? Well, it was like being abandoned in the deep end with no water wings and absolutely no recollection of how to swim.

"Damn doughnut." I scowled and crossed my arms.

"Aw." Milo licked her pink lips and leaned forward, her face inches from mine. A piece of chocolate frosting had found its way onto the corner of her mouth.

"You missed a spot," I said in a husky voice.

"So get it for me," she challenged, her eyes narrowing in on my lips.

The chair creaked as I moved closer; my mouth hovered over hers and then something wet touched my face.

"What the—"

Milo tilted her head.

And more wetness.

I blinked as the dream disappeared and was replaced with what I'd like to say is every guy's nightmare times fifty.

Things were still fuzzy on account that I'm pretty sure I'd been given a pill that I saw on *Nightline* a few nights back could cause sudden death and slight hallucinations—but one thing was clear.

I was getting straddled by Amazon.

And she had just licked my face.

And not in a way that made every male part of my body rejoice in excitement. No, try the exact opposite.

She smelled like pine nuts.

And it just so happened that she was kneeing me in the nuts, which I thought fit pretty well, all things considering.

"Hey there, lover," she purred.

"That work?" I whispered. "Calling a guy *lover*? Does that normally get them all hot and bothered before you knee them in the boys, or is that part of your game? You hurt them and then they finally give up? That turn you on?"

Stop talking, Max, stop talking!

Amazon's gaze narrowed until her eyes were tiny slits. Well, shit, I was about two seconds away from getting neutered.

"Kiss me." She gripped my hair so tight I was pretty sure I'd have two bald spots for the rest of the TV show.

"Um, no thanks." Hey, she might have been crazy but I was still raised to have manners.

"Kiss me, bitch!" She tugged harder, and beads of sweat rolled down my temples. Where the hell was my security? And why was the host letting women attack me? My terrified mind went back to last season, when they'd said they were going to make changes to the show.

Changes, changes, changes.

Money.

Competition.

Game.

Funny, all the tiny little pieces of the puzzle finally settled in, and instead of adding to the fear—it just added to the rage.

I'd never considered myself an angry person, but lately there was a feeling within me that seemed to be building into this horrible thing I couldn't control. I felt anger at every turn—at myself, my parents, even Milo for abandoning me and marrying Colt just when I was starting to get comfortable with my place in the world.

Over the past few weeks, the anger had turned into a simmering rage at feeling worthless because I hadn't been working.

Colt got the girl because Colt had a job. Well, that and Milo had been obsessed with him for years . . . but still, it made me wonder what I had to offer.

What *did* I have? I had money, but no purpose, no real direction for what I wanted to do.

The rage grew.

I literally had so many options I didn't know which one to choose and then felt like a guilty dumbass because how many people can say they have that many good options in life? I had everything handed to me. I should have been happy. Instead I was lost and confused, unsure of my place in the world and why I even mattered. People work for two reasons. To pay the bills and because they like it.

I didn't need to pay bills.

But I wanted to like what I did. I just didn't know what I liked, not anymore.

"Hello?" Amazon snorted. "You alive?"

"I'm breathing, aren't I?" I snapped.

Amazon pulled back a bit, her eyes widening.

"Go sit down," I ordered.

"But—"

"Sit." I lifted her off my lap—a bit impressed with myself that I was able to do so, considering her obvious height advantage—and followed her as we walked toward the back of the plane, where the rest of the girls were sitting.

Amazon ducked into her seat and looked down at her hands while the rest of the group fell into a hush.

A hand touched my shoulder. "Max." Rex chuckled. "Didn't expect you to wake up so soon!"

"Nightmares," I said coolly. "You know how it goes."

Rex squeezed that same shoulder. "We'll be landing in about twenty minutes, why don't you go back and—"

"No." I licked my lips and watched as the girls all shifted nervously in their seats. "I think I'll stay right here."

"But—"

"Thanks, Rex, you can go now." I shrugged away from him and walked up to the first row of girls. Three of them. Each had manicured nails, perfect sleek dark hair, and perceptive eyes. The ones you can tell are calculating your every move.

So I did what I do best.

I played their game.

Because one thing was for certain. I wasn't going to play the victim on the Island—and I sure as hell was going to have my own streak of fun.

Not only were my best friends going to be watching from back home, compliments of the network streaming select episodes online, but apparently my life had made room for some changes.

And this was what a change looked like.

Twenty-five eager women.

None of whom I could trust—because they all wanted to win money. Who knew if love was on the table?

But that fit in just fine with my life plan—because I'd decided a few weeks ago that if I couldn't have someone who could be my best friend and partner, I was going to stay single the rest of my life. No time for the headache that came with relationships, and I'm pretty sure God only made one Milo.

So I zeroed in on the first three girls, purposefully marched over to them, and hovered over their seats so they could get close enough to smell my cologne, near enough to see my smile and the flicker of my eyes. With a smirk I winked. "Hey, girls."

In a fluster they all started speaking at once.

It wasn't until someone nudged me in the back that I realized the camera crew was filming everything.

Game. On.

CHAPTER TWELVE
BECCA

The minute Gina returned I knew something was up. Max didn't look like himself. Not that in the one day I'd known him I actually knew what normal looked like, but he had dark circles under his eyes and a confidence about him I'd missed during our initial run-in.

In fact, his face basically said, "Screw off" to the entire world.

Was it wrong to find the anger marring his face slightly attractive?

I swallowed and tried to look away when he sat down next to the three youngest girls on the show. They'd decided to group together—alliances were getting built and there I was still drooling over the guy who, when we first met, had used the worst pick-up line known to mankind on me and actually appeared to believe the crap himself.

Laughter sounded from where Max was leaning over the girls. One of them reached up and touched his chest. I squirmed in my seat while the girl on the far left whispered something in his ear.

His eyes widened and then he took a step back and looked around the rest of the seats, his face completely white.

"Are you sure?" I heard him whisper to the first girl.

She nodded. "The producer said not to tell."

Right. Like I said, they were the youngest. And HELLO, the producer was standing a few feet away. Surely he'd hear her say that, unless that was part of her strategy. The camera crew focused in on Max. His face went from white to flushed and then white again.

Curious, I watched as he slowly walked up the aisle and disappeared.

Okay. I know I was supposed to stay in my seat. And I shouldn't have cared. I didn't care, I just . . . he looked upset and . . . I was a barista! I made people happy for a living, right? One cup of coffee at a time? Wasn't Starbucks' entire mantra to make the customer happy?

Right, was I really using that as an excuse to chase a guy in a dating game in hopes of winning some money? Howard Schultz would have been so disappointed.

Then again, if I saved the Bachelor, he might just give me one of those fancy cards rumored to give you free coffee for life.

For life.

Sacrifice officially worth it.

I unbuckled my seat belt and hightailed it out of coach toward the first-class cabin.

I greedily searched for Max; he was back in his seat with a few sheets of paper in his hand. He stuck a pen in his mouth and narrowed his eyes as he examined the papers.

"What are you doing?" I blurted. Wow. Smooth. So smooth.

"Thinking," Max said without looking up.

"Finally." I sat down next to him.

"Funny." He tapped the pen against his mouth.

I watched.

Not because I was attracted but because I was concerned that the, um, pen would leak and how embarrassing would that be if he had a blue mouth for the rest of the week?

"Stop staring at me," he sang. "Unless I have something on my face, and then you're obligated to tell me on account that you've been staring so hard it would be embarrassing otherwise, so what is it? Crumb? Pieces of Amazonian pine nuts? Because I'm pretty sure that woman's damn well marked me. I'm surprised she hasn't peed on my pants or something."

"Amazon?" I laughed.

"The tall one." I nodded. "I nicknamed her Amazon, look." He pointed to the sheet he had in his hands, where Gina's picture was located. Underneath it he'd written, "Amazon."

"Clever."

"I thought so." He put a giant X over her face and moved on to the next one.

"So which one is she?"

"Jayne." He nodded.

"But her name's Sarah."

"Right." Max put another X over her picture. "But my trigger word is Jayne on account that every time I hear that name my boys do a little dance in my pants. Not a good dance, so don't slap me, but the kind that makes me kind of wish I was batting for the other team, and no straight man should ever have to utter that sentence aloud. Humiliating. Oh, and P.S.: She's terrifying. I'd take my chances with a goat any day."

"Because goats are terrifying?" I leaned in so I could see the rest of the pictures.

Max dropped the papers onto his lap and turned to face me. "Have you seen a goat?"

"Are you serious?"

Max rolled his eyes. "Goats be crazy. They have red eyes, they'll eat anything, including your shirt, and they have no manners. Plus they're unpredictable. I like my animals . . . slow."

"This is the weirdest conversation I've ever had."

"Whatever, I'm just trying to explain my feelings."

"About goats."

"About Jayne!" Max lifted his hands into the air. "Hey, what are you even doing up here anyways? This is a camera-free zone and we're supposed to be landing soon."

Embarrassed, I leaned back in the seat and shrugged. "I was worried Gina, also known as Amazon, was hunting you again."

"Yeah, well." Max shrugged. "I'll be sure to use my bow and arrow next time she decides to trounce through my forest."

"There's a sexual innuendo somewhere in there, isn't there?"

"Aw." Max winked. "Would you like there to be?"

"So about the goats . . ."

Max shuddered. "If you stay, you have to help."

"Help?" I chewed my lower lip. "Help with what?"

"My strategy."

"But I'm a contestant."

"But I've already decided to keep you," Max whispered.

"Really?" All breath left my body as he leaned in.

"Yeah." He smirked. "Like a little . . . pet."

Deflated, I rolled my eyes. "Wow, thank you, best compliment I've ever received."

"Hey, at least you're not Amazon."

"What's my nickname?" I reached for the sheets but he pushed my hands away.

"No looking."

"Max . . ." I fluttered my eyelashes and licked my lips.

"Nice try." He released my hands. "But I'm the king of playing that game, sweetheart, you can't just go up against the master and expect to come out the victor."

"What game?" I asked innocently.

"Really?" Max licked his lips, then eyed me up and down. "It's amazing what the human body's capable of, like if I lean forward, your breathing picks up, but then again so does mine. That's what happens when you get close to someone else—you pick up on their energy, you pick up on their lust. So right now, I expect you to press your breasts together, to lean down so that I see part of your skin but not enough to actually give me an idea of what you look like naked. I expect your eyes to dilate as if you want to take everything in, and lick your lips one more time. The first time I missed the action of your tongue sliding out of your mouth, which means it wasn't on purpose—it was because you were nervous."

He pulled back and slapped me on the knee.

Holy crap.

I made a move to stand up. I was a bit in over my head, a bit flustered, and a whole lot of curious and possibly . . . a bit . . . attracted.

"Flight attendants, prepare for landing!" the captain said over the loudspeaker.

I tried to stand up but the flight attendant walked by and told me to buckle up.

Before I had a chance to reach for my seat belt, Max's hands were already on it, and adjusting it in my lap. "You heard her." His lips grazed my ear. "She said buckle up."

I closed my eyes and leaned my head against the headrest. So not going as planned. But if Max was planning on keeping me, that meant he knew what we had to accomplish in order to stay.

"Max . . ." I didn't open my eyes. "Did the girls—"

The plane dropped.

At least a few hundred feet.

I screamed.

Max gripped my hand.

And then the plane leveled out.

"That was a rush," Max said dryly.

"Why." Sweating. I was sweating. I hated flying. And it didn't help that I was trapped next to the only guy who had better skin than me and had such a blinding smile that it made you trip on your own feet.

"Why what?" Why did he suddenly sound so controlled?

"Why did you pick me to stay?"

"College," Max said slowly, before the plane dipped again. "You aren't here for me. Admit it."

"I, uh, I want commitment too."

"You're like that new Geico commercial with Pinocchio and his nose just keeps growing, or is that Progressive? I keep getting the two mixed up."

"No, it's just I—"

"You just what?" Max's hands moved to my face, and my eyes fluttered open. "You just want to win?"

"Yeah, but—"

"I help you, you help me," Max said. "We both get off the Island without getting eaten by sharks and women. Win-win."

"I'm not afraid of women," I fired back.

"No, but you're absolutely terrified of sharks. It says right here in your profile."

"Damn you."

"Aw, thanks." There went that smile again. "So what do you say? Partners?"

"But—"

"Make your choice, it's me or them." Max's eyes focused on something behind me. "Fine, I'm making it for you."

"Wha—"

His mouth was on mine before I could protest.

And what was originally going to be my plan—to seduce the man, get the money, get out—suddenly took a drastic turn toward hell, because he kissed like he had all the time in the world. He kissed like I was the only girl for him—kissed me like every girl dreams of being kissed.

When he released me, a camera was immediately shoved in my face.

Too disappointed and irritated to admit my disappointment, I flashed a grin and swallowed.

"So." Max's voice had completely changed, going from seductive to indifferent within the span of two seconds. "How about those sharks?"

He was looking out the window but his hand had found mine underneath the armrest.

I squeezed back and answered, "How about all those women?"

"I won't let the sharks eat you." His eyes narrowed in on my lips. "Swear."

"Don't worry, I won't let the women eat you either." I smiled in return, knowing that I'd probably just made a deal with the devil.

So why the hell was I excited about it?

CHAPTER THIRTEEN

MAX

I'd gone through a prostate exam—one that, P.S., still gives me a little shudder—a dental exam, STD testing . . . I mean, you name it, I'd gone through it. All for a show.

And up until this point, I'd been pissed. I mean, seriously, a doctor had his hands . . . never mind.

But kissing Becca?

Kind of made all that pain and awkwardness worth it. I mean I still wasn't happy about getting tricked into doing the show, and I sure as hell wasn't going to let my so-called friends get away with their little intervention, but still. Maybe *tricked* was too strong a word . . . I probably could have backed out, or at least told the producers I had some sort of contagious disease that meant I couldn't be out in public. I should have just claimed Ebola, which would have bought me at least three weeks.

So I was back to the original issue. Clearly I was desperate enough to have gone along with my friends and their insane idea.

I mean, surely I could have tried harder to fight the contract, right? Was I that bored? That upset about the direction my life was taking?

I licked my lips, remembering the feel of hers.

It had been a good kiss.

Hell, who was I kidding? It had been a damn good kiss.

The only problem? I'd just made an alliance with the one girl I couldn't actually like—because it would work against me, against us. The other women would target her and honestly, what if we had some sort of connection, and the game ruined whatever chances we had because she was so focused on the competition and the money?

And I'd made my choice, taken the show back into my own hands by way of manipulating information out of the weak, and decided to send the ones home who didn't belong—only keeping those who needed either the money or a free vacation.

Yeah, before you get all swoony on me for actually having a heart, just remember, I would still be toying with all their emotions.

Becca bolted when the plane landed. I hoped it wasn't a sign that I was the worst kisser on the planet . . . because she tripped over her own feet to get the hell away from me.

Wasn't the first time.

I made women either swoon or run. Reid on the other hand just made them swoon, the bastard.

Ugh.

"So." Rex appeared out of thin air, his orange skin more orangey now that humidity was starting to seep into the plane. Curious, I wondered if he was melting. Furthermore, if I threw water on him, would I suddenly discover he was albino? I eyed the ocean curiously. "We'll let the girls off first and then you can follow the crowd to the beach house."

Beach house, now that sounded better. After being put through endless hours of torture watching the show with Milo, I knew that at least the contestants were given kick-ass food and a place to stay, not to mention top-shelf liquor.

So it wasn't going to be all bad.

Ten minutes later I realized it was going to, in fact, be bad.

"What do you mean you lost my luggage?" I tried to keep my voice calm, when really I wanted to shake Rex's orange body until his head popped off.

"It won't be a problem." Rex patted his head with a cloth and put on his sunglasses. "We'll have the luggage delivered as soon as possible. Let's get you a nice drink, how's that sound?"

"Fine." I was tired, jet-lagged, and still reeling from that kiss. It didn't help that we were staying on a private island, meaning we had to take a boat ride to get there, and damn I just wanted to take a nap, check the area for wild goats, and have a beer. Probably not in that order, but whatever.

The boat ride took a half hour.

The girls were in the boat ahead of me, but they were staying on the opposite end of the Island, which sounded freaking awesome until I found out the Island was only a mile long.

Which begged the question.

Where the hell did I run?

We were in the freaking Society Islands, somewhere near Bora Bora. The only thing I could do was look at a damn map, find the largest of the islands, and try to swim to it without getting eaten by a shark or taken by pirates.

Ah, pirates. I'd forgotten about pirates.

Ahoy.

"Allergies?" Someone poked me in the arm. What the? I looked up as the on-set doctor poked me with another needle and examined my skin, then looked down at his iPad.

"Um, ouch?" I seriously, seriously, wanted to poke the bastard back.

But then I realized, in my head, that I hated the word *poke*. Who made up that word anyway? One should never poke. Poking assumed . . .

entering someone's skin by force, right? Wow, that pill must have done a number on me.

"Looks fine." The doctor nodded and reached up. I flinched. Hey, not my fault—Grandpops had classically conditioned me to be wary of anyone wearing latex.

Latex . . . what else was made with latex?

"No!" I screamed and fell to my knees.

"Damn it!" The doctor pulled something out of a case, and I felt a tight pinch. "He's having an allergic reaction to the shot!"

"You shot me?" I yelled back, then looked down at my arm and started rubbing it. Wait, what just happened?

"To make sure you wouldn't have an allergic reaction," he said calmly, pulling out another giant-ass needle and flicking it. Without any hesitation he stabbed me again, just in case. His words, not mine.

"And if I would have?" Who was this monster? *I demand to see his degree!*

The doctor flicked the needle. "We would have made sure to give you some medicine to counteract the effects just in case the worst happened."

"Worst?"

"Death."

One of the producers chuckled.

"Ha-ha." I joined in, then pushed the doctor's hands away. "And I'm not having a reaction. I'm fine. I just . . . panicked."

"Oh, yeah?" He peeled off his latex gloves. "You sure?"

I shivered. "Yeah, I'm sure."

"Paradise." Rex slapped me on the shoulder and took a deep breath. "Your hut will be over—"

"Hut?" I interrupted. "You said *beach house.*"

"Ah, the beach house is headquarters, command central if you get my meaning. But you'll be staying on the beach."

"That's not so bad . . ."

"Just be sure the mosquito nets are covering your bed. You don't want any of those little bastards sneaking in and chomping on your parts, am I right?" He laughed and elbowed me.

"Right." I stared hard at the beach as the boat docked.

A hut.

One single hut was on the shore.

It wasn't really small.

But it wasn't big either. In fact it looked like something off of *Survivor*, so that was new. Last year the show had had a penthouse for the contestants. Swear the only thing that got me off the boat was visions of strangling Jason with my mosquito-bite-swollen hands.

I'm leaving a production crew with you and seven others with the girls. They'll be given instructions to explore the Island tonight. Your only task is to get to know them and stay alive." He kept a straight face.

I felt mine pale.

"Ha-ha!" Rex laughed and slapped me on the back. "I'm a kidder, I kid. You'll be fine!" He laughed harder. "The only lizard sighting they've even had was at least fifty years ago."

"L-lizard?" I repeated.

The captain of the boat suddenly dropped what he was doing, made a cross in the air, and then spit behind him and stomped his foot three times.

"You're shitting me."

Rex waved him off. "Silly superstition."

The captain stomped again. Was that a tear? Was he crying?

"Right." I licked my lips and slowly made my way off the boat.

The captain stopped me and put a piece of metal in my hand, then bent over it. "For the ghosts."

"Ghosts?" Ah, even more fun surprises to look forward to.

"The Island is haunted with Polynesian ancestors—ones who are upset about the state of the Island's natural resources." He nodded. "But the metal protects, it wards them off."

"And the lizards?"

The captain proceeded to do the same little spit-and-stomp thing and shuddered. "Only God can save you."

"Awesome." Well, at least there weren't goats!

The film crew followed me as we made our way onto the beach and into the hut. It was actually a lot bigger than I'd originally thought. Kind of cozy and—

"SHIT!" I fell back against the door and froze as the shadow of the giant lizard started moving slowly toward me. "Stay back!" I held up the metal piece knowing full well it would do shit, but still.

The shadow got smaller, and then a small green gecko poked out from the wall and waved. Okay, so he didn't wave, but I felt like such an ass that he might as well have.

A gecko.

Harmless.

"Hey there, little guy." I approached him slowly and held out my hand. The gecko scurried away. "I shall call you Little G," I announced. "My only friend. My only partner."

"Uh, you do know we're filming this, right?" the producer said from behind me.

"If I go insane and get eaten by one of the women, give my seat on the plane to Little G."

"Right." The producer nodded. "Should you sit?"

"What's your name?"

"Al."

"Can I call you Big Al?"

"Whatever gets you to do crazy shit and up our ratings." He smiled.

"Ah, like naming the gecko and adopting it?"

"Nah, like getting a soccer ball, drawing the woman's face on it, and sleeping with it at night because you're so torn up she left half-way through the show. Forty million views on that YouTube."

"Didn't he go insane?" I vaguely remembered the last Bachelor doing something like that, but the details were blurry.

"He got some sort of island sickness."

"It's called the syph." I nodded. "It happens when you sleep with that many women over and over and over again."

"Still recording."

"Still don't care." I sighed. "So where do I go now?"

"The bonfire." Al sniffed. "But until then, why don't you tell us how you're feeling being on the Island, are you excited? Scared?"

I rolled my eyes and looked directly in the camera when I said, "I'm so excited I almost shit my pants."

"Yeah." Al licked his lips. "You're just full of joy, I can tell."

"Or shit." I smirked. "Take your pick. Speaking of picking, I have women to choose."

"Good luck with that, they've been drinking for the past hour."

"So they're dehydrated, drunk, on an island, and desperate?"

"Yeah." Al nodded. "Sounds about right."

"Well, God bless the USA." I made my way toward the door. "Shall we?"

CHAPTER FOURTEEN
BECCA

Going on a show to win money? Officially the worst idea I'd ever had and that includes keeping the whole scrunchie trend alive throughout my freshman year of college.

Well, that and my homemade tie-dye shirt.

"Party!" The three young ones that I'd nicknamed lost sheep were already three sheets to the wind, and Max had yet to arrive. Amazon—damn him for making it so that I couldn't think of her as Gina anymore—was swimming naked in the ocean. One could only hope a shark would catch a whiff of the pine nuts and finish her off—and the rest of the girls were drinking and in various states of undress.

There was enough alcohol to put Arizona State University to shame, and that was saying a lot.

There were five girls to each hut. Each hut had a camera crew and a fully stocked bar. But guess what? No food.

That's right.

Nothing to soak up the alcohol, not unless any of the girls wanted to go hunting through what jungle we had. Pretty sure that if the worst did happen, the animal would be so petrified of the drunk girl it would just give up and keel over and die on purpose. Hey, I know I would if Amazon were charging toward me.

"The fun has arrived!" Max announced, coming around the corner.

"Ah, shucks, I was hoping for food," I said, joining him.

"Have a taste." He winked. "Swear I won't bite back."

I opened my mouth to say something snappy but was pushed out of the way by one of the other girls, whom I hadn't had the pleasure of nicknaming yet.

"Max! I had shots!"

"Did you?" He nodded. "How many? Hold up your fingers."

"Four!" She held up two fingers.

I winced.

Max patted her head. "Let's find you some water."

"Kiss me, Max!"

He shrugged and planted one—directly on her forehead. "Now, let's find you some water."

"Does that count?" I whispered under my breath once he'd walked off with the girl.

"Sure does." The producer stayed behind and wrote something down on a piece of paper. "The rules were vague. They said get the Bachelor to kiss you and you stay."

"But . . ." I touched my lips; they buzzed with excitement. If Max knew that . . . why hadn't he just kissed my hand? Or maybe he wasn't aware of the rules at all?

"Hey, Little B, you coming?" Max called behind him and held out his hand.

I ran up to join him but didn't take his hand. "Little B?"

"Yeah, because you have little—"

My eyes narrowed.

"Hold that thought." He held up his hand and jogged over to the chairs on the beach where around five girls, the shy ones, were lying down. With speed and precision he lifted each one's hat and/or sunglasses and placed a kiss across her temple.

"Six." I applauded when he made his way back to me.

"Seven." His brow furrowed. "You have trouble counting like the drunk one, or are you just checking my math?"

"Sorry." I felt my face heat.

"Whoa!" Max laughed. "And an apology?"

I glared.

"Hold that thought too." He jogged off to another section where some girls were congregating and went down on one knee, pulling their hands to his lips.

I waited.

And smiled.

And tried desperately not to be charmed that he was not only making each and every one of the girls feel kind of special and silly at the same time, but that he wasn't making it a big deal. It wasn't about him, and the thing about the show? It was always about the guy. Even with the money on the line it was always about the guy and how hot he was and how impressive.

With Max, it was almost like he hated the attention. But didn't all good-looking guys like attention? He was a conundrum; on one hand he seemed to be the biggest player on the planet.

But if he were . . . he would have been kissing all of the girls— with tongue.

Rather than going down on bended knee in the sand and taking their hands in his, kissing their knuckles and making them feel . . . like that kiss was better than one on the lips.

I got tired waiting for him, plus he looked like he was having a good time, so I went toward the ocean and dipped my feet in.

"Happy to see the shark phobia doesn't affect you on the shore," Max said smoothly from behind.

"Don't you have girls to kiss?" I asked without turning around.

"I need five more." Max walked up beside me. "Help me make my choices?"

"You want me to help you pick out the next five?"

"Yup. Who do you want to keep?"

Before I could answer, a camera crew came walking in our direction. I tucked the hair behind my ear and pointed so he would know.

"I've got this . . ." Max winked and then I was in the air, slung over his shoulder like a sack of potatoes.

He ran straight for the water. With all of his clothes on.

I'd had time to change into a bathing suit underneath my white cover-up. Max, however, was in low-slung jeans and a T-shirt.

But it didn't deter him from going all the way under and taking me with him. I gasped as the water hit my head. Max's body pushed me farther under, and then he lifted me up just as I was ready to gasp for air.

"What the hell!" I smacked his shoulder.

"You're welcome." He grinned, water dripping from his hair onto his face.

"For almost drowning me?"

"Hey, is that any way to thank me for saving your life?"

"How do you figure?" I splashed water at him. We were a good distance from the shore but I could still stand. The camera crew, however, stayed put.

"We were about to get discovered by the producers. On top of that, I still need your help and I totally saw a shark about two seconds ago, punched it in the nose, and demanded it leave. See? Saved your life!"

"Shark?" I repeated, looking frantically around the clear blue water. "Shark?"

"Aw, Little B—"

I launched myself into his arms, wrapping my legs around his waist. If I was getting eaten, so was he.

Clawing at his chest, I shuddered as the thought of a shark touching me finally became my reality. I was going to die!

Max cleared his throat. "Whatcha doin'?"

"Taking you with me." I squeezed my eyes shut.

"Where we goin'?"

"Hell! Because we're going to get eaten and we went on a reality show and everyone knows reality shows are like a free ticket to hell! They're awful and I'm sorry I wanted the money! You hear me, God? I'm sorry! But I need to finish school and I—"

Cold water hit my face, making me choke. Did that bastard just dunk me? I clawed to the surface and then felt Max's warmth as he pulled me into his arms again. "We done freaking out yet?"

"You son of a—"

Cold water again. Damn, he was strong.

When he lifted me up the second time, I was so pissed my arms and legs went flailing in all directions.

"No sharks," Max said calmly. "Joke, I was joking. Wow, you really must be terrified of them."

"I'm going to name a goat Max, then sacrifice it so its spirit haunts you for the rest of your life."

Max froze. "I will freaking buy an aquarium and name every damn shark after you, then train them to roar whenever they see your picture."

"False, sharks don't roar."

Max's eyes narrowed. "Mine will."

"What, because your sharks are going to be special hybrids?"

"They'll be badass! Just don't sacrifice the goat!"

"I think I'll buy a second goat, and send you picture texts of him in various states of rage in your house, so that you never have peace and—"

"Fine!" Max shouted. "I'm sorry, leave the goats out of it!"

"Then don't lie about sharks!"

"I like you." Max nodded. "You fight fire with fire. I think if we ever get off this island and the world gets taken over by zombies, I want you as my second-in-command."

"Aw." I nodded. "Sweetest thing a guy's ever said to me."

"Comes from the heart." He sighed and then yawned. "So about those girls."

"I don't know their names."

"Sure you do." Max turned me around and pointed at the beach. "There's Angry, Grumpy, Sneezy, Dopey, and Doc. Not gonna lie— kind of on the fence about Doc."

"We're naming them after the Seven Dwarfs?"

"Tell me you don't see the similarity!" Max pointed. The girl he'd dubbed Angry did have a permanent scowl. Grumpy just looked, well, grumpy, she had short hair and was using sticks to try to build a fire. Don't ask me why. Dopey was frolicking across the sand. I imagined she also believed in unicorns and had a pet butterfly. And Doc, well, Doc . . . I tilted my head. "Why don't we like Doc?"

"Nobody likes Doc." Max crossed his arms. "He's like the one dwarf everyone's on the fence about, people don't forget him because his name doesn't even make sense—I mean what does he do?"

"He's the doctor. I can't believe I'm participating in this conversation."

"Um, believe it, and do they ever come out and say oh, P.S., This is Doc, he's the resident doctor for the dwarfs, oh, and he looks like a bazillion times older than the rest of them."

"No, but—"

"Doc." He pointed at the girl. "Her hair looks more white than blond, and she doesn't fit in, she's a bit sketch. Yeah, I'm going with Doc."

"Well, now I feel bad, keep Doc."

"Damn it." Max hit the water with his hand. "The things I do for you, Little B, the things I do."

I rolled my eyes. "And keep Angry, Grumpy looks like Eeyore and we don't need an Eeyore in the group."

"Aw, you're using cartoons as examples." Max clapped. "I'm so proud."

"It's the company I keep these days."

"Badass company," Max replied. "Okay, so that leaves . . . Sneezy?"

"Why is she Sneezy?"

"Oh." Max pointed. "It's not her, it's me. Every time I walk by her I sneeze. I'm not saying it's a sign, but come on, nature's basically telling me I'm allergic to her, imagine what would happen if we slept together and—"

"And let's just not finish that sentence."

"Fine, so I still need three more girls, right?" Max's eyes searched the beach. "Make that two: I'm going to keep Dopey as well. Maybe we'll get lucky, and she'll be shy. So that leaves . . ."

"Sneezy." I smirked. As if on cue, Max sneezed and sent me a glare.

"Fine." He huffed. "And the final seashell goes to . . ."

"Gina." I answered. "I know you hate her, we all hate her, but here's the thing, she's tough. I mean, how many people can say they know how to build a fire with their bare hands? If we get stuck here forever—she's our only ticket out."

"So Gina's our survival." Max winced. "It feels wrong to put our lives in her nutty hands."

"Guy's gotta do what a guy's gotta do."

"What? What do you mean?"

I pushed him toward the shore. "You gotta go kiss your girls, Max."

"Just kidding. We so aren't going to be partners in the zombie apocalypse!

"Pucker up!"

He flipped me off.

But honestly? It felt more like a high five between friends.

CHAPTER FIFTEEN

MAX

And to think I had totally been about to offer the position of best friend to Becca after she used the Eeyore reference! I stomped toward shore, my heart a little bit lighter after our conversation, and turned around to give her one last wave.

She lifted her hand, and it froze midair. Her smile turned to a look of horror and her eyes went so big I came to the only conclusion I could. She'd seen a shark.

Frantic, I looked around my feet, I mean I was in some shallow water but still there wasn't a chance in hell that—

"Maa-aaa."

I gulped and very slowly turned around.

A goat.

Was on the beach.

And the girls were petting it!

"Back!" I yelled. "Get back!"

The goat, clearly taking my terrified yell as a sign of aggression, chose that opportunity to charge toward me, and bits of sand flew underneath its hooves as it galloped in my direction. And I, being the coward I am, ran in the opposite direction.

Toward Becca.

"Remember that zombie apocalypse scenario we talked about?" I yelled, half running and half swimming toward her in the ocean.

"Yeah?" Her eyes were trained behind me.

"Now would be a good time to man up!"

"Goats can't swim."

"This goat can! I can feel him!"

"He stopped at the shore." Becca pointed; I rose to my feet and slowly turned. The demon-possessed goat was peeing on a rock and harmlessly licking its hoof. Bastard. I was going to shoot it, then cook it. For no other reason than that I wanted it dead and the only way was to . . . okay, so maybe I wouldn't eat it. Too far, Max, too far.

"Wait." I scratched my head. "If the goat's up there, then why did I feel something grab my back?"

"Don't move!" Becca held up her hands.

"Okay, you know that makes me want to move, right? That's exactly what people say when you have a giant-ass spider on you or when something's about to drop on your head! Let me move, Becca—I want to move!"

"You can't!" Becca shook her head. "You need to stay."

"I'm not your dog!" I wailed.

"Max," Becca warned. "Just give me a minute to figure it out."

The entire beach was watching. The camera crew was trained on us like there was a freaking shark on my back. Holy shit, was there? Did sharks do that?

"What is this?" I yelled toward the beach. "Freaking *Fear Factor*?"

"Got it!" Becca announced happily. "Phew, that was close."

"What?"

"Seaweed." She lifted it in the air. "Can be very dangerous. Why,

I've read news stories where it wrapped around someone and choked them to death."

My eyes narrowed.

"I'm waiting," she said.

"For?"

"A thank-you."

"It was seaweed."

"Could have been a goat."

I sniffed. "I had the goat handled."

"You almost drowned *handling* it, but yeah, good plan."

"I was going to drown with him!" I shouted.

"So you both die?"

"I didn't say I thought it through, Becca!"

"Is this our first fight?" she teased.

"Only if I win." I grumbled.

"Fine, you win. You're the great goat killer and seaweed's attracted to your power."

"Is it wrong that I actually felt pride swell in my body? That wasn't a metaphor, it is totally a real thing." I nodded. "At any rate, thanks."

Becca's grin was wide; she held out her hand and gave me a high five. "What are friends for?"

"Did you know . . ." I wrapped my arm around her shoulder. "The position of best friend is open too."

"Oh, is it?" Her eyes twinkled. "Would I have to give up my role as your partner in the zombie apocalypse?"

"Never. That shit's real." I splashed water toward her. "Being a best friend does have perks."

"Oh, yeah? What kind of perks?"

"Hi." I held out my hand for her to shake. "Name's Perk."

"Aw, it rhymes with *perv,* don't you think?"

"Not really." I shook my head. "Both start with *P* but it was a good try, amateur. You'll get better the more you're exposed to my greatness."

"You make a girl feel so good."

"Oh, sweetheart, if I had a dollar . . ." We reached the shore, both of us grinning like idiots. Big Al stepped out from behind the camera and asked if I was okay, while the rest of the girls fluttered around me. But my mind wasn't on them, it was on Becca, a new partner in crime, who just happened to kiss . . . very, very, very, very, okay I needed to stop with the *very*s. She kissed well. Let's put it that way.

Which reminded me . . . "Angry, Amazon, Sneezy, Doc, Dopey, you're up!"

The girls looked at me like I was insane, but Becca snorted with laughter. I rolled my eyes and approached each girl, whispered sweet nothings, and kissed her hand.

When I approached Amazon I almost backed away but I needed to put on a brave face. After all I did just try to drown myself because I thought a goat was chasing me. Hey, where was the goat?

I placed the quickest kiss known to mankind on Gina, careful to keep one eye trained on her lest she make another sudden movement and get ahold of my hair again, then searched the beach.

I should have known.

With a curse I stomped over to the tiki bar they'd set on the sand and shook my head in dismay. "Traitor. I knew I offered the title of best friend too soon."

A camera crew followed me but I didn't care. It wasn't like we were talking strategy anymore; we were just . . . talking.

"Aw, look, he's harmless."

The goat reached for my hand.

I backed away.

The goat reached again.

"He needs to smell you," Becca said sternly. "He's afraid."

"That's how they lure you in." I leveled a gaze on the goat. "Huh, big guy? You lure people in with your crazy eyes, then eat them. And what are you, anyway? The damn goat whisperer?"

"Has a sort of ring to it." Becca flashed me another one of her pretty smiles and leaned down. "Come on Max, be brave."

"I choose . . . the opposite of bravery."

"Cowardice."

"I hate that word. It doesn't go very well with Max. Max the Coward. I prefer Max the Magnificent."

"You played way too much G.I. Joe when you were young, didn't you?"

"Stupid Snake Eyes got me every time. Damn you!" I pointed to the sky and then looked down at the goat. "Fine, let it sniff me, but if it bites a finger off we're swimming with sharks."

"Deal." Becca's eyebrow arched.

I closed my eyes.

And felt sniffing. Licking. And . . . no biting. I opened one eye, then the other. The goat was sniffing me and then suddenly lost interest.

"Wait!" I patted his head. "Why doesn't he like me?"

"What?" Becca burst out laughing. "First you're afraid to attract it and now you're mad it doesn't like you?"

"Everyone likes me." I leaned down. "Come on, Billy, give Uncle Max a chance."

"Everything you just said gave me the creeps." Becca held up her hands.

I rolled my eyes. "Maybe he needs a snack?"

"And now you want to feed it?" Becca asked, her voice rising in pitch.

"It's the way to a man's stomach."

"And goats and men are what? Interchangeable?"

"They both have balls."

"I need to find new friends."

"You love me." I winked. "Now let's get him a snack. Actually, we need to find out when they're feeding us because some of those girls look like they could use bread. Lots and lots of bread."

CHAPTER SIXTEEN
BECCA

Finding food proved more difficult then we'd realized . . . mainly because part of the game was locating our food by reading a map. I figured I would be okay, but the others? Not so much.

The producers had already escorted away the girls who hadn't been kissed, even though the forty-eight hours weren't up. Max had made his choices so it wasn't like they needed to stick around any longer. There were some tears, which really begged the question of how dating shows worked. One of the chicks had to be sedated because apparently in her mind the connection between her and Max was so strong that she'd already started naming their children.

I was actually a bit afraid for Max.

But he'd handled the situation with humor and class. Something I'd noticed about him in the past twelve hours. Even when people deserved to look stupid, he didn't allow them to. He was sarcastic, funny, and had such a magnetic personality I almost believed it when girls said they had a connection to him.

How could they not?

I felt connected.

Then again, I was his partner for all things zombie, so maybe that was why. He'd created this "friendship" with me and it made me feel momentarily special.

"Contestants!" Rex clapped his hands and approached us on the beach. He'd changed into a white linen suit, which did nothing but make his orange complexion look more orangey. I cringed when his white smile nearly blinded all sea life behind me and fought to hide my laugh when I noticed that the suit was semi see-through. Huh, who knew guys wore Spanx?

"Welcome to the Island!"

The remaining fifteen of us did a little cheer and waited for the rest of his instructions.

"Deep in the Island there is a feast set up for you and your Bachelor. I'm pairing you off. The Bachelor will be on his own—"

"Um, sorry, what?" Max asked, his laughter forced. "Can't I have a partner? A compass? A horse? Give me something, Rex."

"Our Bachelor will use his skills as a wilderness expert to not only find his own way but try to do so first. Max, if you beat the women's teams, you'll get your first choice of two dates for the next day. If one of the women's teams beats you, they will not only get to pick who you'll go on your date with, but you'll have to get rid of one of the two women on the date. Regardless, one woman will go home, but you have more power if you win because you can choose someone you are already on the fence about to leave or stay."

"So either way I date?" Max asked.

"Right." Rex nodded. "But if you don't win, you don't get to choose who you spend your time with."

A dawning realization appeared on Max's face as he looked around at all the women, most of them just salivating at the prospect of spending time with him. My eyes fell to Gina, aka Amazon, who made a grunting noise and then blew him a kiss. Max choked and then coughed.

"Shouldn't be a problem." Rex laughed. "Max here trained with Bear Grylls for two years! He could do it blindfolded." More laughter. "In fact . . ."

Oh, no. This wasn't good.

"We have so much confidence in Max's skills that we're giving the women a ten-minute head start!"

Max's eyes narrowed. "How . . . gracious of us." His eyes flickered to mine. Yeah, doubtful the man had any wilderness training. He screamed city boy. From his clothes to his perfectly clean fingernails and noncalloused hands. He'd probably never even seen a cow in real life, let alone hiked through the tropics. I had half a mind to feel bad for him.

"All right!" Rex chuckled. "Pair off!"

I made a beeline for Amazon and slapped her shoulder. "Partners?"

Her eyes held mine for a brief moment before scanning the rest of her options. Most of the other girls were jumping up and down, fanning themselves, applying lipstick—right, because that scared away mosquitoes and tarantulas.

"Seems so." Amazon nodded.

I tried to get Max's attention, but he was held captive by Rex, who was explaining more rules. At least they sounded like rules. But he did say something like "Death, bites, creatures" . . . poor Max.

"Hey," a male voice said from behind me. I turned and came face-to-face with one of the most gorgeous guys I'd ever seen in my entire life.

"Um, hi?" I swallowed. "Can I help you?"

He winked. "I'm part of your production crew. The rest of us just got on the Island a few minutes ago and made our way up the beach. Most of us lost our luggage so we were trying to make arrangements."

"Cool." I looked down at the sand immediately.

"So, you having fun?"

"Are you supposed to be asking me these questions?"

The camera was forced into my face by the crew, and the guy smirked. "Yeah, that's kind of my job while I'm here. Now tell me, what do you think of our Bachelor?"

"He's . . ." My gaze flickered to Max. "He's really great."

"He peed the bed when he was little," the guy said helpfully.

"Oh, um, okay."

"Had a deathly allergic reaction to shellfish when he was eight, puffed up like a balloon, swear he still screams when he sees a clam."

"Uh . . ."

"Oh, but he has his strong suits. Did you know his favorite thing in the world is spinach? Seriously. He used to eat it in bed at night because he thought it would make him gain muscle."

"Um, wow, that's a lot of information for you to know."

"Fact sheet." He pulled out a white piece of paper, then tucked it back in his pocket. "So you ready to do this?"

"Yeah."

"Payback," he mumbled.

"Pardon?"

We started walking toward the rest of the groups.

"Oh, nothing," he sang.

When we passed Max he winked at me, then slowly looked at the film crew with us. When his eyes fell on the guy next to me his eyes dripped with hatred, then irritation, then hatred. The guy gave Max a little wave and blew him a kiss. What the heck?

"Damn it!" Max shouted.

"What did you say your name was again?" I inquired once we were a few minutes away from the beach.

"The name's Reid." He grinned. "Nice to meet you."

CHAPTER SEVENTEEN
MAX

I watched Reid disappear into the jungle with Becca . . . my Becca. My friend! The only girl helping me keep my sanity! The gummy-bear-loving bastard son of a SLUT! I stomped toward the edge of the tree line but was held back by Rex. "Sorry, you still got five minutes on the clock, buddy."

Side note. Being called buddy? All it did was made me think of the stupid Buddy movies . . . damn those golden retrievers for making me sob. And right now? The last thing I needed was to think about the golden retrievers who could play all sports with such talent that it made me feel like less of a man.

Stupid dogs. I hated dogs. Well, any dog but my own—but he was more human than animal.

Shh, don't tell. Women say it's a bad sign when man isn't a fan of man's best friend. But I had my reasons. After all, it's a proven point that dogs get more play from a girl when you are in a relationship. When your significant other comes home from a long day? What does she do? She grabs a bottle of wine (women lie when they say they just drink one glass). At any rate, they grab the "glass" (notice I use the term loosely) and sit on the couch. And what happens next?

Man's "best friend" jumps onto her lap.

There's petting.

There's kissing.

There's cuddling.

And where does that leave me? On the other side of the couch with blue balls and a dripping hatred for the traitorous canine.

"You're up!" Rex slapped me on the back.

Gathering my thoughts, steering them far away from dogs, goats, and even Reid, I trounced through the first part of the forest.

"Map me." I held out my hand to Big Al.

"No map." He sighed. "You're supposed to follow the trail of the girls and then when you get close enough, use the power of scent to find the food before anyone else."

"You're shitting me."

"Nope." Big Al grinned. "So, sniff away."

"Right. I'll just . . ." I looked down at the footprints and sighed. At least they led somewhere. I could only imagine what other fabrications Jason had come up with for my application. Why the hell didn't they fact-check? My Facebook profile wasn't set to private! All you had to do was scroll through my many pictures of shopping in Vegas and vacationing in Miami Beach and you'd get the hint.

Max doesn't do nature.

I mean nature's fine and all, and I'm glad we have trees and sure I'll support Save the Rainforest. I donate to the Peace Corps, for shit's sakes! All right? I donate money to those who enjoy dying in the jungle—so I don't have to be in it. Not everyone's made to actually explore, all right? I'm more like the king who sits on the throne and tells Christopher Columbus to get his ass in the ship and discover the New World, while sipping wine and eating grapes.

With a groan I followed the footprints and swore when three sets all went in different directions.

Following those women into the jungle was like following a blind cat that couldn't swim across the Atlantic.

Oh, and P.S., for those still thinking about a blind cat trying to swim across the Atlantic. Spoiler alert. It dies.

You're welcome.

I wasn't going to win. I was going to lose and I was going to find Reid at the campsite flirting with Becca, making her laugh, touching her. I grabbed a tree branch, albeit a small one, and snapped it in half. Then was half-tempted to Tarzan my way through the forest.

He was on my territory. My island—literally. And I could only assume he was hoping to screw things up for me . . . but hadn't the whole gummy bear incident been Milo's fault? Why was he seeking revenge on me? Maybe it was because when Milo's grandma asked for Reid's number I gave her his address and a Garmin so she could locate him. Probably didn't help that I put a tracking device on his car.

Ha-ha. I kill myself.

Yeah, I probably should have hidden the tracking device better.

Damn it!

A flash of color caught my eye.

Red?

Why did that look familiar? There was a piece of red fabric tied to one of the trees to my right. When I picked it up, my eyes fell on the ground next to the tree, where one set of footprints led away from the others.

"This way," I said in my most commanding explorer-like voice, which just so happened to sound a bit British. I went against my better judgment and followed the separate set. After a few feet I noticed another piece of red cloth.

Holy shit! I was like the Hansel to someone's Gretel!

Please let Becca be Gretel because if it was Amazon then I was up a tree defenseless just waiting for her to ax me down. She'd do it slowly too, most women like that did. She'd lure me down with promises of safety, comfort, escape, and then she'd smother me, most likely seduce me, and . . .

I shuddered.

"A trail?" Big Al scratched his head. "You think it's smart to go completely off the grid? The rest of the footprints went in the other direction."

"Shh!" I held up my hand and then went down on my hands and knees, placing my ear against the ground.

It was vibrating.

"I think I hear something."

"Max—"

"Shh!"

It was getting louder. Holy shit, I was officially a badass like Lewis and Clark. For real, I could have been the guy that discovered the Oregon Trail or the Columbia River.

"Max." Big Al grabbed me, pulling me to my feet. "It's a plane."

I looked up, dirt caked to one side of my face. "I know." I laughed and brushed the dirt off. "But there were also footprints, those of an Amazon." I looked ahead. "Bet my life on it."

"I really wouldn't." Big Al sighed.

The camera guy laughed.

"Hey!" I snapped my fingers in his direction. "No comments from the hired help."

He flipped me off from behind the camera.

I glared directly into it, then turned back toward the trail. "We go this way."

"Fine." Big Al sighed.

We traveled inland for around twenty minutes. Finally the smell of food started permeating the air.

"Told you so," I snorted, then stepped directly into hell.

Also known as a circle of rope that gripped my ankle, slammed me backward onto the ground, and pulled me up a tree.

Note to self, don't step over cracks on the sidewalk and never, ever step over rope. Because you'll fall on your ass.

"Got him!" A few female chuckles rang out. I blinked a few times. My mouth watered at the sight of the banquet table. A freaking feast for a king was waiting. But I had a sneaking suspicion I wasn't the king in this scenario, more like the stuffed pig. Oink.

"Sorry." Rex laughed. "You're the last person to cross into the feast! This of course means the girls will battle for the date. This is how it's going to work—"

I raised my hand, or, well, like, lowered it, almost grazing the dirt beneath my head. Holy shit, I was seriously seeing stars. "Can you untie me first?"

"Sorry." Rex did not, in fact, look sorry. He looked excited, piqued, and a bit drunk—where the hell was my alcohol? "You stay upside down until someone cuts you down. In order to be cut down, the dates must be chosen, and since three teams got here at the same time, we'll be doing a tiebreaker." He looked directly into the camera. "It's time to play catch! We'll ask each team a question until one team gets all the questions right!"

"I don't like the sound of that game," I grumbled. Why the hell did they call it catch then? I was afraid to ask and didn't really want to find out, especially if I had to somehow strategically catch something while hanging upside down.

"Aw, have a sense of humor!" Rex laughed louder, and this time the cackle sounded like that of an evil villain in a Disney movie. Great, so I was officially the Sleeping Beauty to Rex's Maleficent.

Don't ask me why I just called myself a princess.

Blood loss. It makes a man say stupid shit, it really does.

"Will the three teams step forward?"

I almost cried when I saw Becca and Amazon take a step toward us. Reid followed closely but sidestepped them so he was closer to me.

"Bastard," I mumbled under my breath.

"Not the thing to say when you're tied to a tree upside down, Brother. I've been put through hell. Do you even realize how many people I had to pay off to be here?"

"Aw, because you love me?" I grinned. Just kidding, I loved Reid. What a good brother. I mean he—"Reid, what's that? What are you doing?"

"Snake." He smirked. "Completely harmless."

"What are you now? A snake expert! Please just put it down."

"You sure?" Reid asked.

"Positive."

"All right, but only because you asked."

He slid the snake into my pant leg. I felt that bastard slide all the way to my knee, then get caught. Thank God for small favors.

Then Reid, the brother I was officially going to cross off my will, gave my jeans a little tug.

It was all the invitation that tiny bastard needed to slide all the way down the middle of my legs and tap one of my man parts.

"Son of a—" I tried to spin, I tried to wiggle, but my actions were in vain. The snake wasn't going anywhere.

"Ha-ha!" Rex said. "Glad our Bachelor's so excited."

"Oh, he's something!" I sang.

"Look at him go!" Reid echoed. "When he comes down you'll all see his moves—his nickname was Chris Brown in high school, according to the producer fact sheet."

The girls gushed.

The snake even seemed to pause. Were those his trigger words? *Chris Brown*? Would uttering those words make the little guy cower in fear?

"All right! Will the first team step forward?" Rex commanded, and Becca and Amazon stepped in front of me. "Your question has to do with pop culture." He cleared his throat. "How many books are in the *Twilight* series?"

"Two!" Amazon shouted.

"WHAT?" I roared. "EVERYONE KNOWS IT'S FOUR!" Damn it. "EDWARD, BITE ME! I JUST WANT TO DIE." Remember what I said about trigger words? I was wrong about Chris Brown and the snake.

His trigger word was *Edward*.

I felt fangs.

And heat.

And then I screamed.

CHAPTER EIGHTEEN
BECCA

Never in my life have I ever, ever heard a man scream so loud. It was like watching a horror film with the surround sound completely turned up. I winced as Max jerked to the left, then to the right, and then, with a horrified gasp, I covered my mouth as something . . . moved . . . in the front of his pants.

Holy crap!

No way.

No way.

I couldn't stop looking. I mean, I wanted to, in the way that I wanted to be totally disgusted that he had the ability to use his parts like a small remote control race car, but wow, I had to wonder if he actually bruised the women he slept with.

"Get it out!" Max shouted.

"Um." I licked my lips.

"Reid, please!"

WHAT? He wanted his producer to . . . unclothe him so his beast could roam free on what would be aired on national television?

"Edward, I'm sorry!" Max wailed.

"He named his penis Edward." Reid chuckled. "Like the vampire. Tell me that's not creepy."

"Question number two!"

"Wait!" Max yelled. "I thought you said the game was called catch?"

At that point a ball was thrown at Max and one of the producers yelled, "Catch."

It hit him square in the face.

"Forget I asked," Max grumbled. "And how is this fun?"

"Each ball you catch gives you a free pass to skip the question for the team if you think they don't know it," Rex explained. "So you can help the team you'd like to win."

"Hit me again!" Max pleaded.

"Next team!" Rex moved us out of the way while Grumpy and Sneezy stepped forward. "Your question is geography."

"If they can't spell it they sure as hell can't answer it, Rex," Max said under his breath. I'm pretty sure Reid and I were the only ones who heard. Funny, watching Max try to cross his arms while his face turned red because of the blood pooling.

Even funnier?

The snake in his pants, not a literal one, but you get my meaning, truly did have a mind of its own. So is that what did it for Max? Was he one of those guys who liked being tied up? Huh, it suddenly made sense. That's why the producers trapped him, to get him so sexually frustrated he'd end up mauling one of the ladies, which would make for good TV.

I made my way over to his hanging body and nudged him, then whispered under my breath, "Just think about your grandma or something."

"What?" His expression turned from pained to horrified. "How the hell is that supposed to help me right now?"

"Well." I shrugged, feeling my own face heat. "I mean, I know that some guys can't control these things, but it has to be kind of embarrassing. I mean, you're, like, really aggressive."

"I'm tied up," he said through clenched teeth. "Any more aggressive and I'd be a paralyzed snail."

I pointed at his pants. "Right, well, tell your parts to paralyze so people don't think ropes and balls turn you on."

"What?" He looked up and let out a defeated sigh. "I can't help that Edward wants to be free. I would too. It's okay, little buddy."

"Um . . ." I swallowed. "Do all guys name . . . things?"

"Oh, he's not my thing. He's a snake."

"In your pants," I clarified.

"Well, it's not like I put it there!" he argued.

"Right, pretty sure God had something to do with that, and you know nature."

"God had nothing to do with what's currently twisting around in my pants. Believe me, if He did, I would so not give money to the church."

"What?"

"The next question!" Rex shouted. "How many oceans border the United States?"

"Catch! Catch!" Max yelled.

But he was too late. One of the girls had already yelled, "One. The Pacific. Duh."

"Good Lord," Max grumbled.

The next pair went and got the question wrong. Then again, was there ever any hope they'd get it right? It's not like they exactly picked the sharpest tools in the shed for this show. I wonder what that said about my own intelligence? Hmm.

"And we're back to the first team!" Rex shouted.

"Free Edward," Max grumbled.

"Stop addressing him." My eyes fell again to Max's pants. "It encourages him . . . more."

"What can I say, when I name pets, they immediately take a liking to me."

"Pets?"

Okay, so, I was officially turned off, no lust, nothing. Wow. Just. Wow. He thought of his penis as a pet? How weird was that?

"Your question." Rex pulled up a card and read from it. "What are the Seven Wonders of the World?"

Max sighed.

But I actually knew it. "Colossus of Rhodes, Great Pyramid, Hanging Gardens of Babylon, Temple of Artemis, Zeus's Statue, Lighthouse of Alexandria, and the Mausoleum."

"Wow." Rex squinted. "Correct! And it seems since you're the only team to actually get one right, you win!"

Max mouthed, "I love you" to me. I was ready to walk up to him and give him a high five. When he was cut down.

The minute his body hit the ground a small snake slithered out from his pants. "'Bye, Edward, be free!"

"Ah." I hunched down next to him. "So that's Edward."

"The things he's seen and survived. We should all be as strong as Edward." He sighed and looked at my torn shirt. "Oh, and P.S.: Thanks for the trail into hell. For a minute there I was going to change your nickname from Little B to Gretel, but then the whole rope incident happened and—"

"And now we feast!" Rex announced.

People appeared out of nowhere with food in their hands and began leading everyone away from Max.

Music started.

And Max visibly relaxed.

We'd officially made it through one day.

Only twenty more to go!

Yeah, he wasn't going to make it.

Then again, I probably wasn't either.

"Shall we?" Max offered his hand. I took it and was followed by Reid and the rest of the production crew. It wasn't until we sat down at the head of the table that I remembered cameras were still on us.

Crap.

I was getting singled out as the favorite.

Which meant only one thing.

I looked around the table as the girls glared in my direction.

Yeah, I was going to be a target.

Max lifted his wineglass into the air. "To the Island!"

"Cheers!" the girls yelled.

We set our glasses down; something touched my right thigh. I looked down to see Max's hand. He didn't move it. Not until it was time to go back to our huts, and even then, I felt the warmth of his fingertips long after I'd left him.

CHAPTER NINETEEN

MAX

All was quiet as I walked back to my hut. Big Al and the camera crew yawned the entire way—but I was anything but tired.

I felt a bit . . . on edge.

Then again, I'd spent the better part of my day getting chased by a goat, choked by seaweed, and attacked by a killer garter snake named Edward, and I'd finally ended said day of hell upside down while that same snake nearly nicked me in the balls, missing by what I can only assume was the grace of God, and biting my thigh.

"You heading in?" Big Al asked, pushing open the door to the hut. "Your call time's at seven, so I'd try to get some sleep if I were you."

"My call time?"

"For your confessional." Big Al yawned again. "We'll go over all the details of yesterday, gauge how you're doing, and set you up for your date tomorrow evening."

"Date." My lips formed into a smile. "With Becca."

"And the scary one." Big Al nodded. "Good luck with that one."

"Right," I grunted and stepped into the small hut. It felt empty. Then again, the past few weeks I'd been not only camping out with Jason but wherever I could. I hated being alone. It made me feel— lonely. And it wasn't because of the typical reasons.

I wasn't abandoned as a child.

My parents didn't lock me in my room.

My dad never raised his hand to me.

And yeah, I had my fair share of friends when I was little, not to mention enough money to go around just in case I needed to buy a seat on the swing set.

I think it was because I was just used to a lot of . . . busyness. The main reason living near Colt, Milo, and Jason worked was that they were the distraction I needed. My days were consumed with making sure Jason didn't physically harm himself or run into anything, and helping out Milo and Colt, who were renovating their house. I was able to supervise.

When I was busy I didn't have to think about all the other things men my age should be doing. Like working or moving on with their lives rather than thinking about where they'd gone wrong with the girl who got away. Or you know, getting a job.

But when I thought about what men did at my age, twenty-one? Most of them started either careers or families. I was pretty sure my career had been decided for me. Take over the hotel business, make millions, be awesome. Maybe I was trying to push back the inevitable CEO position, white picket fence, and trophy wife holding our twin boy and girl while I wined and dined business professionals from all over the world.

Shoot me now.

With an irritated sigh, I walked out onto the terrace that was connected to my hut and led out into the water. I took a seat on the dock. The ocean was just a few feet below, beckoning me to jump in. I looked around, then slowly stripped off my shirt and jeans. With one final glance around the corner, I slid my boxers down to my ankles and jumped into the glassy water.

The warmth of the ocean mixed with the humidity of the air felt like absolute perfection.

I swam toward the dock again and noticed Little G poking his head out from the room. "Aw, little man, you come out for the party?"

"Tell me," a female voice interrupted. "Do you name everything?"

Becca walked around the corner and sat on the dock, pulling her knees to her chest.

"That depends." I swam closer to her. "Is it cute bordering on sexy that I name everything or lame?"

"Hmm." She tapped her chin. "Depends. Why do you call him Little G?"

I pointed at the gecko. "Because he's a gecko and he's small, thus Little G. I didn't say my names were brilliant."

"So." Her eyes narrowed. "You call me Little B?"

I grinned shamelessly. "You do the math."

"Max . . ." Her voice held a warning edge.

"P.S." I swam closer to her and grabbed at her ankles. "I'm naked."

"Oh." Her face flushed, she jerked her ankles away from my grasp and laughed. "That's . . . um, nice."

"It really is." I let my eyelids almost fall closed over my eyes as I scanned her perfect form outlined in the moonlight. "Care to join?"

"Not much of a swimmer." She grinned. "Sharks, remember?"

"Ah," I sighed. "Afraid I'll bite?"

Becca burst out laughing. "Doubtful."

"Excuse me?" Okay, after the snake incident my confidence was a bit shaky, but what the hell, it's not like I'd gotten a personality transplant.

"Max." Becca giggled. "No offense . . ."

Not a fan of sentences that started out as insults.

"But you're kind of harmless."

"Harmless?" I repeated. "As in I'm a badass hunting dog that's just been tamed but can still bark and bite like the rest of them?"

"No." She licked her lips. "More like a blind, very old, old, old—"

"Stop saying *old*," I snapped.

"Lapdog."

"Lap. Dog?"

"Yeah." She grinned wider.

Why the hell was she smiling? Was she mocking me? Me? Max? King of the Jungle? "Grandpops had a lap dog—it used to get the shits around the house and always found the playroom as the best place to hide the evidence. I hated that dog. I wanted to drop-kick it. But it was too damn passive. The one time I yelled it walked right over to my G.I. Joe and dropped a load. So." I glared. "Are you saying I'm like Squeaker?"

"Is that the G.I. Joe or the dog?" Becca dipped her toe into the water.

"Really? The very fact that you have to ask that means you have no idea what you're talking about. Who names their G.I. Joe Squeaker?"

Becca leaned forward, her white tank top catching in the wind, making me stare like a dog, just not one who sat on your lap . . . unless . . . well, at any rate, she leaned forward and said, "What was your G.I. Joe's name?"

"None of your business." I sniffed and grabbed at her foot, massaging the bottom of it and pulling it farther into the warm water.

"Come on." She leaned over farther. Damn, that shirt was low, just low enough too. I cleared my throat and looked away.

"Joe-Joe."

"Like the potato?"

"No!" I released her foot. "Like Joe times two! Like double the badassery!"

"Or like the band K-Ci and JoJo."

"I'm not a lapdog," I said, changing the subject. "And honestly, I'm a bit insulted that you think I'm harmless."

Her eyebrows lifted.

"*Harmless* would mean I haven't been staring at your breasts for the past ten minutes dreaming about what they'd feel like cupped in my hands. Harmless"—I drew out the word—"would mean I haven't been thinking about what you taste like—everywhere." I smirked. "Harmless? Oh, honey, if you think I'm harmless then you're in deeper than you think, but that's okay. I like it that way."

"What way?" She exhaled quickly, then stood.

"Just because I'm friendly doesn't mean I'm not dangerous."

"You named a gecko," she pointed out.

"True." I nodded. "I'm a friend to the animals."

"And a snake was in your pants."

"Right, but—"

"You screamed like a girl."

"Not true!" I yelled.

"And . . ." She held up her hand like she was doing a damn countdown! "You're kind of, like . . ." She leaned forward and whispered, "A bit . . ." Her eyes teased. "Metro."

"As in . . ." I baited her.

"Feminine," she snapped. "Yup, that's the word. And Max, I mean that in the nicest way possible."

"You mean . . ." I licked my lips, then slapped the water. "In the kindest way you can possibly say it, 'Oh, look, Max has boobs'? Or you mean it in the way that says I lack the proper sexual magnetism to get your engine going?"

Becca rolled her eyes. "Hey, I didn't come here to fight. I was just going to go over our date for tomorrow without the watchful eyes of Big Brother."

"Hmm." She was looking down at her feet. So I did what any desperate man who'd just been insulted in the worst way possible would do. I grabbed her feet, dragged her into the water, creating a huge splash, and then, when her head popped up for air, I gave her something else.

My tongue.

Kissing Becca could become a very nice, very addicting . . . pastime. Her lips were soft, pliant, but her hands were beating against my chest. Ah, classic move. Listen up, men: women fight us because they're expected to. They have to put up the fight so they don't come off as easy. So the next time a girl hits you in the chest, go with it, kiss her harder. It just means she wants more, especially when her chest is heaving and her tongue is doing . . . that. Yeah, exactly. Oh. Hell. Damn. Kill me now. When her tongue is doing that? Becca's tongue pushed against mine and then she sucked.

I felt said sucking all the way through my body.

When she stopped fighting me, I wrapped my arms around her neck, pulling her as close against me as I could, and then pulled away.

Her eyes furrowed with confusion as she tried to lean forward.

I pulled back again, and swam her over to the ladder.

"Thanks, Becca," I whispered. "I needed a little motivation."

"M-motivation?"

"Game on." I helped her up and followed. "And by the way . . ." I grabbed her hands and moved her flat palms from my chest all the way down to my waist. "I'm anything but feminine. Have a good night." As I walked away, I did what any sane man would do. I paused so she could get her fill and realize that yes, I was, in fact, still naked. And when I heard her gasp, I turned around and saluted her in more ways than one.

Point. Max.

CHAPTER TWENTY
BECCA

I tossed and turned all night and finally woke up at six a.m. ready to march right over to Max's hut and just . . . punch something. Not him. Because touching him meant . . . touching . . . him and I was pretty sure that after last night I would never be the same again.

His body was . . . tight.

Not just tight. It was tan and tight and . . . not . . . expected? Holy crap it was hot in my stupid hut! Where was the AC?

I tumbled out of bed and made my way on wobbly legs over to the sink to wash my face. Grumpy, one of my hut partners, was snoring so loud you'd think she'd wake herself up. Grumpy was also known as Shel, and no that wasn't short for anything, and no it wasn't a good idea to ask her because, well, Max hit it right on the head: she was super Grumpy.

She didn't appear to be a huge fan of the tropics. At least from what I could tell.

I splashed water onto my face and my body.

It did nothing.

You know how visions just burn into your consciousness? Visions of Max . . . they wouldn't leave! I tried everything! It seemed the harder I tried, the worse they got.

A knock sounded at the door.

I pulled it open and scowled.

"Aw, you're so cute in the morning. Sleep marks on your face and everything." Reid tilted his head to the side.

I glared. "How can I and my sleep-induced puffy face help you?"

"Hey." Reid held up his hands. "You still look hot."

"You're letting mosquitoes in." My eyes narrowed.

"They're not out right now." Reid crossed his arms, and a roguish grin formed across his lips. "Out late last night?"

"No," I said quickly. "Just didn't sleep well."

"Hmm." He leaned against the doorframe. "Interesting."

"Did you need something?" I stepped forward, as if my small frame would do anything to push his six-foot, fully stacked muscular body anywhere.

"You offering?" His eyes did something I'd never seen eyes do. Seriously. I'd heard of guys who knew how to give the look, the "screw-me eyes," but I'd never actually had those eyes directed at me.

"You slut." The words were out of my mouth before I could stop them. Horrified, I slapped my hands over my face and groaned.

"Wow, you weren't lying about being grumpy."

"Go away, you bastard!" Shel yelled from her bed.

Reid peered around me, his face questioning.

"Naw, she's Grumpy—as in, Max nicknamed her Grumpy—so that name's already been taken. Sorry, champ."

"Champ?" Reid's feet shifted, he looked almost confused. "Did you just call me champ?"

"Uh, yeah? What did you need again?"

"You," he whispered. "Only you."

I leaned in so I could smell his breath. "Are you drunk?"

"What?" He reeled back. "No! Hell, no!"

"Then why are you hitting on me?"

"Why aren't you liking it?"

"You're serious?" Was this getting filmed? Maybe it was part of the show. I pushed his muscled chest away and peered around him. No cameras, nothing. Huh.

"Stop that." He blocked my view with his body. "I've never had this . . . happen." He scratched his head. "I'm . . . broken." He ran his fingers through his hair. "Holy shit." He started pacing in front of me. "That's it! She's repelled my sex!"

"Um . . ." I waved. "Sorry to interrupt your freak-out, but did you need anything?"

"Yeah, um . . ." He staggered away from me. "Your call time is eight, for breakfast, games, and then you have your date this evening, so . . . right." He pulled a sheet out of his back pocket. "Here's your schedule and I'll just be . . ." He looked me up and down. "Really?"

"Huh?" I took the paper from him.

His eyes locked with mine. Slowly his tongue reached out to lick his lips, and then his eyes did that thing again where I could have sworn they changed colors. And then he just stared . . . making me feel really, really awkward.

"Hey." I patted his shoulder. "You okay? Do you need to sit?"

"Sit?" he roared. "Oh, hell, no. Take your shit. I need to go for a walk."

Unfortunately the direction in which he turned was wrong, landing his face directly on one of the poles that were holding up our hut. Swearing violently, he staggered out onto the sand, yelling obscenities about grandmothers and gummy bears ruining his manhood.

Huh.

CHAPTER TWENTY-ONE

MAX

I woke up feeling quite . . . pumped. HA, see what I did there? See, I was pumped because of . . . never mind.

Becca, Becca, Bo, Becca, Me, My, Mo, Mecca, Becca! I never backed down from a challenge, and Becca? She was a challenge, a puzzle I could focus my efforts on so I could ignore the drama of the dating show and the sinking feeling that kept inconveniently popping up in my heart and head telling me that I really needed to get my life together.

A knock sounded at my hut, and then the door burst open. Reid came flying in, his cheek swollen.

"Aw, man, did Milo's grandma find you again? Even here?" I jolted off the bed. "No worries, we'll go into witness protection. You, me, Little G, Edward . . ."

"Who the hell is Little G?" Reid roared. "And no! It's not Grandma, I mean, technically it's Grandma, but man, I think it's me. I just . . . repel the opposite sex now."

I grinned, satisfied that his game was finally off. "You don't say?"

"Stop smiling."

"I can't help that I'm a morning person." I yawned and then went over to the coffee maker. "Now, sit down and tell Brother dearest all your problems."

"I think . . ." Reid's hands shook as he paced my floor. "I think . . ."

"Shh, shh." I nodded. "Slow down. Why don't you start at the beginning?"

"Grandma." Reid blurted the word. "She made me do things."

"Yes." I nodded. "She did."

"I thought I was over it, but . . ." Reid shook his head; his bottom lip trembled. "Man, at night, I still see her, I still smell the Bengay. I think the scent is the worst. It's like no matter how many times I shower, I'm still . . . minty."

"Bro . . ."

Reid finally sat on the bed and hung his head. "I hit on a girl and got rejected."

"Which one? Grumpy? Amazon? Sneezy? Ugh, I hate Sneezy. Swear she wears cat hair somewhere on her body, making my eyes itch like a bitch. Hey, that rhymed!" I took a sip of coffee. "So?"

"Becca."

And coffee spewed out of my mouth.

"You hit on my best friend?"

"What?" Reid shook his head. "Um, you've been here two days. You need at least two years to solidify the best-friend spot."

"She's also my partner for the zombie apocalypse."

"Hey, man . . ." Reid looked hurt. "I thought I was your partner."

"Cocaptain." I nodded. "Big difference. Plus she's a chick, we can't have her driving the spaceship, I mean come on."

Reid laughed. "Right? Women spaceship drivers."

We both contemplated that absurdity in silence.

"So it's not Grandma." I sighed and then set down my coffee to stretch. "It's me."

"Huh?" Reid blinked. "What do you mean?"

"Mighty Max gave a show last night."

"The mouse?"

"No, not the—" I groaned. "Reid, focus!" I clapped in front of his face. "I swam naked, I was like a freaking mermaid and Becca—she saw it all. And I do mean all." I winked. "Let's just say it was a really good day to be naked."

"So . . ." Reid still wasn't getting it. Clearly.

"She saw me. Once a girl goes Max she never goes back. We know this. We both know this."

"Ah." Reid snapped his fingers. "So you're under the deluded impression that because she saw your penis—who by the way you've named after a tiny mouse—she's spoiled for all other men?"

I nodded thoughtfully. "Yes, Reid. There isn't any other explanation."

"Maybe I was off my game," he offered. "Bad lighting or . . . something."

"Really? Bad lighting?" I laughed. "Please, she wants me, not you."

"Hmm." Reid stood. "You're that confident?"

"Bro, you've seen it, you tell me."

"Please don't pull down your pants." Reid held up his hand. "But I see a bet in our foreseeable future . . . I mean, if you're so confident, you won't mind that I hit on her? See if I can't be a best friend too?"

"Spot's taken, asshole! We're full up here!"

Reid grinned. "What? Don't like competition?"

"Um, no, I just don't like Reids," I said truthfully. "You cheat, you do the eyes."

"Do not."

"Do it."

"Max—"

"The eyes. Let's have them."

Reid did the eyes. The ones that made women swoon and the elderly offer sexual favors, though Reid wasn't really a fan of the second one.

"If you weren't my brother—"

"Max!" Reid stopped doing the eyes and gave an evil smirk. "It's on. I'm doing it, if only to humble you."

"You will do no such thing!" I yelled. "And if you do, I'll . . . I'll . . ."

"Aw," Reid taunted. "Such a smooth talker. Tell me, do you stutter with Becca too?"

"It's my dating show!"

"For money!" Reid countered. "And it's only a few weeks! Besides, they don't have to fall in love with you to win."

"You're on the crew!"

"Exactly." Reid's eyes gleamed. "So while you're stuck in your hut at bedtime, or dating other women, it frees me up to do exactly what you lack the balls to do."

"Oh, yeah?"

"Get the girl." Reid stretched. "Good talk, Brother. Good talk!"

"You don't want to do this," I seethed. "You really don't want me to bring out the big guns . . ."

"I think"—Reid reached the door and turned—"you're full of shit. Oh, and by the way, your confessional's in a few minutes. Better head over there while I go fetch Becca."

"Bastard!"

"Thank you!"

• • •

"So," Rex asked from behind the camera. "Why don't you tell us a bit about your experience here on Max Island?" He held up fake quotation marks.

"Um, did we change the name?"

"Has a ring to it!" Rex laughed, then sobered. "But seriously, tell the viewers what you're feeling right now."

Stifling a groan, I looked directly into the camera and said, "Hungry. I'm feeling hungry because they make us hunt for our own food, oh, and P.S.: I found a snake in my pants last night . . . folks, maybe censor this little tidbit right now. It nearly bit me in the balls. I hate nature. And a goat, a freaking goat, which I'm still convinced was placed there by some sort of lunatic masquerading as an Oompa Loompa"—I paused and shot a grin to Rex—"Chased me into the ocean, where I was then strangled by seaweed. Oh, and, um . . . I swam naked last night. Yup, I think, I think that's it."

"Er . . ." Rex's mouth dropped open.

"Oh!" I surged forward and looked directly into the camera. "I also kissed one of the contestants last night."

"Well!" Rex looked relieved. "Who?"

"Oh, I can't tell." I put my right hand across my heart. "I signed this weird document about the show not being liable if I get any of the contestants pregnant. Seems there's been problems with that in the past. Hey, I wonder if that's why that one guy jumped out of the plane? Spoiler alert! Bitch pushed him!" I slapped my knee and wiped a tear. "At any rate, it was an epic kiss."

Rex's smile was tight. "Are you looking forward to the date this evening?"

"That depends, Rex. Will there be goats? Snakes? Games? If you say yes to any of those things, then I can say with absolute certainty that I should have joined the army when I was eighteen to prevent this future from taking place. Damn you, Doc! Where's your shiny DeLorean now? Hmm?"

"All right," Rex nearly shouted. "Good interview, we'll, uh, talk again tomorrow."

"Nice." I saluted the crew, and threw off the microphone so I could go for a quick swim before the first game.

I had a sneaking suspicion it wouldn't be anything like chess or water polo.

Hell, no. It was going to be a *Hunger Games* scenario.

And I had a sinking feeling I was Peeta. Just waiting for someone to kill me while I hid in a lame rock costume.

Aw, pipe dream. Should have brought some badass paint so I could blend in with nature.

"Max!" Doc—the girl, not Christopher Lloyd—came surging toward me. See, and this is why I nicknamed people. She was in a white cover-up that seriously looked like a lab coat. "Let's go for a swim!"

"Yay!" I did a fake fist pump. "Let's . . . yes, let's do that." I turned just in time to see Reid escort Becca to the confessional. Damn him.

CHAPTER TWENTY-TWO

BECCA

"Here, allow me." Reid reached behind my tank top and pulled the microphone up my shirt, his hands grazing the outside of my bikini top.

"Thanks." I jerked away from him, my gaze narrowing in on his smirk. Oh, he was good. He knew exactly what he was doing.

"Anything else you need?" He leaned over. I was going to get the eyes again, in three, two, one, bingo. This time I stared, basked, waited. Reid stared and when I did nothing for another few awkward seconds he pulled back and walked off.

"So . . ." A sweaty Rex stood behind the camera. "Tell us about your experience here, Becca. It probably hasn't been easy, leaving your job in hopes to win enough money to finish school."

Reid froze behind Rex, his face hinting that he was a bit concerned about what Rex had just divulged.

"Oh, that." I waved him off. "I made a deal with my parents. They pay for two years I pay for two years. So I thought, why not try to win the money? I'm pretty competitive and I can be sneaky when I want to be."

"So was it you?" Rex asked.

"Was what me?" I looked nervously around the crew.

"The kiss with Max last night, was it you?"

"Um." I chewed my lower lip. Reid made a cutting motion with his hand. Did that mean I wasn't supposed to tell anyone about the kiss? "I have no idea what you're talking about. I was . . . exhausted after last night's win."

"Ah, last night's win. Just how confident are you that Max will chose you over Gina? She's a lovely girl." The camera panned away from me to the girls on the beach. Gina looked like she was trying to fish with her bare hands, either that or she was really, really aggressive when it came to hunting for seashells.

"Yeah." I swallowed. "A regular gem."

"All right," Rex waved at the camera. "That's enough, let's get the remaining girls taken care of and then set up the game. You may go, Becca."

Huh, that was fast. Reid walked up to me, but I'd already started pulling the microphone off. No way was the guy going to put his hands down my shirt for the second time that morning.

When I handed him the microphone, he chuckled. "Didn't want any help?"

"No, not your kind of help at least." I stepped back, keeping my eyes trained on Reid just in case he decided to make a sudden movement. The back of my foot hit something hard and then I was airborne, flying backward, ready to hit the hard sand.

"Whoa there!" Reid yelled, his arms wrapping around my waist as he pulled me down onto the sand. I fell on top of him like a turtle unable to get off its shell.

"Hey, good catch!" Max ran up next to us. "Shocking, since he used to get picked last for little league."

"Did not!" Reid said from underneath me.

"Don't lie, Reid." Max laughed and offered me his hand, helping me to my feet. "Fun fact, Reid was so dedicated to the sport he slept with his helmet on. When Mom told him to take it off he cried. Poor thing."

"Max—"

"Also, he can't hit a ball to save his life. I'm a firm believer that men should be talented in all areas of ball handling . . . aren't you, Reid?"

"Don't you have a shark to feed?" Reid asked from behind me.

"Why?" Max's eyes narrowed. "You offering to sacrifice your body?"

"Only if I was saving Becca!" Reid argued. "Hell, yeah, I'd sacrifice my body for her!"

With a gleam in his eye Max pushed Reid back to the ground and then tilted his head. "Sorry, I was just checking to make sure you weren't a liar. Look, Becca, he fell for you!"

Reid glared from his position on the ground while I rolled my eyes and tried to walk away from all the testosterone. The air reeked of "My horse is bigger than your horse." Or in Reid and Max's case, "My ball is bigger than yours."

A loud horn sounded on the beach.

Oh, no. Either there was a hurricane coming or they were prepping us for the next game.

"Contestants! Gather round!" Rex shouted. The poor guy was still sweating buckets, the man needed to wear something other than linen pants.

A few of the camera crews put down their equipment. Reid hurried off to his crew and started filming; the other two crews were already in front of Rex.

"The game you'll be playing is for a sunrise breakfast with our Bachelor."

"Sunrise?" Max raised his hand. "As in, when the sun rises over the earth?"

Reid chuckled to himself. "Sorry, boss, telling time isn't his thing. Max, remember, it's when the big hand goes—" Max smacked Reid in the stomach and took his position with the rest of the contestants.

"The sunrise breakfast will include local foods as well as a morning boat ride."

That actually sounded really fun. I could be a morning person for some good food and a boat ride.

Throw Max in the mix and . . . yeah, well, it would be nice.

Rex held up his hands. "Contestants, follow me!"

We all walked toward the far end of the beach, where a giant game board was set up on the sand. There were dots of every color—and that's when it hit me, they wanted us to play Twister? Really?

"A giant game of Twister," Rex announced. "Sounds easy enough, right?"

We all nodded and shrugged in unison.

"Wrong!" Rex pointed and laughed. Was it wrong that I had this really strong urge to grab his finger and break it in half? Wow, island life was turning me violent. What was wrong with me? I was the kind of girl who felt guilty when she stepped on a spider!

"This game of Twister has two parts. For the first part, the women will be blindfolded while the Bachelor moves you around himself. When only five of you are left standing, the Bachelor will join the game and play right along with you. The winner takes all!"

Rex cleared his throat. "Max will spin the wheel and call out instructions, and once he joins the game I'll take over. The eliminated girls will also help us referee the game to make sure no cheating occurs."

Max raised his hand.

Rex did his best to ignore him.

But it's kind of hard to ignore someone who starts whistling and then jumping up and down.

"Max?" Rex sighed. "Yes, what is it?"

"If I win, does that mean I go on a date with myself?"

I could have sworn I saw a blood vessel swell and then pop on Rex's forehead as he answered. "No, Max. The final lady will go on the breakfast outing with you in the morning, but if you win you get to pick who you go to breakfast with."

"Gotcha." Max nodded seriously, then winked at me. His winks were too sexy, just like the rest of him. Thankfully he had the mouth of an absolute lunatic so it was easy for all the charm and sexiness to fall into the cracks. Imagine if Max were actually not trying to act like the world was one giant joke?

Yeah, he'd probably be king of the universe.

Women would sob in his presence.

And I wouldn't be able to walk away—maybe it was for the best that he had such a crazy sense of humor. That way I was safe. I could handle his sense of humor because he came across as a harmless flirt.

Right?

"Contestants!" Rex shouted. "Find a dot and stand on it!"

I quickly moved to a red dot and waited for instructions as Reid came up behind me and wrapped a blindfold around my face. "Kinky, huh?"

"Say that again while you're facing me and we'll see just how kinky," I muttered.

"I think I'll keep my balls, but thanks for the offer." Reid playfully shoved me before I could react and walked away laughing. Damn men!

"All right, Max," Rex called. "Make your first move."

And just like that the game started.

I was one of the last to be moved.

I couldn't see any of the other girls or where they were so it was all up to Max to keep me stable so I didn't fall on my ass and lose the game for both of us. I mean, did he really want to go on a morning boat ride with any of those women? And when had I turned into his protector? Since when did it make my chest hurt to imagine him drinking mimosas and watching the sunrise with anyone but me?

"Ready?" Max whispered in my ear. I shivered and gave him a firm nod.

His hands moved to my hips, resting there as if he had all the time in the world. After a few seconds he slid his hands up and then down again. What? What was he doing?

"Right hand," Max said in a commanding voice.

I shot out my right hand and shivered again as he slowly grabbed my hand and whispered in my ear again. "Bend over."

"What?" I hissed.

Max sighed. "I need you to either bend over or get down on your haunches, I figured bending over would be better, trust me, it's not like anyone can see you. Well except, me, Reid, the film crew, and Rex, though to be fair I think he's blind in his right eye from all that twitching it keeps doing. Oh, and there's also Little G, he's in my pocket, and the goat who's watching us creepily from the trees, and always the possibility of sharks and—"

"Fine!" I snapped. "Fine, which direction do I bend?"

Max sighed. "If we were alone you wouldn't have to ask me that . . ."

I licked my lips.

"Pity," he whispered in my ear. Something touched my ear, his tongue? His hands moved all the way down both legs, until finally he picked up my foot and moved it to the yellow dot and then instructed me, once again, in a silky smooth voice, to bend over. What? "Bend down to your right, place your right hand and right foot exactly where I tell you. Yellow."

I hated that my body heated at the sensual sound of his low voice.

It was the blindfold and humidity and, well, the lingering picture I had of him and his nakedness. NOTHING more.

"This okay?" I breathed.

"I'd say more than okay." He laughed softly and moved away. And so went the next hour. I'd love to say it got easier, but really, it was what I imagined hell was like.

For one, it was hot, and I was so sweaty that my shirt was sticking to my body like a second skin. Sweat kept dripping from my arms and legs—it wasn't like I was a gymnast or anything! And there was no way to know how many girls were left because Max had distracted me so much with his words and touching that I hadn't kept track!

"And now our Bachelor will join you. Blindfolds off," Rex commanded.

Finally I peeled off my blindfold and threw it onto the sand. The girls who were left were not the girls I would have picked.

He'd kept the girls he'd originally made fun of. Doc, Amazon, Grumpy, Sneezy, and me. But why keep the girls who scared him? Or the ones who made him want to run and hide?

I didn't have any more time to wonder. Because in an instant Max was placed in the midst of all five of us and the game continued. Only this time he was going to be in the giant pretzel with us.

CHAPTER TWENTY-THREE

MAX

If the roles had been reversed and I had been at home watching this on TV, I would have probably thought, "Lucky bastard." By any guy's standards I was standing in Eden. Every man's utopia. Not only had I just touched fifteen attractive women (according to those who would be watching), but I was smack-dab in the middle of them. They were in bikinis, short shorts, and tank tops, and they were sweaty. And I was the king of their island, for now.

All right, so this is where those rose-colored glasses come off. Don't be envious, you poor couch potato, as you drink your Coke Zero and eat another Twizzler, wishing it were you who had won the chance to be stuck on the Island. Go ahead, eat another chip. I'll wait.

You ready? Because I'm about to shatter your beliefs with one single fact.

I know what these girls eat.

Because when you're on a dating show you want to look your best, right? Take Amazon, the pine nut queen: men, are you aware of what a high-protein, no-carb diet does to the human body? By the looks of your potato-chip-and-Twizzler diet, that's a hell, no. Well, let me tell you.

High protein.

Low fat.

Low carb.

Equals trouble.

Also known as intestinal . . . rockiness. Yes, let's call it rockiness. So the very fact that I have to bend over and stuff my face in all their goodies? Not my favorite thought, not at all. I know what Amazon eats at night. I know what she does with those hands—she crushes nuts and devours them.

And no way do I want my body or my nostrils for that matter anywhere near her ass when she puts her hand on yellow or red. Or damn. Let's just strike out all colors.

I want Amazon colorless. And odorless, but hey, we can't win 'em all, can we?

"Max," Rex shouted. "Right hand, green." I was already standing on green, so I leaned forward and placed my hand on the sand.

"Gina, left foot, green."

Helllllll.

Gina smirked at me and placed her foot right underneath my legs. Really, bitch? Couldn't you have chosen the green spot in front of or behind me? My eyes narrowed, hers matched mine. I mouthed, "Challenge accepted."

She mouthed, "Bring it."

"Becca, right foot . . . well, isn't that the craziest thing, green!"

Hmm, this smelled suspiciously like a setup.

Becca eyed me and then moved her right foot directly in front of my hand. Hey, at least I'd be staring at her ass for the next hour or so.

After ten minutes Amazon made a fatal error and scratched her forehead, her balance was compromised. She fell to the earth much like I imagine Goliath fell to the ground once David shot his head with a rock. Swear the ground shook for a minute as she yelled, "Noooo," in slow motion. Honest moment, I may have given her a little . . . push. Hey, you would too, don't judge me, man. Eat another chip and thank your lucky stars you aren't going on a date with her tonight. She fishes with her bare hands and doesn't shave her legs, and probably beats her bed partners into submission and not the good kind, feel me?

Another girl went down. Poor Sneezy. It wasn't her fault. I'm pretty sure she passed out from low blood sugar and dehydration. Mental note: get her a cookie.

Finally, after another one hit the sand, it was just me, Becca, and Grumpy.

"Becca, right hand, blue."

Becca was still right in front of me but putting her right hand on blue basically meant her ass was going to be pointing toward the sky and her arms would be spread so wide her shoulders were going to hurt for days. With a grunt she moved. Her head was upside down, and she peered at me through her legs.

"Hey, girl," I joked.

Her eyes flared with what I could only assume was hostility. I almost backed up, but I wasn't a fan of losing anything and I figured being a man and all, I would be letting down my entire gender if Grumpy and Becca beat me.

Lose to a woman? I think not. I don't roll that way. Come hell or high water, I would win.

Milo would be so proud.

"Max, right hand, red." Ha, okay, well, that was going to be a difficult maneuver. Damn it! Why hadn't I read that *Kama Sutra* book? Seriously, it would have come in handy, didn't it teach people how to bend better during sex? With a grunt I moved underneath Becca and flipped around so that I was literally getting straddled by her—but hey, I made it.

Her eyes narrowed even more as she glared at me. Safe to say she'd jumped off the "this is fun" train, and was heading straight to the "Twister equals hell" train.

"You have pretty eyes," I whispered, while Grumpy got her coordinates.

"Max." Teeth clenched, Becca whimpered, "You're not helping."

"I like this position," I continued, my eyes roaming over her body. "White bikini? Sexy."

"Max . . ." her voice warned, but her eyes told me something else completely.

A bead of sweat fell from her chin and landed right next to my mouth. I reached out my tongue and tasted the salty sweetness, letting out a little groan. "Damn, you taste good too. Even your sweat tastes like honey."

Her mouth opened and then closed.

"At a loss for words?" I taunted.

"Stop distracting me."

"This isn't me distracting you. Believe me, if I was distracting you I'd do a hell of lot better job than licking your sweat and imagining all the fun Twister positions I could get you in."

"Ah!" Grumpy yelled, and then fell onto her ass.

"Winners!" Rex yelled just as Becca gave out and landed on top of me. I fell onto my back, catching her as her legs straddled my waist.

I wanted to kiss her so bad it almost hurt. Her body felt so good wrapped around mine.

Either she was a mind reader or my thoughts were written all over my guilty face. She pushed away from me, nearly kneeing me in the balls, and wiped the sand off her sweaty body.

"Wow!" Rex chuckled. "We've got ourselves a lead after only two days! Becca, a date tonight and tomorrow morning! Someone better step up or this competition's going to be a sweep!"

Becca's worried eyes darted around the group. The other contestants began whispering behind their hands, their eyes growing more hostile by the second.

Oh, shit, if someone beat her, or worse yet, if she lost a game and had to go home . . . I hadn't thought ahead enough. Chart. I needed to learn the girls' names, their weakness and strengths, and make a chart.

It was the only way to keep the girls straight and make sure I knew how to beat them—so I could keep the one I really wanted. Just this morning I'd decided she was a challenge, something I hadn't had in a really long time. But now I needed her to stay for more than just my sanity—I needed her to stay because I liked her. Plain and simple.

My mind flickered back to memories of our kiss. She'd tasted so good I'd wanted to weep with desire for just one more morsel of what she had to offer.

Body aching, I wiped off the remaining sand and walked toward my hut. Charts first, seduction second.

Only I didn't notice that I was being followed, not until it was too late.

CHAPTER TWENTY-FOUR

BECCA

Being so close to Max had thrown me off mentally and physically. I needed to get away—fast. I scrambled toward the shore peeled off my sweat-soaked shorts and T-shirt, and waded into the warm water.

"So . . ." Reid's voice penetrated my Max-filled thoughts. "You were the winner again. How's it feel?" The camera was pointed in my face and Reid was standing behind it and to the side, where the water reached his knees. So he was talking to me as one of the assistants, not Max's brother, a relationship I'd only recently learned about when Reid had slipped up off-camera and actually claimed the guy. I should have caught it sooner; they both had sexy eyes and mouth-watering smiles. Odd that Max hadn't brought it up before, then again, I wasn't anything to him yet . . . was I?

"Good." I looked away from the camera and waded farther into the water. "I came here to win and that's what I'm doing." But was it only about winning anymore? I glanced back at Max and shivered.

"And the other girls? Are you worried they'll try to distract the Bachelor in any way or possibly even try to win his affection?"

I snorted with laughter, hoping the camera wouldn't see through my insecurity. The last thing I wanted was to lose the money . . . or the budding friendship I was developing with Max. "No."

"Whoa." Reid's eyebrows drew together as he pointed back toward the shore. "Even now?"

Max was locking lips with Doc.

REALLY? Doc, of all people? He couldn't have at least chosen Sneezy?

I mean at least Sneezy seemed frail and insecure and . . .

Doc was . . .

I quickly looked away. Reid's eyes lit up a little too much for my liking. "He can do what he wants." I shrugged, irritated that I had a lump in my throat. Never once had it occurred to me that I'd get attached to Max or that I'd be pissed when I saw him with other girls.

School. My brain reminded me. I was there for money and for school, not Max. He was just . . . an added bonus, a nice added bonus, but also a distraction I didn't need. Right?

"Interesting." Reid cleared his throat. "All right, we're done for now." He sent the camera crew away but stayed where he was. "You holding up?"

"Of course!" I said it way too fast. Licking my lips, I looked down at the water. "It's not like I own him or anything. I mean he's the Bachelor and it's part of the show, right?"

"Right. Actually I meant how are you holding up after playing the game and most likely suffering from dehydration." Reid examined me for a minute, as if he were studying my expressions and trying to decipher me. "But since we're talking about it, off the record, do you actually . . . oh, God, I can't believe I'm asking this, do you actually like him?"

"No!" I snorted, almost choking on the word. "I mean, no, he's . . . he's—"

"Max," Reid finished slowly. "But he's also pretty damn hard to forget. I imagine in another life he was a leech—or maybe even a koala bear—that just attaches himself to you and no matter how hard you try to shake him, he digs in harder. Am I right?"

I didn't answer.

"By your silence and all-around awkward posture I'm going to assume that's a yes, you like him. Damn." Reid splashed the water. "Another one out of my reach."

"When was I ever in your reach?"

"Please." Reid snorted.

I gave him a confused look.

"For real?" he asked, sounding exasperated. "Not even a tiny chance? Not even with the eyes?"

"You're sexy." I nodded. "I'll throw you that bone."

"Why do I feel insulted?" Reid tilted his head to the side. "By the way, he's a good catch, even if he is crazy, a bit unstable, crap in bed . . ." He winked. "Okay, I'm kidding, and for the record there haven't been any complaints in the bedroom department."

I snorted. "How could there be, what with his—"

Reid's eyebrows shot up. "No, please continue. Don't let my shocked expression deter you from saying what's really on your mind . . ." He smirked. "His . . ."

"Er . . . vibrant personality?"

"It's big." Reid nodded knowingly.

I felt myself flush.

"His personality, I mean."

"Right." My throat was parched. "It seems like it would bring you lots of years of—"

"Pleasure." Reid chuckled.

"Yeah." I looked down at the water. "Because it's so—"

"Naturally eye-popping, almost like, so big that you can't help but stare a bit?"

"Oh, look!" I pointed at the water. "A fish."

"I can help you with him."

I snorted. "We aren't in fifth grade, and I don't need help passing notes, thank you very much. It is what it is."

"Fine." Reid went silent.

"But, you know, if I was to ask what his favorite food was—"

"Mexican. We're Canadian, but it doesn't stop him from believing he was adopted and his real father is in the Mexican drug cartel."

"Huh?"

"Because he has olive skin." Reid rolled his eyes. "He likes chips and salsa. One time when he was ten he dreamed that a giant tortilla chip was chasing him and the only way to be rid of the chip was to learn karate and break it apart with his bare hands."

"Please tell me you're joking."

"The man's a god when it comes to hand-to-hand combat. Thank the chip, Becca, don't judge."

I nodded and turned back around to see that Max and Doc had disappeared. My eyes greedily scanned the beach until they landed on Doc. She was sitting on one of the chairs, drinking a margarita and crying.

A smile curled around my lips before I had the decency to stop it.

"Wow, you heartless little hussy." Reid chuckled. "Laughing at another girl's tears. I may as well call you Max."

"Huh?"

Reid pointed to Doc. "White."

"What?"

"He really, really likes when girls wear white." With a wink Reid walked off, leaving me in the ocean all by myself.

CHAPTER TWENTY-FIVE

MAX

Kissing a girl with dry mouth? Not fun. Not fun at all. It was a toss-up between wanting to offer her some of my spit just so she didn't choke to death, and just tripping her in the sand and pretending like a turtle was at fault, you know, because turtles are so fast and they can be sneaky little bastards . . .

"Doc," I started, then shook my head. "I mean, St—" Shit, it was either Stacy or Shannon, maybe Suzanne? With an emphasis on the *ooze*? Damn it!

"Lucky!" She giggled. "My name's Lucky."

Insert mental groan here. I mean, what's a guy like me supposed to do with a name like that? I could spend an entire twenty-four-hour period making up jokes just using her name. But she'd take it as flirting of the sexual nature and I think we've already established that she's grossly dehydrated and in need of food, not Max. Honestly, at this point I was a bit worried that if she saw me naked she'd mistake Mighty Max for one of those giant Costco hot dogs and I wasn't a fan of getting bit, not in that way, feel me?

"Lucky." I said her name softly as I gripped her wrists and pushed her back. "I'm trying really hard to keep things fair."

"Fair?"

"Right." I nodded. "With all the contestants."

Her blank stare said it all. I'd have to spell it out, and even then, I wasn't sure if she knew how to spell, so it was going to be an adventure. Mental note—talk slowly.

"Lucky," I tried again as she took a step forward. I stepped back, Little G quivered in my pocket. I know, little buddy, I know. Swear he was like my robot saying, "Danger, Will Robinson! Danger!" "I'm just here to get to know you girls . . . your heart, not your . . . lips." Round of applause for Max, please. Should I bow after that speech? Because I sure as hell wanted to get to know someone's lips. In an up-close-and-personal way.

"Oh." Lucky's brow furrowed. "I get it, I mean, I shouldn't have come on so strong. It's just, you're really, really hot."

Flattery will get you everywhere. I tried desperately not to do a typical Max maneuver—you know, the type where I made the girl feel like the compliment actually made me feel like I was Superman, by flashing a megawatt smile and puffing my chest out.

"Thank you." A simple response. Straightforward. Add bright smile. End scene. Oscar performance.

"So . . ." Oh, my hell, why wasn't she leaving? "Do you, like, want to hang out for a bit?"

"Um." I stepped back. "I'm kind of tired after all that exercise." Ha, I cut my teeth on boxing training. Yeah, right, I was tired. Try just a bit frightened. I didn't want to spend any more time with her. Little G concurred, if his shivering was any indication. Poor tyke. We'll make it through, buddy. Just a few more feet to the safety of my hut. "So I think I'm going to take a nap and shower and . . . rest."

"I could help you—"

"No thanks!" I chuckled. "Go have a few drinks, and have fun for me, all right? Oh, and Lucky, can you do me a huge favor?"

Her eyes brightened. I almost felt guilty for turning her down, but I didn't like her. Clearly I was changing if I was turning down hot girls—especially ones who didn't have brain cells to spare. "Go eat some food . . . I love a girl with an appetite."

"You do?" She giggled. "Okay, well, I'll go eat then, because that's what you want." Her eyes lowered to my stomach. "And I want whatever you want."

"Awesome," I croaked. "See ya!"

When she turned to leave I looked up just in time to see Becca staring at me. Damn it, I hoped she hadn't seen the awkward kiss.

But judging by the look on her face, the one girls get when they're so pissed they can't help but stare laser beams straight through your body in hopes that you'll spontaneously combust, she wasn't happy.

Damn, I really did need to make that chart. With a wave in her direction, I walked to the hut and started working. I had a few hours before the date and I needed to have a game plan for the rest of the show, the sooner the better.

• • •

A pounding sounded on the door. Panicked, I jolted from the fetal position on the floor and yawned. Must have fallen asleep making my chart. The production crew had brought me pictures of all the girls. I made do without scissors, folding each picture so only the name showed beneath the face, and lined them up on the floor.

Fifteen girls.

I'd set about memorizing their names—their real names as well as their nicknames, so I knew which ones were bad and which were good. For example, Apple, also known as Bang because literally every time I'd smiled in her direction she'd made a gun motion with her hand like she was a sharpshooter from the Wild West. I was still on the fence about her. Not sure if she thought pretending to shoot my face off was cute or if she really did hit the bull's-eye every time and imagined my face as the target. To be safe, I was going to warn Becca about her.

With a sigh I walked to the door and opened it.

Reid stood on the other side, smile huge. "Ready for your big date tonight? You do know you have to pick one of the girls and send the other one home? I wonder who it will be?"

I shook my head and pushed the door open farther so he could walk in. Once he stepped over the threshold I pushed against his chest, stopping him. "The goat, it's stalking us."

"Oh." Reid turned around and pointed. "You mean Hades?"

"The god of the underworld lives on Love Island?" I snapped my fingers. "Damn it! I should have seen the signs!"

"The goat." Reid rolled his eyes.

"You named it!" I roared. "When you name things you take possession of them, jackass!" I smacked him on the back of the head and motioned toward Hades. "Shoo, shoo now, just—just run along!"

The goat stared me down, his jaw moving back and forth as he chewed on a piece of grass. *That's right, little bastard. I'm watching you.* I made a motion with my fingers, pointing at my eyes and then at his.

He stomped his foot.

"Was that a challenge?"

"Max," Reid called from inside. "Stop scaring the goat."

"I'm saving your life!" I yelled back, turning around so I could explain. When I turned back toward the door, the goat was gone.

"Hey?" I took a step outside. "Where'd he go? Hades? Hades?"

"Uh, Max."

"Shh! Reid! I'm working."

"Max—"

"Hades!"

"Naa-naa." I blinked and turned to my right.

Hades was standing two feet away from me.

Reid sighed and walked around me. "He's been like that all day, super silent, scares the shit out of me, but doesn't really do anything except make noise. I think he's . . . lonely."

"When demons get lonely they usually possess someone." I slapped him on the back. "So good luck finding a girlfriend with the mind of that one inside you."

"Max." Reid rolled his eyes. "Conquer your fears."

I smirked, my eyebrows arched, as I crossed my arms. "Wow, really?"

"What?" Reid puffed up.

"One word." I examined my hands. "Grandma."

Reid visibly shook.

"Aw, gonna pee your pants?"

"You're an asshole." He glared, then motioned toward the goat. "Come on in, Hades. Make some friends."

The goat, clearly smarter than I'd given him credit for, waltzed right into the hut and started walking around.

"Son of a bitch!" I staggered back toward the bed. "How dare you invite Satan into my home? Everyone knows you have to invite them, otherwise they have to stay outside!"

"Pretty sure that's vampires." Reid laughed. "At any rate, that's what you get for saying her name." He shuddered. "You doing okay?"

"Sure I am, though I'm a bit concerned that you're actually worried about me. Didn't you make a bet that I'd fall flat on my face during this little escapade, or was that Jason?" I was banking on the fact that they'd made side bets. I knew my friends well—most likely there was at least two hundred dollars in a pool over how many times I'd mess up.

A loud chomping interrupted my thoughts. "Hey!" I ran toward Hades. "Stop that! Stop eating those!"

Ignoring me, he continued to chew on my boxers. I tried to pry them free from his teeth. When I did, he growled. Swear to all that is holy that damn goat growled at me like he was possessed by pure evil.

"Nice Hades." I released the boxers. "Here, take them all!" I dumped my underwear into a pile and scooted it toward the far corner of the room. "Feast, my friend, feast!"

Hades, clearly satisfied with his new arrangement, waltzed over to the corner, plopped down, and went to town.

"Aw, you tamed him." Reid chuckled.

"Why are you here again?"

"Help. I was going to help you, and I was sent by Rex to remind you to get ready. Camera crew's gonna be by the hut in a half hour, so . . . yeah, good luck with what you're going to wear for dinner tonight."

Confused, I stared at him. "I'm the best dresser I know. And I know a lot of people."

"Not a humble bone in that body, is there?" Reid asked seriously. "And I meant the whole underwear situation. You gonna free-ball it during your date? Because I sure as hell wouldn't take that chance, not with Becca wearing white."

It took a minute for it to hit me.

And when it did, I panicked.

"Oh, shit." I sat down on the bed. "What do I do? I need underwear, Reid! I need clothing to conceal! I NEED TO BE INVISIBLE!"

"Says no guy . . . ever." Reid rolled his eyes. "You'll be fine."

"Take your pants off!" I ordered.

"What? No!" Reid stepped back toward the door. "Get away from me!"

"Take them off, damn it!" I launched myself onto him just as the door opened. "Take off your pants or I swear I'll do it for you!"

"Uh . . ." Big Al blushed. "Should we come back later?"

I was straddling Reid. "Uh . . . no, no, totally fine, I mean . . . we're friends like that. We were . . . wrestling."

"Son, I work in Hollywood." Big Al shook his head. "If I had a dollar for every time—"

"It's true!" Reid wailed from underneath me.

"Hey, whatever you say!" Big Al held up his hands. "I didn't see anything."

"Because nothing happened!" My jaw clenched. "I like women and this is my brother. Do you know how wrong that is? Reid, show him your license." Wasn't sure if I was supposed to actually reveal that we were brothers, but whatever, I was desperate. And hey, if he got fired from the show because I was starring in it, it wouldn't be any skin off my nose.

Reid didn't move.

I looked down.

He was grinning like an idiot. Rat bastard! "Reid . . ."

"It's cool, Max, I mean, if Big Al knows . . ."

"I'm striking you out of my will for good now. Just know, at one point I was going to leave you my old Sega Genesis."

"Damn it," Reid muttered as I crawled off of him. "I've coveted that thing for years."

"I'll be ready in ten," I snapped at Big Al. "Oh, and you're going to have to censor what's about to take place." With a grin I dropped my pants to get him out of there faster. Yeah, I was going to be in a world of hurt tonight. Good thing the show wasn't live, because they would without a doubt need to do some censoring, especially with Becca around. Then again, maybe Amazon's all-around terrifying demeanor would cause my balls to cease functioning for a few minutes. One can only hope. Ha, the Erection Killer! Nice. I knew I could have come up with a better nickname!

"All right." Big Al whistled. "I'll just . . ." He motioned to the crew. "We'll be outside."

CHAPTER TWENTY-SIX
BECCA

I almost wore black.

I didn't want to wear white just because Reid happened to mention it was Max's favorite. Yeah, it really sounded like middle school, when you plan your outfit the day before, from your shoes all the way up to your earrings, in hopes that the captain of the basketball team looks in your direction.

Taking a deep breath, I checked my watch and waited. Max was supposed to come pick up the girls.

I was first.

And he was late.

Five minutes later I honestly felt stood up, which was stupid because it was a TV show. It wasn't going to happen.

When a knock finally did sound at the door, I nearly fell off the bed scrambling to get it.

It wasn't real.

Not a real date.

So I let Max knock again.

I finally opened the door after the third knock and almost choked on the humid air.

Max.

Max smiling.

Max smiling, in a white button-down shirt that was slightly open at the neck.

Max wearing linen pants with his white button-down, with a killer tan and megawatt smile.

Swear it was like watching *Ocean's Twelve* when Brad Pitt walks out of the elevator in his cream suit.

Swoon-worthy moment.

"Hey." Max reached for my hand. "Are you ready?"

"Yes," I managed, my legs filling with lead as I stared at him.

"Great." He shoved his hands in his pockets while his eyes roamed over my body. "I really, really like your dress." He drank me in, from the tips of my toes to the top of my head. I did a little twirl. I wasn't wearing anything special, just a white halter-top sundress.

"Beautiful." His smile was so warm, so appreciative, that my heart did a little skip. "Shall we?" His arm was in front of me, and then my hand hooked underneath it, and we were walking to the next hut. The humidity in the air was already causing me to sweat. The thing about humidity? It makes every scent come alive. So walking with Max, even for those few short feet, was pure torture. What the hell kind of cologne did he use? It had a fresh, almost breezy scent mixed with . . . pine? Something piney. It was . . . really, really . . . addicting. I had a sudden urge to taste him, just to see if the taste was better than the smell.

But we were already at the next hut. Gina's hut. One camera was placed to the side so it could watch all reactions, while the other was facing us.

Max knocked.

Gina answered on the first knock, nearly sending Max sailing to the ground, since he'd clearly assumed he'd have to knock twice.

"I'm ready," she announced, barreling out of her room, wearing a camo dress. It had slits on both legs all the way up to her hips. Holy crap. I had to hand it to her, though, with her sharp features, tall figure, and all-around exotic, yet sometimes scary, good looks, it worked. It really worked. And it made me feel kind of . . . vanilla next to her rainbow.

"You look great." Max smiled warmly and offered her his other arm. It was awkward to know we were both on a date with the same guy and at the end of the night one of us was leaving.

Earlier I'd thought for sure I had nothing to worry about.

But Max was talking to Gina like he was actually interested in her.

"Oh, so that's why you like pine nuts!" He chuckled. "Awesome, and when did you discover you wanted to be part of a nudist colony?" Blah blah blah. "Fascinating. Oh, Gina, you're so funny." Laughter, more laughter. Gag me. I chugged my wine and tried to engage in conversation, but every time I opened my mouth Gina interrupted me.

Finally. After our feast of salmon on the beach, it was time for Max to take each of us aside. They stopped filming for a few minutes to let us know exactly how long we got with the Bachelor. We were also instructed to plead our case as to why he should keep us. Were we there for him? Or the money? Or both? What did we hope to gain by staying?

"Why are you here, Becca?"

"Why is the money so important to you?"

"Would you ever choose love over money? What would cause you to choose love instead?"

The questions just kept coming and the more they fired them at me the sicker I felt to my stomach. I was in way over my head. I'd never counted on developing feelings for Max—at all. I mean, I'd watched these shows. I'd made fun of that girl, the one who cried when she got kicked off. If I got kicked off, I wouldn't cry, but I'd be seriously disappointed and not, I realized with a sinking feeling, just because I'd lost the money.

By the time the cameras started rolling again, I'd had three glasses of wine over the course of two hours and was feeling sluggish and sick.

Max had taken a long walk with Gina while I sat and watched. She laughed, he laughed, she laughed again. Oh, look, the wineglass is about to get crushed in my hand.

"Okay, guys." Rex walked up. "Both camera crews on Gina and Max. Becca, go ahead and relax a bit."

Relax, ha.

"So . . ." Reid appeared out of nowhere and sat down. "Killer dress."

My eyes narrowed. "Thanks."

"Nervous?"

"Nope."

"Liar."

"Can you be anything but yourself right now?" I asked. "It would be really helpful."

"Myself?"

"Arrogant and irritating."

Reid smiled. "He doesn't like her, he's just doing it for the cameras."

I tucked my hair behind my ear and looked down at my empty plate. "I wasn't even thinking about Max."

"That's lie number two." Reid reached for a wineglass. "Is this Gina's or Max's?"

"Wouldn't you like to know?" I answered sweetly.

"I'll take my chances." He sipped.

"I really wouldn't."

"So Max . . ." Reid set the wineglass down. "I'm glad I caught you before he got back. He's super embarrassed about this and I wouldn't even bring it up if I didn't think it was going to be a big deal but . . . he has this thing about women touching his leg." Reid leaned in and whispered, "Totally calms him down on dates. It's weird, I don't know why it soothes him but it really does and the fact that you'd make him feel good after he dumps Gina, well, it would mean a lot to me, as a brother."

I eyed him suspiciously while at the same time telling my heart to stop slamming against my chest. Was he really going to choose me over Gina? "Why don't I believe you?"

"My charm." He nodded. "It throws women off, makes them think I'm being flirty and suggestive when really I'm just breathing the same air. I mean, I put my pants on the same way everyone else does, by jumping in with both feet."

"Uh, Reid, people don't really—"

"Sure." He waved his hand into the air. "I date models for fun and my left dimple has its own Facebook page"—he flashed said dimple—"but I'm just a man, Becca. A hot-blooded, well-endowed—"

"Stop." I held up my hand. "You've made your point."

I heard shouting and then a slap cracked through the night sky as Gina ran off toward her hut.

"Shit." Reid shuddered. "Girl hits hard. It's crucial, Becca, you really need to comfort him. I don't care that it's a TV show. Hearts are still involved and as much of an ass as Max appears to be, he hates breaking them."

Reid got up from his seat and gave my shoulders a squeeze before taking off in the other direction.

Max approached with the camera crew, still rubbing his face. By the time he reached the table it was starting to flame red. Poor guy. Maybe Reid was right, Max just needed comfort.

"Ready?" He held out his hand.

"Yeah." I grinned. "I am."

"Let the date continue!" Max pulled me close to his body and wrapped his arm around me.

I breathed a sigh of relief.

It was going to be a good night and I knew just how to put him at ease.

CHAPTER TWENTY-SEVEN

MAX

If Becca's hand wandered any closer to my favorite place, we were going to have a big problem, and not to brag, but it was really going to be a big, huge, large problem. Feel me?

"Ha-ha." I scooted away from her wandering hand and cursed men everywhere for not bringing back the whole hanky trend. Damn, I needed a cloth pressed against my forehead.

"It's pretty out here." Becca put her head on my shoulder. We'd been watching the waves for over an hour, talking, laughing, and, in my case for at least 99 percent of that time, damn near exploding with desire and making a giant ass out of myself.

It would be fine if she had just been patting my leg, you know, in a motherly way.

If mothers did what that girl was doing—it would result in a hell of a long prison sentence, that's all I'm saying.

She didn't pat.

She caressed.

Then slightly pressed her fingers into my thigh, massaging, moving, making my hips want to drive toward her with such hunger that I had to imagine Reid naked to keep myself from having an inappropriate moment on camera.

"It is." I finally found my voice as her hand stopped moving. "Really pretty." I turned and gazed down at her.

She was watching the waves.

I was watching her eyelashes flutter against her cheeks.

When she finally realized I wasn't looking at the same thing, she looked up at me. Her eyes appeared heavy as she looked out from underneath those thick, dark lashes.

Her hand moved.

Ha, so did I.

I mean not my body, but let's just say parts of my body responded in a very . . . cheerful way. Yes, let's go with *cheerful*. Oh, hell, my body was damn near rejoicing and breaking out into song.

Slowly her hand slid up my thigh and squeezed, when she grazed what I'm only assuming she thought was my cell phone. I jerked away from her.

Spoiler alert—I'd left my cell phone in my hut.

It was to remain off at all times. As per the rules.

And I was so damn on.

"Swim?" I choked. "Do you want to go for a swim?"

"But I don't have my swimsuit."

"Me either." I shrugged. "But you're already aware that never stops me, does it?"

Becca blushed.

The cameras leaned in.

"Filming done yet?" I asked, not taking my eyes off Becca.

"We need about ten more minutes of tape. Then again, if you get naked, we'll film till you're done."

Becca's hand moved again.

I was ready to bust out the *bloody hells* and I wasn't even British. See? She was driving me crazy! I was officially changing nationalities! Her hand slipped. Swear it had to have slipped because she was actually now almost copping a feel.

O Canada!

"Done! For the night, done! Ha-ha." I couldn't stop the nervous laughter. Becca smiled and then looked down at my physical tribute to her beauty. Ha, if I weren't so aroused I'd laugh at my own joke.

"Max!" Becca shouted.

I covered her mouth with mine, then let my lips trail to her ear. "Long story."

"Huge story," she whispered against my lips.

"Damn right it is." I pulled her into my lap. Irritated that the light from the camera was two seconds away from making me permanently blind. "Go away!"

"What?" Becca pulled back.

I jerked her against me, my mouth urgently finding hers, before I broke the kiss and said, "Not you, them."

"Not when you give us this." Big Al chuckled.

I kissed Becca's neck. "A little help?"

"Hmm." She tugged my lower lip, then trailed a kiss down my jaw.

I groaned and said through clenched teeth, "That's not the type of help I meant."

"What," she whispered in my ear, "do you propose I do?"

"Not feel me up!" I snapped in her ear, then gave it a little tug, because, you know, I was there and all.

"But Reid said . . ."

"And you listened!" I whispered harshly.

"You don't even know"—she arched her back as I kissed down her chest—"what . . ." she panted, "he said."

"Anything." I gripped her by the shoulders to steady her. "And I do mean anything and everything he says—you take with a grain of salt, or just don't listen." I released my hold on her shoulders, which was a mistake, because it caused her knees to sink farther into the sand on either side of me, making my body damn near explode. "Headgear, Grandma, Reid pleasuring Grandma, Teenage Mutant Ninja Turtles, Garfield!"

"Please tell me that's not dirty talk." Becca gave me a concerned stare.

"I'm trying not to . . ." I held up my hands. "You know."

She tilted her head.

"Your fault." I pointed at her and then stared at her mouth and lost my train of thought.

"Max?"

"Shh." I pressed a finger to her lips. "I'm . . . trying really hard here."

"How's that working out?"

"I said I was trying . . . *hard*, Becca, you do the math," I snapped.

"Guys!" Reid came barreling down the beach to the camera crew. "Rex says to wrap things up."

Big Al grunted and gave a firm nod. The camera turned off, and within a few minutes we were alone.

Except for a grinning Reid.

And the goat that followed.

First things first . . . I was going to kill Reid, and then I was going to do a Google search on the sleeping habits of the goat species.

CHAPTER TWENTY-EIGHT

BECCA

Max slowly helped me to my feet. I tried to avert my eyes so I wasn't looking directly at him and his happy place, but it was almost impossible. Thankfully, things seemed to be going back to normal since Reid's arrival.

"Ah, Brother." Max gritted his teeth together. "How lovely of you to join us on this beautiful evening." He wrapped an arm around my shoulders and squeezed, and we started walking toward Reid.

"No problem." Reid's eyes narrowed at Max, and then lowered. Was the guy seriously checking out his brother? "I mean, I don't have a problem. Do you have a little problem? Anything you wish to discuss? Be rescued from?"

Max shrugged. "Not really. Oh, and thanks for interrupting what I'm pretty sure is going to go down in TV history as the best kiss ever—I should punch you in the throat."

"But—" Reid looked between the two of us, then glanced back down at Max. "I thought that . . ."

"Come on, Hades." Max clicked his tongue.

The goat fell into step beside us as we walked back toward his hut.

"Becca and I were just going to discuss our game plan for the rest of the week." Max said this so nonchalantly that I almost missed it, and then he winked, and every thought flew out the window.

"Right," I said quickly. "That."

"Game plan?"

"Oh, and breakfast in the morning"—Max nodded—"is super early so we really need our sleep. Thanks for nothing, Reid. See ya."

With a tug Max had me in his hut, followed by the goat, who surprisingly stepped around us and went to the corner, where he lay down on what I can only imagine used to be articles of clothing and started chomping down.

"Aren't you afraid?" I pointed at the goat.

"Nah, as long as Hades has underwear I'm his favorite person. Can't tell if it makes him horny or just so damn distracted he doesn't care whether it's me or a stranger he stays with."

In response the goat made a gurgling noise and looked over at us, sighing contentedly.

"I have to say"—I smiled at Max—"I'm proud of you."

"I'm proud of me too." Max beamed. "Now, about that discussion we were having on the beach."

He pulled me closer to his body, but my feet hit something on the ground. Papers fluttered around my sandals. "What's this?"

"Oh, that's my chart."

"Your chart?"

He nodded. "To ward off the crazies."

"Did you actually learn the names of all the girls?"

"Yup, and I assigned nicknames."

"Who's that?" I pointed to one of the girls, one with short-cropped black hair.

"Nicki, but her nickname is Minion. She wore overalls the first day of filming and every time she smiles I swear I hear the theme song to *Despicable Me*."

I covered my laughter with my hand. Yeah, that mental picture was spot-on.

"And her?" I was both curious and buying time. I didn't want to finish the conversation from the beach, because I was pretty sure I would end up . . . naked, somewhere, and I'd only known Max for three days. Three days and he was already making me second-guess all my preconceived notions about the type of guy he was. I'd thought that because he was funny he was harmless, but I'd had no idea funny could be dangerous because it was too easy to let him in and once he was in he stayed there—refusing to budge. He wasn't just funny; he was sexy and had a personality that was electric.

Besides, he kissed like a dream.

An actual dream.

If I could build every dream from here on out, it would include that man's mouth on every part of my body.

"Hey." Max grabbed my hand. "You okay? You're really flushed."

"Yeah," I croaked. "I'm a bit hot."

"If you remember, I did offer to go skinny-dipping."

"Ha!" I hit him playfully across the chest. "So you never answered my question, who's that girl?"

Max didn't take his eyes off me. "Easy, it's Cat, or Catherine, and I actually just use the name Cat because she has super freakishly long nails that I'm pretty sure have some sort of fungus growing underneath them on account that when one broke earlier today it oozed."

"Whoa!" I held up my hands. "Not a mental picture I needed."

"You asked." His smile was bright. Was it really necessary he be that good-looking and funny? "So . . ." He brought my hand to his full lips and kissed it. "Is that a no on getting naked?"

"Again . . ." I rolled my eyes even though the idea made me hot all over. "Does that line work?"

His eyes hooded with desire. "You tell me."

"Nope," I lied. Yes. Hell, yes, it worked.

"Fine." He dropped my hand. Was he seriously admitting defeat so soon? "We should probably plan my revenge tonight anyways."

"Revenge?" Keeping up with Max was like trying to follow the thought process of a first grader on his first day of school. One minute he's talking about pencils, the next he's eating the crayons.

"For Reid, tell me—" Max put his hands on his hips, drawing my eyes to exactly where I had no business looking. He groaned. "Okay, tell me but please don't stare at me while I ask you this question, it makes things—"

"Hard." I grinned.

"You have no damn clue." Max swore violently for a few seconds.

"Garfield?" I offered. "That help?"

"Right, thanks." Breath hissed between his teeth. "Reid told you what, exactly?"

I scratched my head. "He said that you were nervous and having a rough night and that if I just rubbed your leg you'd feel at ease. He said it was one of your things."

"One of my things?" Max's eyebrows shot up as he repeated under his breath, "One of my things, that bastard!"

"I'm guessing it's not?"

"The hell it's not!" Max roared. "Any guy would sell his soul to get a woman to touch him like that. The problem isn't the touching; it's the situation that caused it! Damn it, Reid!" Max's voice rose. "Look at the goat, notice anything?"

Um, yeah. It was entirely too pleased to be eating Max's clothes.

"Look closer."

I looked closer.

"Get there faster."

I blinked. "Holy crap, are those your boxers?"

"All of them. Just in case you weren't aware." Max swore. "Oh, and P.S.: Here's a free anatomy lesson. The better the clothing barrier the less chance you have of a . . . cheerful surprise."

I giggled and then full-out laughed my ass off.

"Yeah, so now it's war, and during wartime, we don't laugh. We get even."

"And how do we plan on doing that? Hmm?"

Max's grin was pure evil. "Oh, I have a few ideas. How comfortable are you with scaring him shitless?"

I pretended to think about it.

"Not the time for hesitation. You're either hashtag Team Max or hashtag Team Reid."

"Did you just hashtag yourself?"

"Yes!" Max threw his hands in the air. "Because what we're about to embark on is Twitter-trend-worthy, all right? You in or out?"

He held out his hand.

I grabbed it. "In, of course."

"That's my girl."

"Who says I'm yours?" I teased.

"That," Max said seriously, nodding toward me. "That look in your eyes. It says it for me." His tone was confident, but something in his eyes gave me pause. He looked . . . unsure of himself.

He tilted his head, licked his lips, then opened his mouth—but no sound came out. Was it possible he was feeling just as unsure as I was?

CHAPTER TWENTY-NINE
BECCA

Max walked over to his suitcase and pulled out a black bag with masking tape across it. Written on the masking tape was "OMRT."

"Uh—" I pointed. "What's that stand for?"

"Operation: Max's Reign of Terror."

"Yeah, and it's not weird you actually labeled something that. That doesn't make me doubt your sanity at all."

Max rolled his eyes. "Please, I'm always prepared for all possible outcomes. I'm like freaking Bradley Cooper in *Limitless* but with better eyes."

Max had finally snapped.

"Pay attention." He unzipped the black bag. "Because this is going to take a type of finesse that can't be taught, although it could possibly be learned if you have someone like me to teach you. Lucky for us I was born with it."

I tried desperately not to roll my eyes. "Fine, what do I do?"

Max pulled out a needle and flicked it with his finger.

"Whoa!" I held up my hands.

"HA!" He laughed. "Freaked you out, right?"

"I'm not laughing."

"Please." He snorted. "It's one tranquilizer."

"Tranquilizer? Where the hell did you get a tranquilizer?"

"Online. What you think? I zookeep on my days off?"

"No," I snapped. "Because having days off means you have days off, meaning you're employed!"

"Who says I'm not employed?" Max asked, his shoulders tense.

I shuffled my feet. "Well, are you?"

"Are you?" he snapped then let out a groan.

I held up my hands. "Whoa there, easy. And for your information, I don't just work at Starbucks. I'm a student, you know, studying to do something with my life."

Max let out a snort.

It was the first time I'd seen his happy-go-lucky façade stripped and in its place something that looked a lot like regret and a bit of anger came to the surface.

"I, um." I exhaled loudly. "I'm sorry, I didn't mean to offend you."

"Damn it, Becca. I can't concentrate with you breathing down my neck! Now, hold the needle while I pull out the Bengay." Okay, so apparently that part of the conversation was closed. Max was back to his oddly attractive self and I was left wondering what the hell had just happened. Clearly jobs were a bit of a sore subject.

"Wow." I took the needle in my hands, careful to point it outward. "There's a sentence I hope to never hear again."

"Shh." Max carefully pulled out the Bengay and whispered, "My precious."

He was either insane or just downright pissed about what Reid had done, whatever that may have been. It was tie between being oddly attracted to his erratic behavior and also a bit frightened that I still wanted to kiss him despite the fact that he was caressing a tube of Bengay and looking like he was about five seconds away from stabbing Reid in the ass.

After a few minutes of setting his "tools" onto the bed he handed me an iPad. "An elephant never forgets."

"You're a man." I felt the need to point that out just in case that needle had pricked him and he was suffering a mental breakdown.

"Hell, yes I am," Max grumbled. "Which is why it's damn near impossible to stand next to you without thinking about ripping off that white dress."

It got very quiet in that hut.

Quiet and tense.

Like, climb-the-walls tense.

"Said that out loud, didn't I?" Max closed his eyes and pinched the bridge of his nose.

"'Fraid so."

He didn't say anything.

"And an elephant never forgets, so . . ."

"Don't toss my words back at me!" He grabbed me by the shoulders and pointed me in the direction of the door. "Now go stick it to him."

"Maybe we should work on a different choice of words." I sighed. "What exactly am I sticking?"

"The needle." Max pushed my body closer to the entrance. "I'll be right outside, all you need to do is stick him in the leg, the arm, any appendage will do."

"Any appendage will do?" I repeated. "You do realize you're asking me to commit a crime?"

"Does it look like we're in America?"

Hades made a choking sound from the corner.

Max ran over and pulled the boxers from his mouth and patted his head. "As I was saying, would this happen in the US?"

"Maybe Canada." I smirked.

"Ha-ha, haven't heard that before. Oh, let's make fun of the country with free health insurance, what do you have?"

I squinted. "You do realize that sex changes are free in Canada but you have to pay out of pocket to get a pair of glasses, right?"

"NOT THE POINT!" Max raised his voice. "Are you going to stick him or not?"

I groaned. "What if I say no?"

"Then . . ." Max's eyes narrowed. "I won't protect you from the girls."

"Oh, really?" My eyebrows shot up. "Is that what you've been doing? Protecting me?"

Max's focus was on my heaving chest, and he shook his head. "Sorry, can you repeat the questions? Your boobs were talking to me."

"They were not!"

"Um, they moved, and I'm pretty sure the right one said hi. Swear it was even ready to pop out and say hi."

"Max!" I squirmed. "Stop being . . . you!"

"Aw . . ." Max looked wounded. "That's hurtful. Now you have to do me a favor to save my pride and all-around insecure self."

"You are not insecure."

His shoulders hunched. "I can't . . . believe . . . you don't like . . . the real Max. The real M-dog, M-money, M—"

"Stop." I waved in his direction. "How about this? I'll try, only because I'm pretty sure if I don't do what you want I'm going to be stuck in this hut arguing with you for the next eight hours and I really want to go to bed."

"Don't we all?" Max sighed. "Sleep is next to godliness."

"I think you mean being clean."

"Same thing." He shrugged. "Now go stick my brother."

"Stop sayin' *stick*!"

"Stick him good." Max winked. "Oh, and P.S.: If he makes a choking noise once the needle goes in, that's totally normal."

"Max!"

"I'll be right behind you!" He shoved me out the door.

CHAPTER THIRTY
BECCA

Was I really going along with this plan? Furthermore, what exactly was the plan? Max still hadn't told me anything, and I still wasn't sure I wanted to participate. Then again, I wanted to hang out with Max. Being with him made me laugh, even if it was at his brother's expense.

I was getting in the way of family drama, but for some reason, excitement coursed through my veins as I approached Reid's hut. What did I do if he was sleeping? What if the camera crew was in there? Last thing I needed was for it to be national news that I'd tried to drug the Bachelor's brother. Sure, that would go over really well with future grad school scholarships and a career teaching little kids.

Yeah, I highly doubted I would get a job at an elementary school if I was found guilty of drugging anyone or anything.

I almost backed out—made an excuse, I mean this was my career he was toying with, and not just that, but what happened if we got caught? Max was already wealthy—the world was his oyster even if he didn't want to work in it. I had everything to lose.

Max turned around and flashed me a smile.

I followed him, like a trained puppy.

I put the needle behind my back and took a soothing breath. I could do this. All I needed to do was knock and then . . . stick. *Damn you, Max!*

With a shaking hand, I knocked on the hut door.

It flew open.

Reid stared at me hard, his eyes taking in my dress and then looking behind me. "I knew you'd come."

"What?"

"I could sense it."

"Are you high?"

Reid's eyes narrowed. "No, why?"

"How are you awake?"

"Aw, sweetheart, you rather I be sleeping so you could crawl into bed with me?" He laughed. "I knew it! Screw you, Max! She's mine!" His gorgeous smile made me want to punch something. "Doesn't do it for you, does he? I can't say I'm surprised. I mean, once you go Reid you don't go Max. That would be like driving a Ford and then ignoring the BMW. It's just ridiculous, and baby, my ride"—he smirked—"is very, very smooth."

"Funny," I said through clenched teeth. "Because I like it rough."

The smile froze on his face.

And then I jabbed the tranquilizer into his arm.

"What the—damn it," he shouted, stumbling backward. "I've been hit!" His eyes crossed and then he tripped over his suitcase as he went flying onto his bed. "I'll get you, Max. So sleepy, oh, look, it's Big Bird." He started laughing hysterically, tears running down his face, and then the tears turned into a choked sob. "I'm so damn afraid of *Jurassic Park*." He shivered. "Hold me, Becca, just this . . . once." He grabbed the pillow. "Oh, that's nice, make the T. rex go rawr! Rawr, T. rex, get your bitch." Cough, cough, cough. "Why don't you love me?"

"Reid—"

"Sing me a song."

I looked around the room. Why wasn't he passing out? Should I just leave him? And where the hell was Max? "Demi Lovato is so damn hot." He sighed. "Noooooo!" he wailed, punching the pillow with his right hand, then his left hand. "My girl! Jonas Brother suck-ass!" He lifted his leg and kicked, then fell off the other side of the bed.

No noise.

Nothing.

Quietly I got on the bed and peeked over the edge, just in time for Reid to shoot to his feet and make a gun motion with his hand. "Put 'em up!"

I held up my hands. I was going to kill Max.

"I'm a cop!" Reid burst out laughing, his eyes were crazy, wild, unfocused, and then he put the fake gun down and slumped. "I never knew my father."

"Good Lord," Max said from behind me. "What did you do?"

"What did I do?" I hissed. "I did what you asked!"

"You broke him?" Max pointed. "Because there was enough tranq in that one shot to make him sleep for at least five hours, and right now it looks like he thinks he's Jack on the *Titanic*.

"Don't let go, Jack, don't let go!" Reid wailed, holding on to the bedpost.

"Or Rose." Max nodded. "No shame in wanting to be rescued."

"Curse you, iceberg!" Reid shook his fist at the sky, and then looked over at me. "Gummy bears kill."

"Max!" I elbowed him in the ribs. "Make it better."

"Oh, shit." Max paled. "Give me the needle."

I handed it over.

The minute Max read it his eyes widened. He quickly ran into the bathroom and disposed of the evidence.

"Max—"

"He's high."

"No shit!" I slapped him across the shoulder. "What did I give him?"

"Er . . ." Max swallowed. "Let's just say Reid feels nothing."

"Absolutely," Reid said slowly, joining in the conversation. "Nothing!" He laughed. "Watch!" And then he punched himself in the jaw.

I winced.

Max laughed.

"Not funny." I glared. "Fix this."

"Oh, I'll fix it, all right."

Max dug through his black bag and pulled out duct tape and the iPad.

"Wait, what are you doing?"

"I don't have a drug past," Max said, ignoring me. "I mean—I experimented, sure, but the thing about being high?" He looked at Reid and smirked. "Let's just say fears are heightened, joy is heightened, and Reid, well, he's never going to mess with me again."

For the next ten minutes I watched as Max adjusted Reid onto one of the chairs, duct-taped him, and then set an iPad in front of him on the desk. I was more confused after he pressed "Play." It was a home video of a sweet old lady celebrating her birthday. How was that scary?

And then that same sweet old lady winked at the camera and slowly licked off the candles. Only to hand them to the person on her right, who just happened to be a trembling Reid.

"Makes sense now, doesn't it? All the little pieces of the puzzle coming together." Max wiped a fake tear and grabbed the Bengay, then started rubbing it on Reid's chest.

"What are you doing?"

"Feels sooo good." Reid laughed. "Harder, bitch, harder!"

"I bet he's so good in bed . . ." Max sighed. "Pity he may lose all ability to perform sexually after this, eh, Becca?" He slapped Reid lightly on the face with the Bengay and sighed. "Our work here is done."

"Wait, that's it?"

"Hey, Reid." Max pointed at the iPad. "Look, a movie!"

"I freaking love Disney," Reid said in a serious voice. "Max, Bro, do you remember *Up*? Damn movie had me sobbing for days."

"Yeah, it was . . . good." Max patted Reid's head. "But this is so much better."

"Why?" Reid yawned. "Yawns are funny, so is breathing." He then made a huge show of inhaling and exhaling so much he started coughing.

"Because—" Max shut off the lights. "Look, you're starring in this movie."

"So cool!" Reid sighed.

"Reid."

"Shh!" Reid snapped at Max and then whispered, "I'm watching my ass."

Max held up his hands. "Have fun, Bro, just remember, I love you."

"Love you too, Brother!"

Max escorted me out.

It wasn't until we were almost back to his hut that I heard a scream pierce the night sky . . . and it was Reid's.

CHAPTER THIRTY-ONE

MAX

"We should go back." Becca grabbed my arm. "He's in pain!"

"So was I!" I scoffed. "Especially with you straddling me and . . ." Max looked away. "Stuff."

"I'm sorry." Becca smirked. "With me straddling you . . . and stuff?"

"It's late." I fake-yawned. "I can't think of big words when it's late."

"It's midnight."

"Your watch is upside down." I pointed at her wrist.

Becca lifted it closer to her face, giving me time to pin her against the side of the hut. "I'm going to kiss you now."

"The combination of Bengay and Reid watching an elderly woman got you all hot and bothered, didn't it?" Her voice was teasing, breathless, but I knew it was a front. She was pretending not to care about kissing or sharing another moment with me.

But she cared.

More than she wanted to admit.

More than I wanted to acknowledge.

So I gently lowered my head and brushed a soft kiss across her lips. "Thanks for helping me torture my brother tonight."

Becca shivered in my arms. "What are partners for?"

"You can be my partner any day. Dibs for when we play laser tag, for real. Those kids won't know what hit them, especially Jimmy, damn bane of my existence. What ten-year-old plays that dirty?"

"Laser tag?"

"One of my many"—my lips massaged hers—"many"—I dipped my tongue into her mouth—"many talents."

Becca pulled back. "What other talents do you have?"

"If you have to ask . . ." I sighed. "Do you really deserve to know?"

"Cocky."

"Extremely insecure." I tried to look humble, making Becca laugh out loud. I would freaking Thor my way through life if I could just hear that laugh every second.

"I should go to bed." She sighed.

"Every sidekick needs his rest."

"Um, sidekick? I'm pretty sure I was the main event." Becca slapped me across the chest lightly.

"Sure, you drugged him." I peeled myself away from her. A few days, I'd only known her a few days. I couldn't invite her in even though I desperately wanted to. "But who taped him to a chair?"

"Right." Becca nodded. "So when the FBI questions us I'll be sure to let them know I was just the sidekick. Glad we got our stories straight."

I grinned.

"Night, Max." She returned the smile, her hand lingering on my arm.

"You know you can stay," I whispered.

"Probably not a good idea." She didn't meet my gaze. "You know, since you have Bengay all over your hands."

I burst out laughing. "Don't knock it until you try it."

"I'd rather not feel that kind of tingle." With a wink she walked off, her hips swaying the entire way toward the huts.

CHAPTER THIRTY-TWO

MAX

To say Reid gave me a wide berth over the course of the next week would be an understatement. Pretty sure he was still planning his revenge, because every once in a while I'd see him glare at me, then scribble something down in a notebook.

Normally he'd be the type of guy to give me hell during all the competitions, but aside from laughing when I fell out of the coconut tree, an incident that would probably cause me to wince when I saw coconuts at the grocery store, he was quiet, the perfect professional.

My head hurt, my ass hurt, everything hurt. When they'd said we'd be competing they hadn't meant that I'd get to sit around and watch the girls vie for my favor . . . um, no, each competition was getting harder and harder, stretching my sanity to the limit until I felt like snapping.

There was the *Survivor*-style canoe race.

The "What type of foreign animal am I eating?" competition that nearly sent me to the set doctor after I had a bad reaction to fish eggs.

The night volleyball—played with oversize balls that had a tendency to break upon being touched too hard.

And finally, my favorite, what would probably be called the *Carrie* episode, where we had to hunt and kill a wild boar.

Blood had been everywhere. Swear mine had no meat, just blood. We were ten days in.

Eight girls were left, including Becca, and, staying true to my promise, I kept all the crazies away from her. We were an unstoppable team. Anyone watching the show would know she was a favorite. But I mean, look at her. She wasn't just beautiful, she was . . . hilarious, intelligent, going to school to be a teacher, she had direction. And I didn't.

I rubbed my chest. I admired everything about her and even though I had a lot of money and what people would probably assume was a lot to offer, I didn't feel good enough for her. At all.

We only had eleven days left . . . so we were close to halfway. But rather than feel relieved, I was panicked because in eleven days I wasn't going to be seeing her daily.

Rex cleared his throat. "Max? I asked you a question."

My confessionals were every morning at seven. I hated freaking seven a.m. I glared at the camera. "Care to repeat it?"

"Sure." I wasn't his biggest fan, and I'm pretty sure he regretted casting me after my very first confessional, where I asked him how to get a spray tan on Love Island.

"Eight girls left . . ." Rex gleamed. "Falling for any of them?"

I cleared my throat and looked down. "A few. Then again, I fell for that goat that hung out by my hut too, so who knows."

His teeth clenched so hard I was surprised a crown didn't come flying out of his mouth and smack me in the face.

"Max." Rex chuckled. "Here on the show we're firm believers in allowing family to help us . . . make those tough decisions in life. Wouldn't you agree it's helpful having friends and family around?"

My eyes narrowed. "Yes?"

"We thought so. And so did they!"

Wait, what?

I heard shouting.

And when I turned around I experienced a full-on panic attack as Jason, Milo, and Colt stepped off of a boat and ran down the dock toward me.

"Son of a bitch," I mumbled.

"Surprise!" Reid said from beside me.

I glared.

Little G poked his head out of my pocket; I shoved him back in, nobody needed to see what was about to take place. Because if I knew my friends, they weren't going to make these last eleven days easy. They wanted to win their damn bets, and they wanted me to finally get my head out of my ass, by any means possible. I was pretty confident they didn't really think any sort of law applied to them, and the thought of prison clearly wasn't a deterrent if our past circumstances were any indication.

Milo had been sending me job applications via e-mail for the past month.

Jason had been worse, actually setting me up on a job interview, which I'd thought was a date. Let's just say I didn't get the job, especially since I told the lady interviewing me that I liked the way her dress hugged her hips. How the hell was I supposed to know I was interviewing to be the new HR manager for a hotel chain?

My friends were ruthless.

Which meant only one thing.

Becca was going to see the real Max, all right, because they brought out the worst in me, and she would either run screaming in the other direction or find me endearing.

My money?

Was on the screaming.

"Max!" Jason was the first to reach me. He held out his arms, and I seriously contemplated gut-punching him but hugged him instead and may or may not have wrapped my leg around his waist and grabbed his ass.

"Hate you," I whispered in his ear.

"Love me." He jerked away from me and laughed. "Besides, Reid's been saying you've . . . found . . . someone."

"Oh." I nodded. "Little G, he's cool." I pulled him out of my pocket and showed everyone.

"He has no tail," Milo pointed out, clearly unaware that Little G had recently suffered a trauma to his little body via Hades chasing him. She tilted her head in my direction. "You look awful happy for being so against doing the show."

Ignoring her, I shoved the little guy back in my pocket. "Don't be so insensitive, Milo! God, not all animals can have tails! All right? Just drop it!"

"You a little tense?" Colt smirked.

"I'm totally and completely in control." I managed a very tight shrug.

And then Becca walked by.

And my heart did that irritating little flip thing where it starts beating really fast. Even Little G started squirming in my pocket.

"That her?" Milo whispered to Reid.

"Only one way to find out." Jason looked at all of us, then jogged in her direction.

"Noooo!" I ran after Jason and tackled him to the ground, thankfully not squishing Little G in the process.

"What the hell, man?" Jason swore from underneath me.

"Sorry." I quickly got off of him. "Island fever makes people"—I coughed—"weird."

"I'll say." Colt eyed me up and down. "What the hell's wrong with you, Max?"

"He has no underwear." This from Reid.

"Helpful." I glared. "Thank you."

Milo squinted. "Why don't you have underwear?"

"Oh"—I shrugged—"Hades ate it."

Milo's face fell. "Max, you know I love you, but do you think you've been on this island maybe . . . too long?" She gave my arm a little squeeze.

"He's real!" I argued. "He's in my room! In the corner!"

"Aw, champ." Colt shook his head. "We had no idea this show would cause you to go insane."

"I'll prove it!"

Reid crossed his arms, his brows knitting together in concern. "Should you maybe ask Poseidon if it's okay? Since we're standing by the ocean and all?"

"Hades," I announced, "is a goat."

"Wait." Milo held up her hands. "You named a real goat, or your hallucination of Hades manifests itself as a goat?"

"He feeds his goat his boxers. It's how he gets off," Reid commented, then yelled, "Hey Becca, come over here!"

"Swear—" I shook my head. "Every time I tell myself to wake up, the nightmare just gets more real. Why are you guys here?"

Becca jogged toward us.

Milo opened her mouth to speak. We were still on the dock, so I did what any sane person would do in my situation. I pushed her in the water and then yelled, "Quick, sharks!"

Colt swore and dove in after her, followed by Jason, you know, because I tripped him, and then I made a cutting motion with my hand to Reid, who held his hands in the air and stepped back just as Becca approached.

"Sharks? Are you serious, Max?"

"Don't think I don't remember!" Reid pointed at Becca. "Don't think I don't . . . know things, about what you and Max did."

She shrugged innocently. "I have no idea what you're talking about."

He pointed at her slowly and then walked off.

"No sharks." I crossed my arms. "They just looked . . . hot."

"Who are they?" Becca watched in fascination as Colt and Milo dragged themselves to shore. Jason started swimming around happily.

Hmm, could I disown them? Probably not. What was a good lie? I finally went with the truth. "That's Milo." I pointed. "We used to be best friends until she made me pretend to be her fake boyfriend, then gay fiancé, and then she had the audacity to go and get married to that tool"—I pointed to Colt—"who slays dragons and shit and thinks that means he deserves the title of Milo's best friend." I sighed. "Oh." I pointed at Jason. "And that's Satan."

"Color me crazy, I feel like there's a story there?" Becca's cute eyebrows shot up as she nudged me.

"He signed me up for the show and said I was mourning the death of my fiancée, oh, and abandoned me when I was getting a prostate exam. Thanks, jackass!" I yelled at him as he got out of the water and flipped me off.

"You didn't want to do the show?"

"Do sharks have teeth?"

"Max . . ." She laughed. "I thought you were happy to be here."

"I am . . ." I grumbled. "Now."

"So what you're saying is I should go thank him?"

"I'm sorry, what?" I cupped my ear. "You want to engage in conversation with the Prince of Darkness why?"

Her smile made my heart slam against my chest. "To say thank you."

"For?"

"Had he not signed you up, I would have never met you . . ."

"You met me at the coffee shop," I pointed out.

"Right." She rolled her eyes. "And you also used five lame pickup lines on me. Had it not been for Jason, that would have been both your first and last time talking to me."

"Cocky?"

"No." she mimicked my voice. "Extremely insecure."

"Fine, you may speak to him, just make sure you talk really loud because he's eighty percent deaf in his left ear."

"Aw," Becca sighed. "Poor guy."

"Yeah, but his manhood more than makes up for all of his faults, at least that's what he claims. Then again, I'm pretty sure he has an undescended testicle, because he worked for years to get his voice to lower."

I wasn't done listing all the things wrong with Jason. By the time he made it to us he'd suffered through herpes, cholera, a bout of H1N1, two bat bites, halitosis, and an unidentified mass on his chest also known as a third nipple.

Don't judge me. I had to make him as unattractive as possible.

Because he was competition. He was a male and now he knew I was interested in someone, and didn't that bring out the competitive nature in all guys?

He would pay attention to her just like Reid did.

I wasn't going to have it.

CHAPTER THIRTY-THREE
BECCA

After meeting Max's friends, I gathered with the rest of the contestants for a giant feast to welcome them to the show.

Apparently they were there to help turn the tables. Each of his friends was going to pick out their favorite girl and plan a date with Max. Everything had been going so well between us that I tried not to be worried. Honestly, the show wasn't so much about the money anymore. I mean, I still needed it, but somewhere along the way it had turned into something more. It was about . . . finding someone I genuinely had fun and chemistry with.

Yeah, if the chemistry was any hotter I was going to go up in flames.

But Max hadn't pressured me in any way. Oh, he'd kissed me plenty, but that had been the extent of it. He'd invited me inside his hut, but he'd never . . . tried anything.

Did that mean we were just friends who kissed? Was he toying with me? Just a flirt? His behavior made me want to rethink my priorities. One minute I felt solid in my decision to see where things were going with him, but in that same breath, I'd start to panic.

What if he was just being friendly and I lost the money? All of it? How would I finish school? I could always take a year off.

I chewed my lower lip.

Would I do that? Just for a chance with Max?

Now that his friends were there I was a bit worried that I'd lose his attention, but when he arrived at the feast clad in hot white shorts that showed off his tan legs and the tightest gray muscle shirt I'd ever seen in my entire life, his eyes roamed the crowd until they landed on me.

The smile that curved his lips could only be described as one of pure excitement and then . . . lust.

He didn't even talk to the other contestants as he made his way over to my table and sat down next to me.

A few of the girls started whispering among one another. One of them glared in my direction, but I was used to that by now. We were in a competition, but none of them had crossed the line into being hostile. The producers probably hated that. The girls were civil to me; then again, I was nice to them, so I didn't see what the problem was.

"My lady."

"My lord."

"How badass would we be if we owned a castle?"

I laughed. Max was ridiculous. Everything that came out of his mouth was random. He made no sense, but was so entertaining. I was never bored. One could never be bored around Max. I never knew what he was thinking, which was both a good and a bad thing.

"Would our castle have a moat?" I asked.

"Of course." Max poured me a glass of wine. "Where else would we put the gators and Little G's family?"

"And what will we do with Hades?"

"I'm already convinced Reid's never going to find love, since I highly doubt he can keep it up, if you get my meaning, so we'll gift Hades to him to keep him company so he doesn't turn into a cranky old man."

"Wow." I laughed. "You've thought of it all."

"What can I say?" He shrugged, leaning his head toward mine. "I'm a giver."

"Good, because I'm a taker."

"Take all you want. As king of the castle, I order you, my fair lady, to take . . ." He kissed me softly on the mouth in front of all the contestants.

Too stunned to do anything but react, I kissed him back.

When the kiss ended, Max gave me a look of utter panic. "I just kissed you in front of everyone, didn't I?"

"Yeah," I said breathlessly.

"They're going to want to beat you even more now."

"Because you're such a prize?" I teased.

"Prize bull with the balls of—"

"Stop, I'm eating." Colton walked up behind Max and took a seat opposite me. "Hey, I'm—"

"The jackass who took Max's place as Milo's best friend?" I shook his hand.

"Cool, so he's already brainwashed you." Colt shook his head. "And you were so young, so full of potential."

"He says I have to drink red wine and wear only black and white until we consummate our blessed union." I nodded.

"Wow." Colton chuckled. "Cheers, apparently Max found his doppelgänger in the form of a hot-as-hell chick."

That earned Colton a swat to the back of his head as Milo made her way to our table. Apparently she didn't like him calling me hot? "You ass." She rolled her eyes.

"You and the missus fighting?" Max asked Colton.

"She's just mad because I wouldn't let her invite the turtle into the hut."

"Aw . . ." I nodded to Milo. "Aren't they pretty?"

"They're possessed!" Colt shouted. "And it snapped at my foot!"

"He probably thought your pinkie toe was a shrimp." Max shrugged.

Jason chose that moment to walk up. "Turtles don't eat shrimp, those badasses love a good burger, though."

"What?" we all asked in unison.

He shrugged. "I saw it on Animal Planet, they like ground beef. Sue me for being educated!"

"Are you guys"—I cleared my throat and pointed at all of them—"always like this?"

"It's the Max effect." Colt sighed. "Drops everyone's IQ and maturity. Tragic, really. I always wanted to have friends that made me smarter."

"Not a hard feat, I'm sure." Max grinned.

"Contestants!" Rex clapped his hands, gaining everyone's attention. "Welcome to the halfway-point feast!"

Cheers erupted around the table.

"Now, this is the time to get to know the Bachelor's friends. Remaining women, this is your chance to impress them. If they pick you, you'll get a private date with our lucky Bachelor. After each date, if he chooses to keep you, his kiss will be a sign of his consent for your continued participation. No kiss means you're going home."

Kiss? I tried not to squirm in my seat. The last thing I wanted was for Max to be kissing girls. Any girl but me.

Then again, it wasn't just a competition; it was a dating show.

"Hey," Max whispered into my hair. "I don't have to kiss them on the mouth."

I squeezed his hand and smiled.

"And each kiss will need to be . . . on the lips."

"Just kidding." Max released my hand and slumped in his seat.

"Why are you pissed?" Jason elbowed him. "Some of these chicks are pretty hot. No offense, Becca, I know you and Max have . . ." He pointed. "Whatever this is, but still, I sent him here to find love and get out of my hair, not fall for the one girl who signed up so she could say, 'Screw you' to the Bachelor and take the money, breaking his heart in the process. And you have that written all over your pretty little face." He rolled his eyes. "That's just what we need, a sad, jobless Max."

The smile on Max's face froze while the rest of the table fell silent. "Jason, don't . . . I already know she's here for the money. I knew that from day one. And I'm not jobless because I'm stupid . . . I just want to do something . . . you know what, never mind."

Jason opened his mouth but was elbowed by Colt.

What was going on? What were they talking about? Of course I'd told him the truth, I was there for the money, but now it was more. He had to know that! And why were his so-called friends acting like parents? So what if he wasn't working?

Reid sauntered up to the table, followed by Hades.

"Aw, you're like a mama bird with her little chick," Max teased.

Reid ignored Max and sat down at the table, pouring himself a large glass of wine before saying, "Whatever you do, do not pick that Grumpy chick."

"My roommate?" I asked.

"Dude . . ." Reid swallowed. "Okay, confession time, remember how I had to bribe a few people to be on staff here? Well, my old theater coach is friends with the producer, and one of my jobs is to"—he turned a bit red—"flirt with the contestants who don't get as much attention, so that they'll be happy and then more confident around Max."

The table fell silent.

Max burst out laughing. "Holy shit, you're my fluffer!"

Reid's eyes widened. "I am no such thing!"

"What's a fluffer?" Milo asked.

Colt groaned and laid his head on the table.

Jason coughed and looked away.

Max grinned. "I'm so glad you asked, Milo. I may reinstate our friendship based on that question alone. A fluffer is . . . wow, how do I put this sensitively?" Max pressed his fingertips to his lips. "Oh, right, in the porn industry there are certain . . . individuals . . ." He squirmed in his seat a bit.

"Who," Colt said from his muffled position against the table, "help."

"Yes." Max snapped his fingers. "They help . . . excite the actors."

"Excite?" Milo squinted in confusion. "Like they cheer them on?"

When all the guys groaned, Milo winked in my direction. I loved that girl. No wonder she was Max's best friend.

"Yeah," I joined in. "I don't get it either."

"Shrimp me." Max raised his hand and Jason passed the shrimp.

"So the daddy shrimp"—Max picked up one of the crunchy brown delicacies—"sometimes isn't as turned on by the mama shrimp." He nodded to Colt, who picked up another shrimp, that one a bit plumper.

"So"—Colt swore—"in order to aid in the *excitement*, a third party . . ." He eyed Jason.

"Hell." Jason picked up the third shrimp and cleared his throat. "The third-party shrimp comes onto the scene to . . ." His shrimp jumped between the other two. "Help."

"In a sexual way," Max explained in a low voice. "Jason's shrimp gets Colt's shrimp hot for my shrimp and—boom! Orgasmic experience that er . . . produces . . ."

"Cocktail sauce!" Milo blurted, clapping her hands.

"Oh. Hellfire and rainbows." Max stared longingly at the shrimp. "You just ruined one of my favorite foods."

"Thanks, guys. I think I get it now." Milo sighed. "So should we start to talk to the other girls?"

"Yes." Colt dropped the shrimp and grabbed the entire bottle of wine. "Lead the way."

Everyone dispersed but Max and me.

"So . . ." Max dipped his shrimp into the sauce and took a huge bite. "Truth or dare?"

"Truth." I laughed.

"Does my shrimp get you saucy?"

I dipped my finger in the sauce and licked it off slowly. "What do you think?"

"I think," Max groaned, "that we should leave. Like, right now."

"And leave your friends and the feast?"

"Run away with me!" Max gripped my hand. "We can live off love alone!"

"But where will we live?" I gasped. "What will we eat?"

"We'll live off the land," Max grunted. "I'll hunt! I can shoot a bow!"

"But the children."

"Damn them!" Max shouted. "Curse you, offspring."

"It was worth a try." I patted his knee.

"Yeah." He grabbed another shrimp and winked. "It really was."

CHAPTER THIRTY-FOUR

MAX

I liked Becca, not just a little bit. A lot. A lot. A lot. More and more I was hating the fact that I couldn't do anything about it, meaning I couldn't sneak off into the bushes and have my way with her. Not that I would do that in the first place because with my luck we'd roll around in poison ivy or something and I'd discover a rash that looked like an unfortunate case of the mumps on my favorite appendage.

I watched in dismay as my group of friends made their way around the tables, chatting up the girls, laughing with them, engaging in conversation I should have been engaging in. But I was rooted to my spot. I was rooted to her.

"You should probably make the rounds," Becca suggested in a soft voice.

"Like a doctor," I joked.

Becca rolled her eyes. "Yes, like a doctor."

"Be my nurse?" I said in a low voice, eyeing her up and down.

"Saw that one coming a mile away."

I smirked and just . . . stared at her. She was so pretty, and I wanted nothing more than to sit across from her until . . . well, until either I fell asleep or it was so dark I could only see the outline of her lips and even then, yeah, I'd probably still fight so damn hard to keep staring.

"Stop." She blushed and tucked her hair behind her ear. "Go mingle."

"Fine." I sighed heavily. "But know that when I mingle the only single girl I'll be thinking about is you, Little B." Before she could pull away I grabbed her hand and kissed it, then walked off in the direction of doom.

"Max!" Grumpy shouted. It was always a toss-up whether she was yelling at me or yelling for me. Let's just say she was a yeller, and leave it at that.

"Hey." I forced a smile.

She had Jason's hand in a viselike grip and he was giving me the "help me" eyes—also known as the eyes that show when a man's worried about the ability of a woman to hold on so tight to his person that he's afraid if she ever gets close enough to other parts of him they'll suffer such an extreme bout of blood loss that they'll fall off.

"So Jason here was saying he'd really like to see us go on a date and I agree." She licked her lower lip. "I really think it would be fun if you picked me, right, Jason?" She squeezed harder; swear I heard something pop in his hand.

Jason let out a little whimper.

"Dude, you okay?" I put my hand on his shoulder.

He nodded.

"Of course he's okay!" Grumpy laughed in her usual terrifying way, where she threw back her head and forced the laugh out of her mouth so loudly it sounded as if she were birthing a chicken in a cow-shaped suit. You know, because it sounded like a chicken, but with the way her face was strained no chance in hell was it any smaller than a cow.

"So . . ." I took a step back and brought my hands in front of me to protect all parts not solid at that moment. "Jason, I take it this is your choice?"

"Ah, ah!" Rex came up behind me and slapped my back so hard that I almost turned around and decked him in his orange face. One day he was going to get his and I was going to smile while I hovered over his Cheetos-stained body, feel me? "No announcing until the end of the night."

"Aw." Grumpy's shoulders slumped. Her grip on Jason, however, was still as strong as ever. Poor guy was going to lose a thumb. I almost felt bad for him, but then again, he was getting his just reward.

"I'll just . . . go talk to . . ." I pointed behind me, which meant I was actually pointing at the ocean, so yeah, I was going to talk to nobody, but I didn't want to stay. I rushed off in the direction of Milo, who was talking to Minion. Ah, lovely. Minion wasn't wearing her usual overalls but a cute little black dress. Aw, she put on a dress for me. What a nice girl! At least she would be seminormal and—

"I have dreams of eating him," Minion whispered in a hushed voice. "My psychiatrist says I fantasize about eating things because I feel powerless in my own life and to consume another person's soul is like owning them, you know? So if I could eat him, then I could understand him."

Please let the *him* be the goat.

"Oh." Milo nodded. "That's, yeah, that makes sense."

"Girls," I croaked, wishing I hadn't approached.

"Max!" Minion yelled. "You look so great tonight. I like your hair. I've always liked brown hair, you know, because mine's brown too. And I hope you like my dress. I picked it out just for you. I hope when you choose me that you realize what a catch you're getting. Not only was I an Olympic gymnast, but I'm in excellent shape for any sort of . . . activities you may have in mind."

"Olympics," I repeated. "So you're in retirement, then?" Wasn't touching the whole "activities" comment with a ten-foot pole, no matter how much fun it was to poke the bear. It always woke up and attacked.

"Well—" Her brow furrowed. "Apparently it's frowned upon to trip a girl when she's getting ready for her floor routine. Honest mistake."

"Right." That wasn't as bad as I'd assumed.

"I may have also . . . caused an entire team to get food poisoning." She shrugged.

"Awesome."

Milo's eyes widened a fraction of an inch in my direction. "Um, thanks for the chat, I'll be right back."

She grabbed my arm and led me away from the group. "She's crazy."

I nodded. "So crazy that I'm pretty sure the only reason she ended up on the show is because the producers probably needed some entertainment. Last night she ate a cricket."

"No!" Milo gasped.

"And she swallowed."

"Max." Giggling, Milo wrapped her arms around me and hugged. I missed her hugs, how stupid was that? It had always been her and me for the past four years, and now it was just . . . me.

"You doin' okay?" she whispered, still holding on tight.

"Define *okay*?" I sighed and closed my eyes, feeling at peace for the first time in a few days.

"Max." Milo pulled back and looked into my eyes. "Are you okay with this whole process? I feel like I owe you an apology. When Jason suggested you do the show I thought he was kidding and then you started acting so strange. You seemed so lost after graduation, almost like you didn't know what to do with yourself anymore."

I narrowed my eyes at her. I hadn't been acting weird. I had been acting sad. That's what guys did when they had no passion for anything. But it was lame to tell her that for the four years we went to college my only purpose had been to be her best friend. That was me.

I was one half of a friendship, and I was okay with it. I thrived off of it. But things didn't stay the same.

She got married.

She graduated.

She got a job.

She moved on.

I stayed stagnant.

And staying frozen in place, when you're a man of action, or typically a man of action, sucks.

"You know what I mean, Max, a purpose beyond hitting on girls, sleeping with them, abandoning them the next morning, and making up stories about sick family members so they don't call you ever again, or worse yet, stalk you."

Wincing, I shrugged and broke eye contact. "Yes. To answer your first question, I'm fine. I'm glad I came." Milo had that look in her eyes that meant she wouldn't stop pressing until I divulged more. "Look, I've just been in a bad place. For the last four years it's been you and me against the world, right?"

She nodded.

"And then you moved on and I stayed . . . on my ass. I graduated but realized upon getting that fun little diploma that I had no idea what I wanted to do." I sighed. "Doing the show hasn't been the worst thing that's ever happened to me. Besides, I met Becca and was able to give Reid yet another reason to sleep with a night-light." I flashed a smile.

"She's cute." Milo grinned. "Have you slept with her yet?"

"What?" I roared. "No! What the hell, Milo?"

"Just checking. She's cute, she's fun, she plays along with your insanity, and I wouldn't want you screwing anything up just because you like to play night games."

"Bed sport"—I rolled my eyes—"is a real thing."

"Whatever." Milo shook her head. "So what's the plan? Get

through the next week and a half, kick off the girls, and then what? Get the girl? Ride off into the sunset?"

I suddenly felt hot all over. My mouth dry. My nerves shot. Becca looked in our direction and waved. I had no choice but to wave back with a stupid grin on my face, while I said through clenched teeth, "That's the plan, then again . . . she may not want what I want."

"Max . . ." Milo looped her arm through mine. "Any girl who doesn't want you is insane."

"You didn't." The words were out before I could stop them. Holy shit, did I just say that out loud?

Milo froze, then looked up at me. "But you said, I mean you always acted like—"

"Gay?" I offered. "Stupid? Like I didn't care? Like I was the sexless best friend without any feelings? Or just all of the above?"

"Max—"

"Milo." I laughed and shoved my hands in my pockets. "It's over and done with. I'm over it. I love you, not like that, but as a friend. Honestly, it's my fault. I liked you too much to care. I just wanted to be in your solar system even if I was Pluto."

"Pluto?"

"The last planet." I sighed. "The furthest away from the sun, the most unliked, the cold planet, the one nobody can reach, the—"

"Stop comparing yourself to Pluto."

We walked back in Becca's direction. The minute we approached the table her face lit up when she saw me.

"Huh, interesting," Milo whispered.

"What?" I felt my face light up.

"You may be Pluto, but she's not the sun. She's Neptune."

"Huh?"

Milo rolled her eyes, "Look it up . . . Neptune's right next to Pluto, genius. You do the math."

With that, Milo walked off.

CHAPTER THIRTY-FIVE

BECCA

In typical Love Island fashion, the winners of the individual dates were announced with pomp and circumstance, meaning they had to walk through a tunnel of fire if their names were called.

It wouldn't have been such a big deal.

But one of the girls had used too much hair spray. The night was almost ruined because of that hair spray.

As Rex announced each name, Jason, Milo, and Colton grinned from ear to ear. Milo even winked in my direction when I walked through the fire—unharmed.

I should have been excited.

But I felt . . . unsettled.

When I'd decided to do the show I hadn't intended to fall for the guy. My head had been fully engaged in the game, in the competition. And the competition had been good to me. I'd been winning. Each game earned the winners either dates with Max or points toward prizes at the end of the week, when we could cash out and get things like cell phones, shopping sprees, and gadgets.

But at some point, my motivation had changed from money to Max.

Rex instructed all the girls to return to their huts. The first of five dates would take place tomorrow morning. Each girl was given three hours with Max, and during those three hours he could choose if she stayed or went home. Those three who weren't chosen for the individual date would go on a group date.

At the end of the day three girls would stay and two would go, so only five of us would be standing at the final ceremony.

"Pssst!" A noise came from the bushes.

I whipped around and stared at the trees. What the heck?

"Psst!"

"Okay, stop freaking me out," I said out loud, slowly walking backward.

"Damn it! Let me be romantic!" came a male voice.

Max slowly emerged from the bushes, all smiles. "I was going to capture you, pull you under the coconut tree, and have my way with you."

"Ah, darn, and I missed it. How come?"

Max shrugged. "Simple. You didn't come close enough to the tree line. Oh, and also we aren't close enough yet to where we can read each other's thoughts, but no worries, all good things come to those who wait."

"You always like this?" I asked seriously, crossing my arms over my chest.

"Like this . . . meaning?" Max squinted. "Awesome and good-looking? Yes, yes I am."

I laughed and looked away. "No, I mean, are you always this sarcastic?"

"No," he said quickly. "How silly of you to ask." I looked up into his dark hooded gaze. "Was I being sarcastic when I had you straddled across my lap? Or how about when I gave you a naked show? Or kissed your neck and dipped my tongue into your mouth? Was that sarcasm? Or something else?" He started stalking toward me. I didn't have enough good sense to back up. "What say you, Little B?"

"What's Little B stand for again?" I asked.

"Aw, smooth transition from subject of sarcasm to lust to nicknames, I tip my hat." He offered his hand. I took it. "Little B means . . . Little B."

"You just repeated yourself."

"I think we should do something crazy."

"You mean like go on a dating show and then drug your brother so he sees visions of Milo's grandma and the Jonas Brothers when he closes his eyes?"

"Right . . . that." Max sighed. "It's unfortunate that I mixed up the needles, but to be fair I never said I was a medical professional. I mean he can't sue me because I never made any promises to make his penis bigger or his eyes smaller."

"Why would he want smaller eyes?" I ignored the other comment.

"So when he sees Grandma he only sees a fraction of her. I imagine it would take away some of the shock."

"I see."

He gripped my hand, the smile reaching his gorgeous eyes, and yeah I was in so much trouble because he was pretty, easy to talk to, hilarious, and he . . . was smiling at me like he wanted to get into trouble, and I really, really wanted to join him.

"What did you have in mind?"

"I'm so glad you asked, Little B. First let's drop off Hades at the hut."

"Huh?"

Sure enough, I turned around and Hades was following close behind.

Max sighed. "He's my kin."

"So you've conquered your fear?"

"Of course." Max stopped walking and released my hand, only to touch my face. "Then again, it's kind of hard to be afraid of goats when my mind is otherwise occupied."

"With revenge?" I teased.

"That"—he returned my smile—"and a girl with blond hair."

"Milo?"

"Who's being sarcastic now? I've created a monster." He laughed. "Maybe I should just call you Frankenstein."

"Right, because that will get you laid."

"It will?" His eyes widened. "The secret formula! By Jove, I've discovered it!"

"You're insane." I couldn't stop laughing.

"I know." He kissed the top of my head. "Let's go be insane together."

And that invitation right there . . . was the beginning of the end. Because I knew I would never say no to him. He could ask me to bungee jump, and even though I was terrified of heights, I'd do it. I'd do it because it was Max asking and he made me feel like I could do anything.

After eleven days.

I tried not to worry about how fast I was falling and reached for his hand—not letting go until we reached his hut.

Once he dropped off Hades, he grabbed my hand again and led me to the water.

"Strip."

"Sorry?"

Max lifted his shirt off his head. "I said strip." With a wink he removed every stitch of clothing he had on and dove.

CHAPTER THIRTY-SIX

MAX

One point Max, no points Becca. I mean, you can't earn points when you're frozen in place.

Should I yell? Clap my hands in front of her face?

I decided to splash her.

Mouth open, she didn't even say anything. Holy shit, was she having a stroke? Concerned, I jumped out of the water and pulled her face in for a soft kiss. "Hey, you okay? Need CPR or something?"

I was kidding. I wasn't serious. I mean, I just wanted her to laugh.

Instead the joke was on me. As I stood there, naked, water dripping off my body, she gave me one sultry look and lifted her arms high into the air.

Rather than my breaking out into song and dance like I wanted to, my hands moved to the halter part of her dress. One pull. And the dress pooled at her feet, leaving her naked.

Because, apparently, I was back in God's good graces.

She wore nothing underneath.

Nothing.

NOTHING.

I'm sorry, I don't think you understand, let me rephrase, underneath her dress, there was nothing but skin. Really, really, really soft skin.

I let out a moan and just . . . drank my fill.

"So we doing this insane crazy thing or not?" She placed her hands on her hips.

I shuddered.

"Nervous?" she asked breathlessly.

"Naw." I pulled her tight against me; we fit perfectly. "Just hoping they aren't filming this from the bushes over there."

"Aw, you don't want to be naked on TV?"

"Do I look like I have a problem being naked?" I pinched her ass. "No, but my little cousins are watching and I'd hate for them to see the little censor blocks across my parts. I mean the natural assumption would be that I was sexless and I'm kind of a big deal in their eyes. I don't want to give them the wrong idea."

Becca shook her head. "I have no response to that."

"Good." I squeezed her ass harder. "I wasn't really looking for a response, now a moan? I could use a moan. Maybe a slap." I pretended to think about it. "Some kissing would be nice too, but first we have to get you wet."

"But—"

I fell backward into the ocean and pulled her with me.

The water was warm and inviting. The minute we hit, she moved away from me and dove deeper.

And like a man totally obsessed I followed her deeper and deeper until we were out where we couldn't touch, just treading water.

"I think I like your crazy ideas." Becca let out a breath and rubbed her eyes. Damn, she was beautiful.

"Yeah, well, there's more where that came from," I teased. "Then again, that means you'll have to spend copious amounts of time with me to discover all of them. Hope you don't mind."

She was quiet, then her eyes met mine. "I don't mind."

"Good," I whispered. "That's good . . . you know, considering . . ." I swam toward her and then tugged her arm to me. Within minutes we could touch again. Once we were back to the dock I pushed her against one of the wooden legs and kissed the hell out of her.

With a gasp she kissed me back, and her hands dove into my wet hair and then slid down my neck as I deepened the kiss. She hooked her legs around my waist.

With a groan I switched positions so I was leaning against the dock pulling her harder and harder against me.

"What if we get caught?"

I immediately stopped kissing her neck and looked up, my chest heaving. "Then we get caught."

Her smile grew. "And then what?"

"We wait." I drew her mouth into a long sensual kiss, slowly tasting her before pulling back. "And then we do the same damn thing again."

"What?" Breathless, she pushed against my chest.

"Getting caught means that we're doing something wrong." My hands slid down her arms and gripped her hips. "Truth or dare?"

Moonlight caught her skin, causing her features to glow. "Truth."

"I'm sure, no, I'm positive, that up until this moment I have been doing life wrong." My hands gripped her hips harder. "Because I haven't been with you. It hasn't been with you."

She gasped. I took her mouth again, plundering it until I was so out of breath I couldn't think straight. We were in the ocean. But no matter how many times my brain kept screaming at me, my body had other ideas, so when Becca guided me to exactly where I wanted to be, I not only almost drowned, but had little to no self-control left.

"Are you sure?" I groaned, knowing that even if she wasn't, I was too far gone. I was tipping over the edge of sanity. Swear the roller coaster just kept going and I had no desire for it to stop.

Our eyes locked.

"Yes," she whispered. "I'm sure."

I didn't wait for another invitation. I'd like to think I'm the type of guy who knows how to be patient in order to get what he wants.

But that's the thing about these moments, the ones that steal your breath away, you aren't in your right mind, and you sure as hell aren't patient.

And I couldn't have walked away even if she'd wanted me to.

I slowly inched into her, I mean we were in the water and to be fair I'd never actually done anything remotely sexual in the water, it just seemed unclean and I was a clean guy and I didn't like . . . "Shit!"

I blacked out.

Okay, fine, I didn't black out. But it sure as hell felt like it, because before I knew what was happening, before I could get the car ready, she'd hit the accelerator and I was powerless. She'd stripped me of everything as I moved inside her, as our eyes locked.

"This changes things . . ." I whispered as she tilted her head back in ecstasy. "Let me take care of you."

Becca nodded, then let out a slight moan as her nails dug into my back.

"After the show"—her head fell back as I kissed her neck—"this doesn't stop when the show stops."

"No," she agreed, her voice hoarse.

Our bodies rocked into one another, fitting perfectly.

Everything felt right.

"Tell me you're mine," I demanded, my voice urgent as I felt her tighten around me.

"Yes." Her forehead touched mine. "Yes. I promise."

I wouldn't fail her—I wouldn't be the same Max. I'd be better, starting now. I moved my hand between our bodies and watched her.

Every breath.

Every moan.

Every movement.

I had it memorized.

And when she found her release, I took that moment as a treasure, one I'd keep forever. If she'd have me.

CHAPTER THIRTY-SEVEN
BECCA

I didn't have time to regret sleeping with Max—and it was all the goat's fault. I opened my eyes and rubbed them, then tried to lean up and yawn. The minute my hands reached above my head the goat made a noise and then huffed at me. Okay, so I finally understood why Max had been so terrified. The damn thing could sense my terror or something!

"Max," I hissed, smacking him in the shoulder. It really was a shame waking him up. His dark tan looked so . . . pretty against the white sheets. I wanted to stare. Again, let's revisit, he was beautiful. A beautiful man I'd had the pleasure of exploring all night long.

Not once.

Not twice.

Three times.

So not only was I officially a whore, but I'd gone and done the ONE THING I'd sworn to myself I'd never do. I'd had a one-night stand with a guy who in the heat of the moment made promises to me, but outside of that moment, nothing. We weren't even really dating. For crying out loud, we were on a dating show! And he was going to be kissing other girls today. Four of them!

Crap, I really should have thought things through.

But then Max had gotten naked, and his kisses had made me forget everything but the moment, and I'd wanted to hang on to it forever.

"Stop biting your nails," Max grumbled, his eyes still closed. "And stop staring at me. And stop hitting me with your pillow. I get it—it's morning. No need to keep reminding me over and over again."

"Aw, you remind me of my roommate."

"No!" Max's eyes burst open. "She's a terrible excuse for a human being and most likely put Jason in a thumb cast last night."

"Thumb cast?" I repeated.

"Hey, you're naked." Max reached for me.

I slapped his hand away.

"Ouch." Max grinned. "But it's cool, I'll play."

I rolled my eyes. "Hades is upset."

"Uh, wouldn't you be upset too? He lives with dead people."

"Max," I warned.

"Fine, why's the goat upset? And how do you suddenly read minds? Holy shit, did you read my mind last night? Is that why you did that thing with your tongue, because I have to admit—it was hot."

"Max!" And I was officially bright red. "We can't . . . I mean, we can't do that again . . ."

"Define *that*." Max pulled me into his arms and kissed my mouth. "Or better yet, can you show me?" He easily moved on top of me so our bodies were literally inches from being joined again. "Or how about"—he leaned down and kissed me softly between my breasts—"I just keep guessing until you moan, or yell or say yes Max, no Max, more Max—"

"Max, you better not be talking to that goat!" Reid shouted.

Max froze on top of me.

I froze beneath him.

We shared one look and I dove under the covers.

Max propped up the pillows around him and fluffed the bed just as the door to the hut swung open.

CHAPTER THIRTY-EIGHT

MAX

Son of a possessed goat. I was screwed. Oh, wait, no, that's what I would have been doing had my satanic brother not knocked on my door and barged in.

Becca moved slightly, her face planted against my stomach. Her breath hot on my skin. Shit, I was in a bad place, a very bad place. She would be the death of me and the last thing I needed was for Reid to think I was getting all hot and bothered because Hades had eaten another pair of my underwear.

"'Sup, Bro?" I tried to act casual as I placed my hands behind my head and exhaled.

Reid's eyes narrowed. "You look funny."

"I just woke up." I faked a yawn. "You're no perfect male specimen in the mornings either, my friend."

"Right." Reid looked around the room, his eyes wildly searching for something. "Have you seen Becca? I went to her hut to remind her about the morning confessional and also make sure she knew what time her date with you was, but she was gone."

I shrugged. "Maybe she died."

Becca pinched me in the ass.

My body jerked.

"Maybe. She. Died." Reid repeated, his eyes narrowing more and more by the second.

"I was kidding!" I laughed nervously. "She's probably just . . . swimming. You know." My throat was drier than the desert. "With the fish."

"Becca hates fish."

"She hates sharks," I corrected. "Fish aren't sharks. Do you even watch the Discovery Channel when I turn it on?"

"Swimming, huh?"

"Yeah, she loves swimming, one of her favorite things to do, next to, you know . . ." *Me*, HA! "Art."

"Art?" Reid looked confused. "What kind of art does she do?"

I can neither confirm nor deny that Becca was actively squeezing something that should never be squeezed in that way. Ever. And I do mean. Ever. Ever. Ever. "Er . . . she does nude art."

And the squeeze just got worse. I kicked my feet, hoping to land one on her, but she kept squeezing.

"Nude art?" Reid laughed. "Wow, that's kind of hot."

"Everything about Becca's hot." I shrugged.

The squeezing stopped. Hey, I'd done something right!

"You really like her, don't you?"

"Yeah, man, I really do. She's . . . incredible."

Was it wrong to be a bit sad at the loss of her hand?

"Hmm." Reid scratched his head. "Hey, what's Hades have in his mouth?"

I followed the direction of his gaze and felt my face pale. Becca's dress. Hades had somehow grabbed it in the middle of the night and was now apparently trying to find the best way to deface it, if the way he was sitting on it was any indication.

CHAPTER THIRTY-NINE
BECCA

Getting back to my room was like something out of a James Bond movie. Seriously. I ran to one palm tree and hid, then ran to the next one. I knew I had to avoid Reid at all costs because I wouldn't be able to keep a straight face, and the last thing I needed was more steamy footage. Reid was scouring the beach with binoculars! Seriously? Swear Edward the snake was following me, I mean when Max set him free I'd thought he'd run away. But nope, he was sitting outside Max's hut just waiting for the inevitable invitation to join the farm.

"Shoo!"

"Becca?" Reid shouted from his position a few hundred feet away. He waved.

Luckily Grumpy was already ready for the day and most likely eating breakfast so she wasn't going to pester me about where I'd been all night. I quickly showered and threw on a pair of shorts and a black tank top just in time to open the door and see Reid standing there with his hand raised.

"Oh!" He stepped back. "Weren't you just on the beach? Could have sworn I saw Max's old football shirt on you."

"Max played football?" I blurted. I mean, come on. He so did not look the type.

Reid laughed. "Of course he played football. Max plays all sports. Hmm, I'd think that with all you've"—he tilted his head—"shared recently you'd know that about him."

"Yeah, well . . ." Heat invaded my face as I blushed. "We haven't had much time to talk."

"Talking is overrated." He grinned.

"Did you need something?"

"Just making sure you're safe."

He didn't move.

"Well." I lifted my hands in the air. "I am. Totally. Completely safe."

Safe. Why did *safe* make me suddenly freak out? Safe, safe, safe, ho-oly crap! My eyes widened just as Reid's did.

"No! No, I didn't mean it like that! I mean whatever you do in private time with men or my brother or anyone for that matter, you're a responsible, consenting adult who—"

"Move!" I ran past him and jogged back to Max's hut. I knocked twice, three times—the bastard didn't answer!

And then I remembered his confessional.

Stupid Becca, stupid, stupid Becca! We'd had sex. In the ocean, of all places. Of course we hadn't been safe!

I hadn't been thinking.

He clearly hadn't been thinking.

I found Max talking to Rex using wild gestures.

Yeah, so he was acting normal.

I waited patiently.

Finally Max turned.

I motioned him over while Rex shouted, "Becca, just in time for your confessional."

"One sec!" I yelled back as Max approached.

He sighed. "I miss the nakedness."

"Max!" I gripped his arm. "Last night, in the ocean—"

"I'm going to stop you right there before I have to excuse myself and take a cold shower."

"No!" I gripped his shoulders. "Max, listen!"

"O-okay." He sat down on the sand with me. "What's wrong?"

"We . . ." Oh, my gosh. I couldn't say it. Why couldn't I say it? "You know how with the shrimp . . ." Awesome, and I was officially turning into Max. It was only a matter of time before we had our own nickname, BecMax or something stupid like that.

"Did the shrimp make you sick?"

"No! Okay, you know how you cover the shrimp with, er, sauce? And I mean not everyone likes sauce so sometimes it sucks that you have to dip it, but whatever, the sauce keeps you safe, Max!"

He leaned in. "Am I the shrimp or the sauce?"

"You're the shrimp and something else"—I held out my hands—"is the sauce, and while most guys don't particularly enjoy eating with the sauce it's necessarily to prevent . . . types of . . . disease."

"Okay." Max nodded and then his gaze shot to mine. "Ohhhhh, okay. Gotcha. So you're worried because the first time you ate the shrimp there was no sauce."

"Right." I exhaled in relief. Because yeah, sure, I was on birth control, but still!

"My sauce is boss." Max grinned and then gripped my hand. "Becca, you have nothing to worry about. Granted we could have been smarter and were when we got back to the love hut . . ."

"Please don't call it that."

He winked and flashed me that gorgeous smile again. "But how do I put this carefully . . ." He nodded. "Right, so before the show I was examined by a complete monster, who did everything within his power to keep it so that when I wanted to eat shrimp I cried instead.

Classically conditioned me to hate all doctors and men over the age of fifty, but the point is, my shrimp is awesome, even without the sauce my shrimp is still perfectly fine and yours . . . is . . . too . . . wow, this conversation would have gone a lot better had you straight-up asked me if I'd been tested for STDs."

I sighed and leaned my head against his shoulder. "Right, but I was trying to do it the Max way."

"Always more complicated but tons of fun, mainly because there's usually props," he agreed. "We okay?"

"Yes." I swallowed. "A lot better."

"Good." Max kissed my cheek. "Because I'm buying stock in shrimp and probably going to tie you to my hut so you can't escape."

"Empty threats." I waved him off.

"See you on the last date. I may have convinced Rex that we should save the girl I liked for the very end."

"And he was okay with that?" I asked, surprised that Rex even cared.

"More than okay." Max winked. "Let's just say I promised him that if they filmed it, I'd finally kiss one of the girls like I meant it."

Warm fuzzies radiated through my stomach. "Oh."

"See you later." He kissed my cheek again, then lingered. "Damn, I don't want to go." When he rose he put on his sunglasses and sighed. "Dream of shrimp, Becca, because I know I will."

CHAPTER FORTY

MAX

Becca walked off toward Rex to do her confessional and I stared . . . I mean, it wasn't one of those creeper stares that get a lesser man arrested; it was more of an appreciative . . . glance. Now that I'd seen that body of hers up close and personal, well, let's just say I was going to try my damndest to convince that girl we should join a nudist colony, you know, to save money on clothes.

"Hey," Reid yelled from behind me. Sadly I stopped watching Becca and turned around.

"Yes?"

He tapped his fingers against his mouth, then leaned forward and sniffed.

"What the hell!" I pushed him away.

"You had sex."

"I did not!" I did, I did, I did. My body rejoiced, Little G popped up in my pocket, and I'm pretty sure had Hades been on the beach I would have given him a significant head nod.

"Did too." Reid scowled. "How'd you manage to escape the cameras? Was it with Becca? Wait, does she know?"

"Um, she was there," I said defensively.

"I knew it! You did have sex with her!"

"Keep your voice down!" I smacked him in the shoulder. "And of course she knows it happened."

"You never know." Reid huffed. "Apparently you snuck drugs into a foreign country so yeah, I wouldn't put it past you."

"When have I ever needed to use pharmaceuticals in the bedroom?" I squinted. "Furthermore, if we're laying our cards all out on the table, between the two of us, who do you think's going to need help getting it up during future . . . activities?"

"Please." Reid rolled his eyes.

"Grandma."

"Shut up. I hate you!" Reid pushed against me and whispered under his breath toward his . . . manhood, "He didn't mean it."

"You talk to your penis now? Things that bad that you need to verbally affirm your man parts so that they don't have to wither and fall off when I speak her name?"

Reid glared. "Speaking of parts withering off."

Jason approached and slapped Reid on the back. "Whose parts are withering off?"

"Colt's," I said, not missing a beat. "On account he's nailing your sister every night."

"Low blow," Reid whispered.

"Ah, blow." I grinned.

"I'm sorry I walked over here," Jason grumbled.

We started walking toward the breakfast hut. Reid wrapped his arm around my shoulder. "You get to hang out with five pretty girls today and, no worries, they're hand-picked so you're going to have a wonderful time."

"Is it just me?" I shrugged out of his hold. "Or does *wonderful* sound more like *terrible* coming from your mouth? It was like you hissed it, you slut."

"Self-proclaimed reformed slut," Jason piped up. "And Reid's right, some of the girls are nice."

"How's your thumb?" I asked.

Jason winced and squeezed his hand. "A bit sore."

"She's a strong one."

"I imagine she ties people to bedposts and has her way with them and then gives them Advil afterwards or maybe even a shot of morphine. Really it's a toss-up, and with my background? Bound to happen, which is why I'm carrying Mace." Jason patted his pocket. "No chick's going to surprise me and I won't have to worry about, shit, I don't even remember her name."

"Ah, no worries, I have nicknames for them all."

Reid and Jason stopped walking.

"What?" I threw up my hands. "Do you really expect me to remember all their names? It's so much easier using words like Minion, Grumpy, and—"

"Ah." They nodded in unison and pointed at the two girls I was talking about.

"Damn it, those overalls need to be burned." I sighed and kept walking with them.

"Surprise!" A girl popped out from one of the trees.

I was fast enough to have stopped Jason from making an epic mistake; instead I watched, because, well, I was a huge fan of self-destruction and Jason was always the main attraction in that department. I even mom-armed Reid so I could see better.

In slow motion Jason yelled, "Aghhhh." It was gurgled, which I could only assume meant he'd choked a bit on his spit out of terror. It was terror spit. He reached into his pocket and pulled out the Mace and sprayed.

Sure I could have stopped him.

I could have pushed him out of harm's way.

Hell, I could have yelled.

Instead I groaned, and smirked, as Jason sprayed himself in the face.

"Well, that's one way to do it, I guess." Reid snickered.

Jason, now just discovering the pitfalls of panic and why rape whistles are always a better alternative, fell to his knees looking much like Russell Crowe in *Gladiator* after his final kill.

"Nooooo!"

I felt like jumping up and down and screaming, "Are you not entertained?"

But I restrained myself.

Mostly because I didn't want to look like an insensitive ass; well, because of that and the fact that I was pretty sure most chicks wouldn't get the movie reference.

"Reid"—I pointed at Jason—"cold water and towels, stat!"

"Ohhh, did you train to be a doctor?" Minion clapped her hands.

"Yes," I said through clenched teeth. "It goes really well with a poli-sci degree."

She giggled.

And I sighed as I saw a brain cell fall out of her ear, give me a hopeless look, and combust.

"My eyes!" Jason screamed. "Hell, that hurts!"

"Can I help?" Minion got closer.

"Er, yeah." I licked my lips. "Why don't you go try to find us some Acidifalide. Do you think you can remember that? It takes the sting away."

"Acidifalide. Got it!" She ran off, zigzagging like someone was shooting at her and she was escaping. Clearly she was confusing her self-defense classes with first aid.

"Max, no chance in hell am I putting Acidifalide in my eyes! Dude, the first syllable of that word is *acid*!"

I smacked him on the back of his head. "You try thinking of a fake drug on the spot!"

"Oh." He tried sitting up. "It's not real."

"I hope not." I shuddered. "Because if she finds it, good luck prying yourself away from her."

"Thanks," he said through clenched teeth just as Reid returned with some cold water and rags.

"Here." I dipped the rags in the cold water and slammed one on Jason's face. "So maybe next time, look before you spray."

"Like a dog." Reid nodded helpfully. "They always look before they lift; it's just common sense, man."

"Holy shit!" Colt ran up to us. "Someone said Jason was crying, you guys okay?"

"I am not crying!" His voice was muffled from the rag.

"There, there." I patted his back and winked at Colt.

Colt, being Colt, took the opportunity to fall to his knees next to Jason and start yelling loudly, "Let it out, man, just let it out! She's not worth it!"

"I can't see you guys." Jason swore. "So when I lift my middle finger please assume I'm directing it towards all of you."

"Jason?" Milo jogged up to us. "Are you okay?"

"Do I look okay?" He threw his hands up in the air as the rag fell off of his face. His eyes were so red, his face so puffy, that honestly it looked like a giant spider had decided to bite every inch of skin it could.

"Oh." Milo put her hand over her mouth.

Little G quivered in my pocket, so I lifted the rag and dropped it back on Jason's head. "You're scaring the gecko, man, not cool."

"As much fun as this is"—Reid grinned—"you have your first date in a half hour, Max."

"I need food." I stood.

"What about me?" Jason asked from the ground.

"Do you want me to get Hades to sit with you or something?" I offered, thinking it a kindness.

I received the middle finger again.

"See if I let you goat-sit," I muttered, and walked off, leaving Jason on the ground, rubbing his eyes.

CHAPTER FORTY-ONE
BECCA

"So, how does it feel to be the favorite?" Rex asked, grinning from ear to ear.

"I wouldn't know." I shrugged.

"You have to know." Rex sighed. "You've been spending a lot of time with our Bachelor. Some of the girls even said you're with him during every free moment you have."

"I highly doubt he takes me to the bathroom," I said through clenched teeth, hating that he was right.

"Any jealousy?" Rex sighed. "A lot of the girls are very beautiful."

Right, but they were also clinically insane. "It's all part of the game, right?" I tried to keep my voice light. I was a woman, which basically meant I harbored insecurities like any other living, breathing female out there. Of course I was worried, because as much as Max said he didn't like the other girls . . .

I still had to wonder.

I mean, clearly they'd made it on the show because they offered something unique. What if Max discovered whatever that was and fell for them?

"All right." Rex clapped his hands, causing me to jump. "Any last confessions for the camera?"

I could have easily said something like "Max is mine, bitches, back off," or any other type of threat. Hey, I'd watched the show before so I knew how crazy the girls got. Instead I shrugged indifferently and said, "Max is a grown-up, he can do whatever he wants."

"Perfect." Rex's teeth snapped together.

I took off the microphone and made my way toward the breakfast hut just in time to see Jason on the ground, Reid hovering over him, Max yelling, and Colton grinning.

"I need food," Max grumbled, leaving Jason on the ground. His head lifted, his eyes zeroing in on me. "Care to join me for breakfast?"

"That depends." I glanced down at Jason. "Will I end up like that?"

"That depends," Max repeated. "Do you actually know how to use Mace?"

"You point and shoot, what's so hard about that?" I shrugged.

Max laughed. "Apparently the shooting part."

"Aw, Jason."

"I'm fine!" Jason yelled from a sitting position with a rag draped over his head. "I'm just a cop who panics in the line of fire, no big deal. That doesn't mean I'm going to die before I hit thirty."

"There, there," Max said gently. "Come on, Little B, I gotta carb up, this day's going to be—"

"—Fun?" I offered.

"Yes, if the definition of *fun* is getting your teeth pulled by a blind dentist who doesn't know how to use pliers."

"Even my date?" I squeezed his arm.

"Your date?" Max licked his lips and wrapped his arms around my waist, pulling me against him. "Is going to be epic."

"How epic?"

Max pushed me behind the hut and into the shadows. "Epic enough"—he nipped at my lower lip—"that we're either going to have to hide from the cameras or there's going to be a hell of a lot of censoring."

A warm blush crept over my face.

"Aw, don't go getting all shy on me." Max licked my lower lip and then sucked it. "I could taste you all day."

"B-breakfast," I said lamely.

"You." He nibbled harder, his teeth digging into my lip. "I'll snack on you all day."

My body trembled.

"I love it when you do that." His hands moved from the small of my back up my sides. "I promise."

"You promise what?"

Max grabbed my hand and led me around to the front of the hut. "I promise that when I kiss the girls, when I keep who I'm choosing to keep, it won't be their lips I'm touching. I'll be imagining it's you and even then I'll make it brief, so at the end of the night? You better be ready to pay up . . ." He pinched my ass. "Because I'm collecting."

CHAPTER FORTY-TWO

MAX

Breakfast was over too soon, which meant only one thing. Date number one. I waited on the pier for the first date to show up and was momentarily bummed and a bit jealous as I watched Jason, Colt, and Milo laughing on the beach. Becca soon joined them, with what looked like a mimosa in her hand.

I'd never imagined what it would look like. Being a part of a relationship or the other half of a couple. In my mind it had always been Milo and me as friends, and maybe at some point something more.

But now? I only had eyes for Becca.

And she fit.

She fit so perfectly with my friends that it almost freaked me out. I mean, after next week, what would happen? I'd never been the insecure guy. But I was suddenly panicked over my future, and not because I was so concerned for myself but because I finally saw someone sharing it with me.

"All ready?" Rex sniffled and snapped his fingers at the cameraman. "Max, why don't you tell us what you're feeling right now?"

"Er, excited," I answered in a totally lame voice as my attention was again captured by Becca's laughter on the beach.

"Right." Rex laughed. "You seem unable to control your excitement."

"That's me," I said dryly.

"Oh, look, your date's walking towards us. You kids have fun and remember, we're not really here."

Ha, like I could forget Rex, the camera guy, the sound guy, one of the producers, and a makeup artist. Sure, but they weren't there. I turned and pasted a smile on my face as Nicki came running up the beach. At least Minion had dropped the overalls and replaced them with jean shorts and a cute tank top that said, "Baller."

Ten bucks she has no idea what it even means.

"Max!" she yelped, and then launched herself into my arms. I had no choice but to either catch her or let her flail into the ocean. I chose to catch her, you know, being a gentleman and all. "I'm so excited for our date!"

I placed her on her feet and continued to give her a fake smile as she jumped up and down right in front of me. And not in a cute "Aw, bless her heart, she's excited" way, but in an obnoxious "Holy shit, what pill did you take before coming?" way.

"Er . . ." I placed my hands on her shoulders, willing her to keep her feet planted on the ground. "You ready to go?"

Her eyes widened. "We're leaving the Island?"

"Sort of." I sighed wistfully. "It seems they've found life on another one of the islands. The zombies haven't made it that far and we're the first explorers to go out and scan the area for food!"

She blinked.

"Nothing?" I squinted. "Nothing at all?"

A tear ran down her cheek before she wiped it away. "I, um, I'm really scared of zombies."

"Because . . ." I sighed. "They're real?"

She nodded.

"Do you also happen to have one of those doomsday shelters and enough food and water to last for ten years?"

"How'd you know?" she gasped. "Daddy says not to tell anyone on account that the government may want to shut us down."

"I highly doubt they'd shut you down, I mean it's your property, right?" Okay, fine, I could engage with crazy.

"Yeah." She nodded. "But I'm pretty sure the guns are illegal."

"Guns?" I choked, then looked into the camera.

Yeah, ten bucks said Daddy was gonna be shut down a lot sooner than she realized.

"But shhh," she whispered. "Don't tell. It will be like our first secret."

"Ha-ha." I smiled. "On national television."

"Exactly!" She smacked me across the chest. "Max, you're funny."

"I'm not," I disagreed, "at all."

She giggled anyway.

Never in my life have I ever—HA! Hey, that's a game! Sorry, refocus: never have I ever tried to sound boring. I mean, for shit's sake, being boring is so . . . boring. I'm not boring. I don't like boring people. I hate libraries because they're too quiet. I thought it was stupid to have silent time in preschool and I'm pretty sure that I was the reason for recess being reestablished in high school, feel me? But in that moment I tried, I desperately tried to sound like Jason. Oh, don't roll your eyes. You know what I mean . . . cop who eats doughnuts and drinks his coffee black and only likes sex in like two positions.

Okay, fine, so maybe I was judging him.

But still.

I tried channeling Jason.

But apparently I was too damn interesting.

Swear, had I told Nicki/Minion that I collected potatoes for a living she would have gasped and thrown her arms around my neck screaming, "I love them mashed!" She wasn't a challenge, she was passive and agreeable, and nothing about her inspired me.

And maybe that was the problem.

Becca not only made me want to be a better man, she made me think that it was possible to want better for myself, to take time and actually think about what I wanted for my future. And she'd done all of that in two weeks.

An hour into the date I contemplated jumping off the boat or faking my own death. Then again, I had Becca's date to look forward to.

I still had to choose three out of the five girls.

And sadly, Minion was not a front-runner.

I realized this not at first, which I know sounds shocking. I mean for shit's sake she believed in zombies! I mean, I do too, but I don't take it far enough to stock my house with illegal firearms and weaponry.

They had freaking ninja stars and astronaut food.

No, the straw that broke the camel's back was when Minion picked up her fork during our midmorning snack and proceeded to comb her hair.

I, thinking she was channeling the Little Mermaid much as I was channeling Jason, burst out laughing and said, "Ariel?"

To which she replied, "Who the hell is Ariel? My name's Nicki!"

I stared, openmouthed, and then laughed, because SURELY she was joking, right? Finally she was showing a sense of humor.

Nope. Not joking.

She then proceeded to burst into tears. When I tried to calm her down and explain who Ariel was she called me a whore and Ariel a bitch, and tried to impale my cheek with said fork, all before getting up from the little picnic and stomping all the way to the boat and sitting in the corner.

It took me ten minutes to get her to respond to me because she was so upset, she'd somehow reverted to childhood and would only respond if I said, and I quote, "Baby girl, come out, come out, wherever you are." Mind you, we only discovered this after Rex made a phone call to the on-set shrink, who then explained that when Nicki was upset she went back into her other personality.

Yeah, I'm going to stop right there and give you a moment to let that sink in. Her other personality.

Also known as Baby Nicki.

I'm being serious as a heart attack.

Needless to say Baby Nicki did not earn a kiss, and I got an earful about how I should never, under any circumstances, call my dates by someone else's name.

Clearly she still didn't get the *Little Mermaid* reference.

I waved good-bye once we got back to the beach. Pretty sure even Rex was a bit mystified, because for once he had nothing to say and merely shook his head and said, "Next."

CHAPTER FORTY-THREE

MAX

I'd like to think I'm an optimistic individual, so when Cat came barreling down the beach, nearly colliding with a crab and getting tangled up in a piece of seaweed, I thought to myself, self, there's a real winner right there.

Even when she started screaming obscenities into the otherwise peaceful morning air about how nature sucked the big one, I smiled.

Because at least we agreed on something.

Nature sucked balls.

I was done with nature.

Through.

I wanted Becca and a fifth of whiskey, preferably served over her hot body.

Damn nature to hell! I shook my fist and sighed as Cat finally made her way to me and smiled.

Her smile scared me. It was wide and not inviting, and swear on Reid's life she had two very sharp teeth that looked a hell of a lot like she'd filed them down so she'd look like Edward's sister, the vampire, not the snake. Note the difference.

"So . . ." She reached toward my arm, and I watched in utter horror as her long talons latched on, much as a mama eagle latches on to its baby bird and never lets go. "Where are we going?"

Hell. Ha-ha.

"We're going to go scuba diving." I sighed. "You up for it?"

"I'm up for anything!" She smiled brightly and then winked at the camera.

I tried to engage in typical date conversation: *What's your favorite food? Do you like goats?* (Hey, no judgment, Hades was a permanent fixture in my life now.) *What do you do for a living?* Things seemed to be going pretty well, I mean pretty well given that she didn't eat goat meat or cheese, score one for Hades, and when she said her favorite food was spaghetti I was like, sure, I can dig that.

But things clearly couldn't last that long.

Going on a date with these women was like playing Candy Land with a small child. You think you're going to win because you're smarter and you keep missing the Molasses Swamp and whatnot. So when you get to the end, you're all *What's up bitch! Winner!* Except you played way too fast, so the damn kid wants to play again.

Meet every single woman on Love Island.

I stepped through each ring like a monkey on a pole (ha, because monkeys on poles would be hilarious) and after I was done doing the whole dance they wanted to repeat the same process.

So what should have lasted . . . oh, I don't know, maybe a few minutes? I mean how long was small talk supposed to last?

Well, it lasted a hell of a lot longer.

In all my dating experience, you have small talk, you laugh, you touch, then you move on. These girls? They talked in absolute circles about nothing that made sense! I wanted to end Candy Land once I reached the final card—they wanted to start over and talk about their favorite color again!

Oh, and here's my favorite part. Plot twist! This girl? Her job is *to be.*

And no, I did not forget to finish my sentence.

That's her job.

To be.

Or, according to Cat, "I merely exist to bring pleasure to others." Right, let that sink in a bit.

I'll wait.

Jury's still out, but who wants to bet she's a prostitute? Anyone? Anyone?

"Oh, I'm scared!" Cat hissed.

"It's fine." I pried myself away from her clutches. "See?" I dipped my fin in the water and offered an encouraging smile. We were out on the boat in around twenty feet of water. We'd been hanging out there for the past thirty minutes, and each time our instructor asked us to jump in, Cat got scared.

The instructor jumped for us. Land on your feet, bitch! Seriously, someone get me alcohol.

My date was officially a scaredy-cat. See what I did there?

"Cat." I licked my lips. "Would it make you feel better if I go first?"

She nodded.

Cool. Fingers crossed a giant shark ends my life so I don't have to go through with the rest of this date. The old Max would have liked the attention.

The old Max would have kissed every single girl, gotten into their pants, made no apologies or promises.

But apparently I'd started to change, because not only was I bored out of my mind, but every minute with these girls seemed like a waste of time—when I could be with THE girl. The one I really wanted.

Cat giggled.

It sounded like nails on a chalkboard.

I glanced around, my eyes hoping to find a shark. Then again, I was pretty sure Becca wouldn't want me going out like that. Now, death by whiskey? She'd probably high-five my corpse and take a shot over it. I mean she was cool like that.

The splash of water was warm, inviting, a bit soothing. Hell, if Cat didn't wanna go scuba diving, I was perfectly fine entertaining myself.

"See?" I swam around a bit. "Totally fine out here."

Cat smiled.

And then that same smile froze.

The instructor's eyes bulged nearly out of his head as he held up his hands and said in a strained voice, "Don't move."

I thought I'd gone over this with people. Worst thing ever to say to a person who was voted most likely to panic in tense situations. I was the dude who ran into the burning building not to save someone but because I was so freaking disoriented I just ran toward the light, feel me? So saying, "Don't move" was like waving a red flag in front of a bull.

So I moved.

Cat screamed.

Our instructor paled.

And something nudged my leg.

Please let it be Hades.

I looked to my right.

A shark.

Not huge.

Not small.

Just right.

Like the three bears, it had found the perfect spot, a sweet spot, so to speak, and it was nestled right next to my left nut, also known as Mighty Max Jr.

"I'll never sire children," I whispered.

"Hit its nose." The instructor made a sweeping notion with his hand.

"How hard?" I asked.

"Who cares?" Cat screamed. "Just hit it, Max!"

Ah, I knew she had a brain in there somewhere. With a curse I moved with deadly precision and hit the shark right on the nose.

It let out a war cry, or maybe that was me. At any rate there was a lot of splashing, someone pulling me back into the boat, and then Cat's mouth was on mine before I could do anything.

"Breathe!" She pounded my chest. "Breathe, damn it!"

"I'm—"

"Breathe, Max!"

Finally I turned to my side as she smacked my back, hell, why hadn't I pushed her in with that shark? She would have terrified the shit out of it.

"Thanks," I muttered, voice hoarse, pretty sure she'd done more damage than Sharky.

"He's alive!" she yelled to everyone on the boat.

There was applause and because it was a date where my date at least cared enough to want to save me, I quickly turned and kissed her across the mouth. "You stay."

She beamed.

And I instantly felt guilty for being such an ass.

But what was worse? I'd just kissed a girl who wasn't Becca and I hated it. I hated every single part of it. What should have been easy was hard because as much as I wanted it to be her, I still had two more dates to go.

CHAPTER FORTY-FOUR

MAX

It was lunch.

I was starving and I was in some serious need of alcohol.

With a sigh I waited for the third date. At least after this I was halfway through the individual dates, right?

Rex handed me a protein bar and patted my back. Holy shit, was he actually soothing me? Did he suddenly see the error of his ways?

I looked down at the protein bar.

It was called Aphrodisiac Delight.

Um. No.

I was half-tempted to chuck the bar at his head. Instead I mumbled a thanks and tucked it in my back pocket. No way was I letting any of those girls near that thing.

A pretty girl started walking toward me. I semirecognized her and tried to channel the whole chart in my room but I kept coming up with a blank, so by the time she reached me all I really had to go off of was my charm.

And let's be honest, I was practically dripping with charm. I held out my arm and said, "You look lovely."

Her eyes narrowed as she looked behind me at the camera and made some obscene gestures with her hands. Holy crap. What did I do?

"She does not speak English," the producer said. "We thought it would be fun to show some diversity in the show."

"Well, I know some Spanish," I offered lamely. How the hell had I not interacted with this girl yet? I'd met her when we'd gotten on the Island and I'd waved, but when she hadn't talked I'd just thought she was shy!

"You know Portuguese?" the producer asked, an amused grin plastered all over his shit-eating face.

I laughed. "Aren't they the same thing?"

The producer groaned. "You're lucky she doesn't understand you."

"Wait." I held up my hands. "How are we supposed to communicate?"

"And that," Rex said from next to the camera, "is part of your date. You woo her with your native tongue—"

"My tongue isn't native. I mean it's been some pretty crazy places but I wouldn't necessarily say it's in possession of a passport or anything."

Rex rolled his eyes. "You use gestures to show her how you feel."

"So is the middle finger to her as it is to me?"

"What?" Rex's eyebrows furrowed.

"Hey, I'm just being cautious. Hand gestures mean different things in different countries, like a thumbs-up can actually mean 'up yours.' I don't want to insult her by being encouraging!"

"Then don't use gestures," Rex said in a strained voice.

"But you just said—"

"Max!" Rex barked, and then regained his posture of control. "We're running out of time and have two dates left after this. Could you please carry on?"

"Fine." I clenched my fists. "What's her name?"

Rex groaned. "We'll edit that out."

"What?" I roared, "It's not like they're wearing name tags and I haven't spoken to her once!"

The girl gave me a concerned look so I flashed her a smile and wrapped my arm around her while I said in perfect English to Rex, "Look how good I'm doing with positive body language. She probably thinks I'm saying she's hot and here I don't even know her name. Point Max."

"Good Lord." Rex patted his head with a hanky. "Her name is Ella."

"Ah, *Ella Enchanted.* Anne Hathaway, terrible film. Pretty sure it got a few rotten tomatoes on account that she was the only one in the entire damn film that spoke in an American accent. Hashtag stupid Americans."

"You done?" Rex asked.

"Yup." I winked and then strolled along the beach with Ella. I pointed at seashells. I picked one up and then handed it to her like she was my queen.

Honestly, it was the perfect date. I got to talk all I wanted about things that were important to me like Hades, golf, football, the Costco hot dogs with green relish, and she had no choice but to smile encouragingly. I imagined this was what it would be like to be married to the perfect woman.

But an hour into the date, I started getting bored.

So I may have, possibly, started getting slightly . . . inappropriate . . . not with my gestures. Nah, my gestures were solid. I held her hand, I smiled, I waved. I was awesome.

My words? Not so much.

"So if I told you I had a secret clown fetish, would that be a deal breaker?" I asked.

She smiled and nodded.

"Oh, good." I sighed. "Because I have a clown fetish."

Her smile brightened.

"No? Not scared? Not running in the opposite direction?"

She nodded.

"Last year I ate my best friend's goldfish. She'd named it and everything, and well, you know about eating pets that have names. It's basically like stealing their soul, so the soul of Goldy resides right there." I placed her hand on my heart. "Forever."

I then made a fish face.

Which she took as an invitation to kiss me.

I pretended to trip over my own feet and managed a solid blush and shrug.

She laughed.

I laughed with her and made a cutting motion with my hand toward Rex. Our date was supposed to be a picnic lunch while riding on horseback.

But we never made it to the horses.

Because I wasn't going to keep her—and even I wasn't so heartless as to make her go through with the rest of the date.

"Look," I said, and sighed. "You're really pretty, but you gotta go."

She smiled.

I patted her hand. "Mm-kay, pumpkin? It's time . . . oh, wow, how do I say this in Portuguese?" Instead I just waved bye-bye.

She waved back.

I groaned and looked at the producer.

Finally she was escorted away from me.

She waved the entire way back to her hut.

"She's a strong one, didn't even shed a tear." I sighed.

Rex rolled his eyes. "She thought you were proposing when you tripped, just FYI, so remember you can't hold us legally responsible if she sues."

"I hate you."

"Next date." Rex slapped me on the back and walked off.

One more girl.

And I was Becca free.

Not home free.

Becca free.

Way better.

CHAPTER FORTY-FIVE
BECCA

I was on my third mimosa and it was only one in the afternoon. I saw the beginning of each date. Max was a perfect gentleman to each of the girls. I hadn't been worried about any of them until Colton decided to inform me that he'd actually chosen a girl who was normal.

"You what?" Milo roared, smacking her husband in the shoulder. "You chose a normal?"

"As opposed to . . ." Colton looked at all of us, his brow furrowed in utter confusion as to why he was getting beaten by his wife. Yeah, I was one bad choice away from grabbing a voodoo doll of Colton and poking it with something.

"As opposed to"—Jason slurped his drink; poor champ had had at least seven but was still able to have a complete conversation without slurring. It was impressive—"a cray."

"Cray?" Colton repeated.

"Or as Max calls them"—Jason took another sip—"a cray cray."

"Like Jayne," Milo explained.

"Ohhh." Colton blinked. "But why would I choose a crazy when it's all about finding love and—"

"Colt!" Milo shouted. "He likes Becca!"

My body erupted with a fiery sensation—my skin had to be bright red by now.

"I know." Colton rolled his eyes. "I'm not stupid."

Jason snorted.

Milo gave him a pointed look.

"I have my reasons for choosing another normal. Wanna hear them?" Colton leaned forward.

"Doubtful they're good reasons, but sure." Milo grabbed another drink from the bar. "Hit us."

"So this whole scenario makes you think you're falling in love when really you're not given a choice. Most of the girls that are here are absolutely bat-shit crazy, making it so Becca's an easy choice, and if I know girls, which let's be honest, I'm like a master at reading the female mind . . ." Yeah, that earned a lot of laughter and pointing. "Whatever." Colton rolled his eyes. "Becca doesn't want to be the best option out of the crazies, she wants to be the best option period. Max has to see it and Becca has to see it." He smirked. "You're welcome, world."

"Wow," Milo sighed. "You almost made up for being an ass right then."

"Aw, babe." Colton smiled. "Nicest thing you've ever said to me."

I watched and tried not to be jealous as they cuddled and kissed. Jason made eye contact with me over their heads and made a gagging motion with his hand, then promptly fell out of his chair. Right, so he was three sheets to the wind already. Clearly the alcohol had affected him more than I'd thought.

The wind picked up a bit; I glanced back at the beach just in time to see Max's fourth date approach. Out of all the girls, she was the one I was most worried about. Quiet, pretty, normal.

Great.

I silently prayed she had spinach in her teeth and was defeated when I noticed Max's face light up when she gave him a warm hug and grabbed his hand.

Pangs of jealousy attacked me from all sides.

"Hey." Milo squeezed my arm. "It's going to be fine. He likes you."

Right. He liked me. I'd slept with him already because, what? I was that convinced that what we had was going to last past two weeks? Suddenly nauseated, I ordered another drink.

It had taken me two weeks to not only fall for the guy, but also to sleep with him. I hadn't kept my cards close, if anything I'd laid them all out in front of a complete stranger in hopes he'd love me.

But Max was . . . Max. He had everything—what if I wasn't enough to keep someone like him entertained? What if I wasn't enough to keep him, period? Clearly he'd had lots of dating experience and when guys were that experienced they bored easily. Insecurity hit me again square in the chest . . . what if this was just an infatuation for him, brought on by the show? What if, once we were back to our normal lives, whatever there was between us proved to be too normal for him?

CHAPTER FORTY-SIX

MAX

Thank Hades. They chose a normal. A normal! As in someone who doesn't have multiple personalities, a fetish for sharp nails, the inability to speak English—a normal.

Little G popped up from my pocket and froze. He was so astonished that we weren't getting attacked by another crazy girl that he'd stopped breathing altogether.

"Hey." The girl smiled. And it wasn't scary. You know what I'm talking about. Some girls have the creeper smile where you're not sure if they are going to attack you or just say hi. She meant to say hi. And I actually liked the smile. So I returned it with one of my own.

"Hey." I pulled her in for a hug. "You ready for our date?"

"Sure." A blush tinted her cheeks, making her look really young. Damn, was it possible she was younger than me? Great, so now I was the old creeper. "What are we doing?"

"We are . . ." I looked around. "Honestly, I don't remember. I mean I think they'd like you to think I totally plan these dates on my own but spoiler alert, today they've actually been doing it for me. But can I get points for dressing myself?"

She laughed out loud, throwing her head back a bit. "Yeah, you get points for color coordination."

"And not wearing socks with sandals," I felt the need to add. "Because I'm pretty sure that's a deal breaker."

"That and men who hate goats. I have a goat farm so . . ." Her voice trailed off as she winked.

"Fine, how'd you know?"

"How'd I know?" Her eyebrows shot up. "The first day you ran into shark-infested waters when a goat looked in your direction."

"Well . . ." We started walking, the camera crew followed. "You'll be happy to know that Hades and I have settled our differences and now he sleeps on my underwear."

"Ah, a goat paradise. How nice."

She smiled again.

And honestly, I could not stop smiling. And it wasn't because she had cropped blond hair and wore absolutely no makeup but still managed to look fresh-faced and cute. I didn't feel lust for her or anything, just companionship. She was no Becca. Then again, Becca was in a league all her own. But this girl? I could hang out with her and not want to kill myself in the process.

She smiled. "My name's Sam, just in case you forgot."

"Sam?"

"Well, Sammy." Her nose wrinkled.

"Sammy." I tried out the name. "I think Sam fits you better."

"Me too." She reached for my hand.

Rex made a motion with his hands for us to go out to the docks. So I took Sam with me, falling into easy conversation. That is, until we stopped at the end of the dock and noted the Jet Skis.

I loved sports. All sports.

But water sports? Let's just say I didn't have any experience with them except for the one time when I was sixteen. I went Jet Skiing and had to be freaking rescued by the coast guard because I couldn't get back on my Jet Ski. Fine, so back then my upper body strength was that of a wet noodle. I developed later in life!

"You know how to drive those things?" She pointed.

I laughed. "Please, girl, I drive them in my sleep."

And by *them* I meant cars.

Not the Jet Skis.

"So"—I pointed—"I guess we just get on our own . . . jets . . ." I nodded. "And race."

"Race?" She perked up.

"Aw, how cute." I patted her head. "Scared?"

"Of a metrosexual on a Jet Ski?" She snickered. "Watch me."

So I did.

I watched her get on her ski and tried to mimic the movements. All was well until I was asked to turn it on.

A girl asked me to turn it on and I drew a blank, so I defaulted. "Aw, that's not the first time someone's asked me to turn them on." I winked.

Her response was to take off on her own Jet Ski, splashing me in the process.

"Rex!" I said through gritted teeth. "What do I do?"

He winked. "Why, Max, you turn it on. Having trouble with your engine?"

"You're dead to me!" I pointed at the camera crew. "Every single one of you! No Christmas presents."

They stared blankly at me.

With a roar I turned the key, gripped the handles, and went back so fast my feet kicked said handles as I landed ass-first in the water.

Coughing up a lung, I made it over to my Jet Ski and managed to get back on before I tried again and took off after Sam.

Three hours later I was sore in places no man should ever be sore. I was so frozen to the seat that it took both Rex and the camera guy to help me get off the Jet Ski. Even then I walked like I had balls the size of a prize-winning bull as I made my way very slowly down the dock.

"So that was fun!" Sam jumped up and down next to me. I needed a drink and she looked like she was ready to go another round. Damn high schoolers.

"Yeah, it was righteous," I said dryly.

"Wanna race?" she asked, getting into the ready position.

"No." I shook my head. "I want a newspaper, a snifter of whiskey, house pants, and a chair." I paused. "Holy shit, I'm my father!"

"How old are you?" She examined me from head to toe.

"Too old for the likes of you," I grumbled. "Run along and climb a tree, and the old man will watch and take pictures."

"Um . . ." Sam cringed.

"Poor sentence choice." I nodded. "But to be fair I'm extremely dehydrated."

"Right." She tucked her hair behind her ear; it fell across her face anyway. "So do I stay or?"

"Oh, sorry!" I managed to pull her into my arms and press a chaste kiss to her lips. "You stay."

"Woo-hoo!" She jumped again.

"Stop jumping, you're making me tired." I yawned.

She pushed me. "You're old."

"Truth." I nodded. "See ya later. Thanks for the date, Sam."

"Bye, Max!" She ran off.

"If only I could channel that youthful energy." I sighed out loud.

"One hour until your next date." Rex slapped me on the back. "Just think, after this you only have a few girls left!"

"Then I get off the Island?" I said in a hopeful voice.

"Yes." Rex nodded. "Only to get on the roller coaster called marriage. Welcome to life."

"That wasn't encouraging," I pointed out.

"If I meant to encourage you, you'd know it." Rex smiled. "Now, how about you go refresh yourself and grab a drink."

"Or ten." I saluted and walked off toward my hut.

With a yawn I opened the door and locked it behind me. Rubbing my eyes I made my way to the bed and noticed that the sheets were pulled back, and slowly my head lifted.

Becca.

Becca naked.

Becca naked in my bed.

"Shit," I grumbled. "I drowned, didn't I? And this is heaven?"

Becca tugged me onto the bed. "I don't know, does this feel like heaven?" She nipped my lips and then used her teeth to bite and lick me from my jaw to my ear.

"No." I jerked toward her. "In heaven my clothes would already be off."

"So . . ." She shrugged. "What's stopping you?"

"Oh, you know." I sighed. "My morals."

Her eyes narrowed.

"Which I happily threw out the window the first time I got you naked." I pushed her down on the bed. "Carry on."

CHAPTER FORTY-SEVEN
BECCA

I'd had four too many mimosas, which was the only explanation. Who in their right mind sneaks into a guy's hut and hides in his bed naked? This girl. Apparently champagne and orange juice make it so that your moral compass doesn't even work anymore!

It was too late to back out.

I realized this the minute the doorknob turned.

And then I was kind of . . . done panicking.

Because it was Max. And I liked Max. He was . . . just . . . incredible. He was smart, funny, gorgeous, and yeah, maybe I was acting a little slutty, but again, I was a bit inebriated, so what would normally be a terrible idea felt so right, especially when I saw the look of pure adoration cross his face. He wanted me as much as I wanted him.

Anything beyond that my mind wouldn't let me focus on, because I was pretty sure my heart was screaming at me to stop before it got broken, but I couldn't help it.

Max's kisses made me forget myself, which at this point? I needed. I didn't want to think about the weeks after the show, the money—anything. I just wanted to focus on Max and how everything felt so perfect when we were together. He kissed me harder. Those kisses of his were dangerous, because they made me focus on everything all at once—but that everything was him and only him. He made me feel on fire, yet safe at the same time.

"I really like you, you know," Max said a half hour later. His clothes were everywhere. Hades was facing the wall, clearly embarrassed at the free show he'd just received, and I was happily relaxed against Max's shoulder, rubbing his chest, his golden-bronzed chest.

"I like you too," I said softly.

"More than the others," Max added. "More than anyone."

"Not because of the show?" I asked quietly, not wanting to make eye contact lest my heart shatter into a billion pieces if he joked or said that we were only together because of the show.

I hated how vulnerable I felt in that moment. Like one wrong sentence coming from his lips would destroy my world, altering me forever.

"Becca." Max shifted and then tilted my chin toward him. "The show brought me you, but it doesn't define what this is." He pointed between the two of us, then pulled me in for a kiss. "Speaking of the show, we should probably get ready for our date."

"What are we doing?"

"Told you"—he winked—"I saved the best for last."

I sighed as he slowly got out of bed and did the naked walk to the bathroom, where he turned on the shower. I was staring like a lunatic but he was just so . . . firm everywhere and sexy and . . .

"Becca?" Max grinned. "You okay?"

"Yeah?" I said breathlessly. "Why?"

"You're about ready to fall off the bed and I could have sworn I heard a moan, but hey, it could have been Hades."

Wasn't Hades.

My skin went hot all over.

With a grin Max walked over to me and kissed my head. "Join me?"

"Huh?"

"Shower," he whispered against my ear. "Join me."

"But—"

"Come on, just a few minutes."

"But the date is in a half hour and—"

Max silenced me with his lips and then lifted me into his arms and walked into the bathroom, slamming the door behind him. Hot water cascaded down my back as he walked us both into the shower and then pressed me up against the wall. "You were saying?"

"Good idea?" I opened my eyes.

Water dripped down Max's dark hair and across his full lips and strong jaw. Damn, the man was so good-looking it hurt.

"So . . ." With one hand he kept me firmly placed against the wall, with his other hand he gripped my fingers, interlocking them with his, and then gently pressed them against the wall, sliding me higher until he was able to position his body beneath me. "Let's start this date off right, shall we?"

No speaking took place over the next fifteen minutes. Some laughing, a lot of moaning, and a few slaps, but that was it. The shower was over too soon. Just like our time on the show would be and I was left to wonder.

Would it always be like this?

Or was I just another sucker falling for the lie that was reality TV?

CHAPTER FORTY-EIGHT

MAX

Because of my impromptu shower session with Becca, I'd had no time to get ready. Then again, she was the type of girl I figured I'd never actually be ready for. She was more like a hurricane-force wind blowing in my direction. You can duck and take cover, but it's best to just stand out in the middle of the road and embrace what's happening.

If I thought about it too much, my man card started getting shaky. Every guy has one. Trust me, I don't lie. When little boys are brought into this world they're given what I like to refer to as a list of instructions. A boy must always chase things. A boy must always reference bodily fluids when he is uncomfortable. Until the age of eight, boys by their birthright are allowed to throw rocks, grass, or any itchy object in the direction of little girls. By age twelve all boys are allowed to bathe in Axe body spray in order to deter their own body odor. The list goes on and on, but the point I'm trying to make is that guys go through stages. When they finally get to the stage where they're faced with the rules about commitment, a guy does one of two things. He commits and gladly hands over his man card, receiving a new one in the process titled *husband*, also known as *whipped*. Or the man hesitates, trying to hold on to his card while also trying to reach for the husband one.

Doesn't work that way, my friends.

I've seen many a man lose a limb because he overestimated his ability to reach and hold on at the same time.

So at this point? As I was walking toward the beach to join Becca? I was stuck in the middle zone. If I stepped into commitment it meant I was leaving everything behind.

It meant uncharted territory.

And I think it's already been established I would have been a terrible explorer.

The film crew followed me down the beach. Becca was wearing a long, black halter cover-up and that same white swimsuit that made my entire body heat on sight.

I needed to focus on this date. There was no future, no past, only the present. Me and her . . .

"What the hell?" Rex called out, and pointed behind me. I turned to see Hades trot in my direction.

"Hades!" I scolded. "Go back to the hut, I'll be home soon."

Hades hung his head.

"Buddy." I shuffled toward him. "I know I haven't been paying much attention to you, what with"—I looked behind me and lowered my voice to a whisper—"Becca staying over, but I swear, we'll do stuff when I get back."

His little head popped up.

"Like that, do ya?"

Hades smiled. Okay, so he didn't smile, but he nodded his head a bit.

"We'll watch Discovery Channel, I promise. I'll find you a nice lady goat and who knows, maybe one day you'll have kids!"

Hades looked like he was grinning, so either he'd just passed gas or he was as horny as I was and the whole idea of procreating had merit. Satisfied, he trotted back toward the hut and sat.

"That goat is . . ." Rex didn't finish his sentence; he just scratched his head and cleared his throat. "All right, last date of the day before the group date. After this all bets are off. You ready, Max?"

"My mom says I was born ready." I shrugged. "It's the truth. Apparently I clapped my hands five minutes after being born. I was a child of promise and all that."

Rex stared. "Good for you." With a sigh he ran his hands through his greasy hair and pointed to the beach. "Remember, you get the same amount of time with Becca as the rest of the girls. This date is going to be more . . . intimate than the rest. We need to catch some of the evening on camera, then the rest of it is yours, all right? But, remember, this is TV, so . . ." He elbowed me and waggled his eyebrows. "If you extend past the allotted time . . . allow us to film."

His eyebrows looked like caterpillars just ready to bolt from his overly large forehead. Gross.

"Yeah, thanks, Rex." I slapped his back. "I'll just go get the girl now."

"You do that." Rex motioned for the cameras to roll.

"Hey," I called out, and my voice cracked. Someone shoot me now. Becca turned and then ran toward me.

Let me repeat.

The girl? The really hot one who allowed me to see her naked and then allowed it a second time, ruling out drunken mistakes and insanity? Running. Toward. Me.

I suddenly had a vision of Becca in a red bathing suit.

She'd do *Baywatch* good, just sayin'.

I caught her just as she flew into the air and wrapped her legs around my waist. When we fell into the sand, I just took her with me. Not caring that yes, our kissing was going to be recorded for the world to see. I wanted her and fine, okay, I was ready to release the card.

Funny how when you finally make a decision to do something, it's no longer hard, but extremely easy, and then you wonder why the hell you were so stressed out in the first place.

So as my man card fluttered away I didn't even glance up and wave good-bye. I simply kissed Becca harder, knowing that I'd made the right decision.

She was mine. I was going to keep her. I mean, I'd probably have to divide my time between her, Little G, and Hades, considering I'd gained a freaking animal family on the Island, but still.

I was going to make it work.

When she pulled back and looked into my eyes, I had trouble finding my voice.

"You okay?" she asked.

"I'm great." I licked my lips and kissed her mouth again. "Now stop attacking me so we can get started on our kick-ass date."

"You attacked me." Her eyebrows lifted.

"Not true. I believe it was you that launched yourself through the air and landed on my hotness. I merely caught you. I was afraid you'd sprain your ankle or something."

"My hero," Becca said dryly.

"Aw." I placed my hands on my heart and sighed. "If I had a dollar . . ."

Rolling her eyes, she grabbed my hand. We walked down the beach toward the rock formation on the other side of the huts.

"Did you plan this date?" Becca asked once we'd reached the rocks.

"Yes. All by myself. Can't you tell? Doesn't this just scream Max?" I pointed to the rocks.

"I'm confused." Becca looked around the area. "Where's the date?"

"Oh, that." I nodded. "We have to go up."

"Up what?"

I smiled. "The rocks."

"As in, we have to . . ." Becca tilted her head. "Climb?"

"You can spider-monkey on my back if that makes you feel better. I'm big enough to carry us both but don't get pissed if I drop you. I can't be held responsible if something bites my hand and I lose my grip."

"Has anyone ever told you how brave you are?" Becca asked. "No?"

"I get so tired of compliments." I sighed.

"Okay." Becca clapped her hands together. "I can climb. I can do this. I mean, it's not like there's sharks waiting for us up there."

"If there were, would you scream?" I asked as the professional climbers started putting us in our gear.

"Probably. Why?" Becca pulled off her cover-up and stepped into the harness. Swear she looked like every dream I'd ever had in high school about Xena, warrior princess. White swimsuit with harnesses and rope? Good golly Miss Molly, was there anything better?

"Just curious what it takes to make you scream." I sighed.

"You should know—"

"Believe me." I cut her off. "I do."

Her eyes heated.

"I just want to cover all my bases, you know, just in case I lose my touch."

She flushed and looked down.

"But by the look of red on your cheeks I'm not in danger of that happening just yet, am I right?"

"So climbing." Becca exhaled and put her hands on her hips. "Do I just go up?"

"You can go down too," I assured her. "I'll allow it."

"And then I place my hands on the edges of the rocks and pull?"

"Pulling is always advised," I said seriously. "Some say that the little tug is the best part."

"And what? The ropes help pull me to the top?"

"Peaking." I thrust out my chest. "Think of climbing like an orgasm."

Becca started coughing wildly.

"What?" I shrugged. "I'm a guy, I use sexual references, sue me. It's a cliff."

"The rocks?" Becca placed her hands on the rocks and waited for me to follow.

"Right." I stood behind her. "And the higher you get, the better it feels, because you can see the top, you can feel yourself reaching it. And I guarantee that the minute you finish your climb, you'll want to do it all over again."

Becca's body trembled beneath mine.

"Or we can zigzag-run through the sand, try to lose the camera crew, and lock ourselves in the hut."

Becca's eyes went wide, as if she was really contemplating not climbing.

"I was kidding." I sighed into her hair. "You're going to climb. Besides, who knows what's waiting for you at the top, hmm?"

"But you're behind me?"

"Baby." I trailed my fingers down her jaw. "Haven't you realized it yet? I'm everywhere." I placed my hands on her hips and lifted. "Now shimmy up so I can get a good view of that ass."

"You're an ass!" she fired back.

"Thank you!" I chuckled, climbing up after her. "And if you get nervous just think orgasm."

"Or," Becca called back, "I could just slip and you could break my fall."

"I need my face, Becca, it's all I have. Men can't live off of sparkling personalities, you know."

"You'd survive."

"Duh, because I'm Max, but I don't want to have to survive off my wit and charm. Without my looks I'm only half a man."

"I think you mean without your balls." She climbed higher.

"You thinking about removing them or something? Because I have to admit, right now, watching you sweat while threatening me, kinda hot."

"Max!" she yelled, I could tell her teeth were gritting together because my name was strangled.

"Orgasm!" I shouted.

"National TV!" she fired back.

"Say it!"

"I hate you!"

"Almost there!"

"Stop yelling at me!"

I laughed and kept yelling.

Becca started cursing.

But finally she reached the top.

When I joined her and sat next to her on the rock, I didn't have time to speak, she quickly straddled me and then attacked my mouth with hers. When I was finally allowed air, she whispered, "Was it good for you?"

"The best." I grinned. "But how about we make it better?"

CHAPTER FORTY-NINE
BECCA

"What did you have in mind?" I was still trying to get my mind off Max's bare chest and focus on his eyes when he helped me to my feet. He really was a cocky piece of work but I had to wonder if he truly realized how beautiful he was.

"Oh, you know." Max wrapped his muscular arm around my body. "World domination and all that."

"I can dig it," I agreed.

"Zombie partners for life, yo."

"So." I looked around. There was absolutely nothing except for a really pretty view of the ocean. "This is nice."

"Deep breaths, Little B, deep breaths."

"I'm fine," I explained. "I'm not really afraid of heights. I mean, I'm not exactly thrilled that we had to climb, but that was more of me not being a fan of lifting my body a few hundred feet into the air."

"Fair enough." Max led me to the edge of the cliff and pointed. "See that beach down there?"

I followed the direction he was pointing. There was a private beach on the other side of the rock. A small bonfire was going and there was a beautiful hut built around it in a half circle. The entire scene looked like paradise, especially since the sun was starting to set.

"Hungry?" Max kissed my head.

"Yes!" I bit down on my lower lip. "So do we just climb down the other side of this giant rock, or . . ."

Max's eyes teased. They taunted. Shit.

"You see that down there?" Max pointed below. Rocks ringed a large pool that was protected from the splashing waves of the ocean, creating a lagoon.

"No," I lied. "So about that climb . . ."

"Halt." Max grabbed my arm before I could walk away. "Now we fly."

"Can we just maybe . . . climb instead?"

"The only way up is down. Fun, right?" Max tilted my chin toward him. "You afraid?"

"A bit." I looked over the edge. "I mean, that's at least a forty-foot jump."

"It's nothing."

"It's something."

"You're going to be no help at all during the zombie apocalypse if you cower in the face of danger."

"Max." I leaned over and placed my hands on my knees to catch my breath. "Look around you, do you see any zombies chasing us?"

"True." Max sighed. "Rex is at the bottom of the cliff, otherwise that may actually work." He tapped his chin.

The camera crew that seriously followed our every move busted up laughing.

"Want me to chase you?" Max offered.

"Please don't."

"No, really." Max moved away from me, then started staggering toward the cliff edge, making groaning noises. "Should I drool? I think zombies drool."

Laughing, I reached for him, just as he wrapped his arms around me and whispered, "Let's do it together."

"We already did that," I teased.

"That"—his eyes darkened—"we'll do until I'm so dehydrated Hades has to bring me his milk."

"Nice visual, what, you gonna suck on his nonexistent nipple, Max?"

"Guys have nipples, Becca. Or didn't you notice? Aw, poor soul, tell the truth, were you raised Amish?"

"No."

"Did you have one of those sexy little hats with the strings?"

"Max—"

"Holy shit, tell me you wore braids. I'm such a sucker for braids. I freaking ruined the *Heidi* VHS my parents had for me when I was little."

"No words."

"No, none, just lots of singing. It's weird, right? At any rate, saddle up, Amish B. We're going under."

I didn't have time to respond.

Because Max grabbed my hand and pulled.

Soon we were free-falling in the air.

And then warm water cascaded all over my body.

When I swam up for air, it was to find Max's mouth already on mine. Breathing for me.

"So," he whispered. "How's the date so far?"

"Goats, orgasms, climbing rocks, stories of zombies, and *Heidi*? It's normal . . . for you it's normal." I smiled. "Wouldn't want it any other way."

"Oh, good." Max's wide smile made my stomach flip. "Because there's more where that came from."

"Oh, yeah?"

"Girl, I could talk *Heidi* all day, try me, just try me."

I rolled my eyes and swam with him to the edge of the pool and into the ocean.

CHAPTER FIFTY

MAX

By the time we reached the beach, I was famished. And not your normal famished where your stomach politely growls and you smile shyly. No. Hell, no. Since we actually had food in front of us, I can't be sure I would have gone as far as to eat a bug, but the very fact that the thought appeared in my head . . .

Well, it tells me something, doesn't it?

I'm no good when I'm hungry.

I'm like those Snickers commercials. Swear I'd be the dude that goes all bat-shit crazy on his friend, turning into a weird celebrity, until he has the chocolate in his mouth.

"This is so pretty." Becca released my hand and walked over to the table where our first course was already set out. "I'm starving, can we eat now?"

"Thank God." Have I mentioned how much I love a girl who loves food? There's a reason Carl's Jr. makes a killing off those stupid commercials, people. A girl biting into beef? Sauce dripping down her . . . whoa there, boy, whoa. Sorry, I almost blacked out for a minute imagining licking barbeque sauce off Becca's stomach.

"You okay?" Becca asked from her spot at the table. She'd already sat down and was drinking some wine.

"How do you feel about barbeque sauce?" I sat down next to her and watched as her eyes peered through mine.

"Hmm, considering it's you asking and not a sane individual, I like to eat it, and I'd say that the world is a better place because of it, and, well, if I had to choose between swimming in a tub of barbeque sauce versus ketchup I'd probably choose barbeque."

"You"—I nodded and lifted my glass in appreciation—"are a true American. Tell me you own a cowboy hat and I'm proposing at midnight."

"It's pink."

"Good God, you're perfect."

"Why midnight?"

"Silly." I winked. "Midnight's the only time where you can be both in the past, present, and future."

Becca leaned forward, her smile growing wider by the second. "How do you figure?"

"The clock strikes twelve. Your cell phone's always on time, my watch is always late by one minute, the clock in my car is early." I shrugged. "So I exist in all time, and come on, isn't it romantic that the proposal would be part of your past, present, and future all at once?"

Becca's breath hitched before a pretty blush stained her cheeks. "Yeah, that's, um, actually pretty romantic."

"And you doubt me." I scowled.

Becca tilted her head. "You do realize not thirty minutes ago you were pretending to be a zombie and accused me of being Amish."

"Details." I waved her off. "So, food. We have salad to start and oh, look, Reid . . ." I did a double take. "Son of a barbecue-sauce-drinking slut."

"What?" Becca looked up.

"Surprise, bitch," Reid mouthed. "I'll be helping this evening since I'm part of this camera crew."

Side note, we changed camera crews because the other crew was shooting from the rocky cliff. It only made sense to have one waiting for us while we approached from the beach.

"Tell me the truth, did you poison the food?" I asked. "Don't lie, Reid. It tarnishes the family name and Pop-pop always told us he'd haunt us if we lied."

"Pop-pop's dead." Reid rolled his eyes.

Something howled.

I lifted my hands in the air and pointed at Reid. "Cool, so when whatever that was comes to get you tonight, remember those words."

"Romantic." Reid nodded to Becca. "Am I right? He talks about his dead Pop-pop over a candlelit dinner—nearly stole my breath away."

"He's hungry," Becca explained.

"I'm marrying her," I announced. "Not only does she realize that I'm not myself when I'm hungry, but she owns a cowboy hat."

"Got any boots to go with that hat?" Reid asked, his interest piqued.

"I'll do you one better." Becca leaned back and took a long sip of wine. "I've got a rope too."

"Oh, God," I moaned.

Reid patted me on the back. "I think you just gave my brother his first orgasm."

"Why do they let Reids in this joint? It's supposed to be a classy establishment!" I pushed off his hand. "Now bring us food, damn it!"

Reid walked off behind the hut and helped the cook bring out the first appetizer.

"*Bon appétit!*"

I looked down.

Becca tilted her head.

"I'm not gonna lie." I poked around with my fork. "I don't need this . . . I'm already there."

"Huh?" She looked up.

"Oysters for my oyster," I explained.

"What are you talking about?"

"You sure you're not Amish?"

"Do Amish people not eat oysters?"

"Horny." I nodded. "They make guys horny. It's said to aid blood flow to certain areas of the body."

Becca snorted. "Like you need help with that."

"Aw." I winked. "Care to find out? I promise I won't tell if you won't."

"Cameras." Becca coughed.

"Free show!" I shrugged. "Besides, it's dark."

Becca's gaze met mine. "I don't care if its pitch-black. Some things you just can't hide, Max, especially if they're big enough."

"I want to paint you." I nodded. "It's the biggest honor I can think of next to making a statue in your name and honestly, that's just too far."

"Amazing." Becca picked up an oyster and used her fork to remove the inside. "That you even know the definition of *too far*."

"*Too far*." I cleared my throat. "When you cross the line and have sex. *Too far*. Next question, please."

Becca smirked and rolled her eyes. Pretty sure we were about to go through an entire bottle of wine before the second course.

Luckily, Reid brought bread, which was good because I hadn't been drinking much water and the wine was going straight to my head, making me feel more brave, which, if we're all being honest, is just a bad idea all around. For everyone.

Myself included.

Two salads.

A loaf of bread.

Two bottles of wine.

Chicken and vegetables.

Laughter.

And finally . . . dessert.

Our date had officially lasted longer than the rest of the dates put together. I got up from my chair and held my hand out to Becca. We walked over to the fire and sat on the cushions placed around it. A tray of different types of chocolate and strawberries had been placed next to the cushions. And, of course, more wine, because apparently they wanted us completely smashed before the night ended.

"I'm tired." Becca yawned.

"I seem to have that effect on people."

"You are pretty exhausting."

"I count that a victory." I laughed, picking up a piece of white chocolate and holding it to her lips. "Now bite."

Becca bit into the chocolate and moaned.

Damn chocolate.

Why didn't I think of rubbing my body down with chocolate, then asking her to bite?

"So good." Becca opened her mouth again, like a little bird. I had no choice but to keep feeding her, and lusting after every little movement her tongue made across her lips. Self-control be damned.

"You're killing me," I said in a hoarse voice. "But if I had to choose a way to go, this would be it."

"Feeding me?" Becca laughed.

"Watching you eat." I sighed. "I could watch that mouth all day long and never get bored. In fact, you're my favorite when you're this way."

"What way?"

"Don't move." I pulled away and stared. "Exactly like that."

"Hardly breathing and so full of dinner I want to sleep?"

"Yes." I nodded. "Sitting by the fire. I could watch you eat chocolate, drink wine, I could just watch you all day because everything you do is so unique, so part of who you are." I sighed. "It's possible

I drank a bit too much wine, but you're absolutely, astonishingly beautiful." I cupped her face and brought my mouth close to hers. "Mmm, white chocolate."

"Do I taste better with or without chocolate?"

"If you tasted any better I'd be dead, and where's the fun in a dead Max?"

"No fun at all," Becca agreed.

"So . . ." I leaned back. "The last part of the date."

"Is this where you kill me?"

"Damn it! I always give away the endings!"

"It's okay; just do it fast."

"Can't." I sighed. "I have a thing for slow torture." I licked my lips and started inching my hands up her thighs. "It's more . . . pleasurable that way."

"They never warned us about Maxes in school." Becca groaned as her eyes fluttered closed. My hands kept moving toward her hips, then slid to the sides, cupping her ass.

"Silly, of course they didn't," I murmured against her neck. "It's rare to see one in the wild, even more rare to be able to catch it."

"To see a Max in the wild." Becca tilted her head toward the sky as an awe-filled expression crossed her features. "Must be a glorious thing."

"Dangerously attractive," I agreed. "Seductive, truly a feast for the eyes."

Someone cleared his or her throat. I pulled back reluctantly and glared at the producer. Fine. I'd do the dance, then I was taking Becca into the hut.

"Becca, I want to keep you." I said it in a no-shit voice and shook my head. A person would have to be blind not to know that. "Also, we're sitting so conveniently by this hut, would you care to go inside and look around? You see it's an overnight date." I gasped and put my hands on my cheeks. The producer rolled his eyes. I'd only recently discovered that little tidbit during our confessional break. "And, well . . . I know you promised to save yourself for the right guy, and golly gosh, I think I may be him."

"Shucks." Becca snapped her fingers. "But my daddy always taught me never to go into a dark room with a man. He says they only got one thing on their minds."

"Not I!" I stood. "I swear it!"

"Oh, Lord!" Becca stood and wrapped her arms around me. "I found a good one! Mama would be so proud!"

"Dude," I whispered in her ear. "We would have killed at theater camp together. Literally slain them."

I took her hand and led her to the door of the hut. Rex said he needed to film some of the scene, which was fine. But later tonight? She was all mine.

CHAPTER FIFTY-ONE
BECCA

I was a bit uncomfortable as Max led me into the hut. I mean, there was an entire camera crew following us. A bit weird? Yeah, a bit. I understood that it was a show, but I was thankful in that moment that Max and I had been able to sneak away so many times before. How embarrassing it would have been to actually have all those moments on tape.

Holy crap. I would officially have had my own sex tape! My parents would have killed me, and I'd never have been able to work at Starbucks again. I never saw anything about it in the training manual, but I was pretty positive sex tapes for Starbucks employees were frowned upon.

"So . . ." Max cleared his throat and held up his hands. "This is it."

"Fancy." I looked around the room and crossed my arms. A bottle of champagne was cooling on the table with more dessert. I pointed. "Are they trying to get you to seduce me?"

"Depends." Max shrugged. "Are you seducible?"

"Guess you'll have to find out."

Max groaned and made his way over to the small couch and patted the cushion next to him. "I think not."

"Not?"

"Seducible." He sighed and then wrapped his arm around me when I sat down. "Want to know why?"

"Even if I said no, you'd tell me."

"Truth." He toyed with my hair. "You're too pretty for the likes of me."

"Is this where we part as friends?" I joked.

"Never. I could never kiss my friends the way I want to kiss you and I'm pretty sure I'd get arrested if I tried to kiss Pop-pop that way."

"He's dead."

"See? You get me." Max's fingers continued combing through my hair. The rhythm was hypnotic. "Besides, I'm a Sagittarius."

"What?" I yawned.

"Sleep," Max whispered in my ear. "At least take a small nap and I'll get them to leave."

"Then what?" I whispered as low as I could so the camera crew couldn't pick up on it.

"Oh, I thought you knew." Max kissed the top of my head. "Then Max gets dessert."

"Max won't get anything if Max keeps referring to himself in the third person."

"I feel you," Max said in a serious tone. "Care to feel me too?"

"Had to add the last part."

"I'm Max."

I rolled my eyes and snuggled into his chest. Soon sleep overtook me.

The smell of chocolate woke me up . . . my eyelids felt heavy as I tried to open my eyes. A piece of dark chocolate was placed right in front of my face. I blinked a few more times and then opened my mouth.

Max dropped the piece of chocolate onto my tongue. The taste of dark chocolate mixed with salt exploded in my mouth. What a way to wake up.

"That was nice," I whispered, still chewing.

"Well, I almost let Mighty Max wake you but I figured it would probably scare you. I know how girls are with big objects in the dark. I mean, what's to say you didn't mistake it for a snake? Or a bear!"

"Or a worm." I smirked.

"Or the largest piece of PVC pipe a girl could see!"

"Because you know us girls, we're really scared of tools and such."

"I offer you my services, madam. You may play with my tools any which way you please. I know just the one to start with."

"Max." I pushed myself into a sitting position. "I'm not playing with your—"

Max gripped my hand and placed it across his chest. "Start here."

"Huh?"

"My heart . . ." He grinned. "What? You thought I was talking about something else? Geez, Becca, get that pretty little head out of the gutter. I would never, and I do mean never, force you to put your hands on me."

I grinned. "That's sweet."

"Now asking . . ." He winked. "I'd probably do that."

"You're impossible."

"I could have starred in that movie . . . I'm way more badass than Tom Cruise. Besides, I have better hair."

"Speaking of hair—" I reached for another piece of chocolate. "Where's Reid? And the production crew?"

"You like his hair?" Max's eyes narrowed.

"It's nice," I teased. "So thick and wavy."

"Not funny."

"Silky."

"Becca . . ." Max warned.

"Running my fingers through it would feel like—"

"One more word and I'm putting Nair in his shampoo." Max flipped me onto my back and pounced on me, straddling my body. "Then again, the guy would probably look good bald too." He closed his eyes. "Damn you, Reid!"

"I like your hair too." I reached up and tucked his dark hair behind his ears. "It's . . . nice."

"Hmm." He leaned down. "We can do better than *nice*, can't we?"

"Sexy?"

"A word that starts with *sex*?" Max seemed to think about this for a minute. "Sold." He jumped off me and held out his hand. "Now for the second part of the date. The film crew got the footage they needed, and you and I are going on an adventure."

I placed my hand in his. "Where?"

"To the moon." Max grinned. "Where else would I take the girl I like?"

"Go big or go home?"

"See!" Max wrapped his arm around me and led me outside. "We get us!"

"Us?"

"A couple." Max kissed my forehead. "That's what we are."

"Oh." I felt my face heat. Had he just . . . declared us an *us*? Did that mean he wanted more time once the show ended? I decided not to approach the subject. Instead I leaned farther into Max's embrace and calmed my rapidly beating heart. I had him for now. We were an *us* . . . and I loved the sound of that.

CHAPTER FIFTY-TWO

MAX

"Becca!" I yelled over my right shoulder. "Hurry up!"

"Must. Get. Water!" She heaved, leaning her head against the rock.

"Water's for wimps," I scolded. "A few more feet, come on, I know you like climbing things . . . remember what I taught you about rock climbing."

"Orgasms," Becca muttered. "The last thing on my mind."

"Funny." I laughed. "They're always the first thing on mine."

"You're a guy."

"Hooray! You noticed." I lifted myself up to the top of the rock and turned around to offer my hand. "I was afraid I was going to have to drop my shorts or something."

"Keep"—she heaved—"pants on."

"Where's the fun in clothing if you can't take it off?" I offered an easy smile and lifted her the rest of the way to the top of the cliff. The climb had been close to thirty feet. To be fair, I hadn't realized it would be so hard, especially after drinking all that wine and taking a power nap, but I was desperate for romance. No, not true, I was desperate to romance her.

And Becca wasn't like normal girls. I couldn't bring her flowers; she'd probably sneeze into them and be like, *Oh, cool, you got me weeds.* I couldn't give her chocolate because the show had already done that. I was big on the gesture thing, the only issue was that the minute I realized I wanted to do something . . . another thought occurred.

I'd never actually dated a girl beyond a few weeks.

The big gesture?

Hadn't ever taken place.

I'd never wanted to invite a girl into my life. In my mind it was like inviting a vampire into your house, all of a sudden they had free rein to come and go as they pleased, meaning they could redecorate while you were out golfing and you couldn't say shit about it because *ding ding ding*, you're the jackass who invited them in the first place!

But if Becca was a vampire . . .

I'd totally invite her in.

Let her bite me.

Hell, I'd bite back—pretty sure it would be hard not to . . . biting into that supple skin was what dreams were made of.

"Max?" Becca touched my shoulder. "You okay?"

"Just thinking about vampires." I shrugged. "Sexier than zombies."

"True." She nodded. "Plus vampires bite."

"So do zombies," I pointed out. "But I'd rather be bitten by a vampire."

"Why?" She grabbed my hand as we walked toward the edge of the cliff and up to the last peak.

"Easy." I helped her up the rock, placing my hands on her hips. "I'd be a badass vampire. Super fast, sexy, able to lure women into my den of iniquity."

"Do you even know what *iniquity* means? Just curious." Becca's foot slipped; I caught her, allowing her to gain her footing again, then helped her the last part of the way.

"We think alike." I nodded. "Just in case you were on the fence about the whole *us* thing."

"I'm not on the fence." Becca smiled. "I'm jumping over the fence, then jumping right back onto my own lawn."

"I guarantee my lawn's nicer than yours . . . I keep it freakishly green. It's one of my things, and if the reason for your hesitation is that my lawn is new and scary . . . well, just know I wouldn't be worth it, we wouldn't be worth anything, if we weren't a little bit terrified."

Becca put her hands on her hips and peeked at me from beneath heavy lashes. "It amazes me how you can go from talking about vampires to speaking philosophy."

I nodded. "I'm a strong personality so I try to mix it up a bit as to not overwhelm people into having seizures."

"How kind."

"I think so." I grinned. "Now close your eyes."

She closed her eyes as I led her to the edge. The moon was just starting to rise above the water, giving everything a silvery glow.

"I give you," I whispered in her ear, my tongue sliding along the outside curve, "the moon."

Becca opened her eyes and gasped. "It's huge."

"Not me, silly." I rolled my eyes. "The moon."

Becca elbowed me in the stomach and continued to stare. "So, you bring all the girls here?"

"First, I can't." I sighed. "We're halfway across the world and for a first date that's kind of spendy, feel me? Second, the timing has to be perfect. And third . . . well . . ." I moved behind her, wrapping my arms around her middle and leaning my chin on her head. "The moon is for lovers."

"W-what?"

"For lovers." I moved my hands down her arms, interlocking our fingers. "It's for lovers. I would never bring someone the moon unless I was planning on giving them the sun and stars as well. It's kind of a package deal; therefore, the moon is for lovers. The stars are for partners. The sun . . . for best friends. Package deal . . . you get one, you get all, just like a real relationship."

"Are you asking—?" Her body trembled. "Are you asking what I think you're asking?"

"For your firstborn? Yes, yes I am," I joked.

Becca laughed, the tension easing from her body.

"I'm asking for something much more scary," I whispered in her ear, "Your trust . . . and that giant muscle between those perfect breasts."

"Classy."

"You wouldn't want me any other way." My lips found her neck. "I want it all . . . past this week, past two weeks from now. The only question . . . the one I won't make you answer, not yet . . . is how much are you willing to give?"

I stepped away briefly, then turned her around to face me, tilting her chin toward my mouth. "I'll wait for your answer . . . praying to the moon, the sun, the stars, that it's the one I want to hear, because you've managed to lay your soul next to my heart, and I've discovered it doesn't want to let go."

CHAPTER FIFTY-THREE
BECCA

We didn't talk much as we hiked back down. My mind was whirling with possibilities. He'd said everything I'd wanted to hear and yet . . . it didn't feel real. Maybe it was the atmosphere? Or possibly the circumstances. I needed him to say those things to me in the grocery store, or after work when I smelled like coffee beans and was having trouble paying my electric bill because my textbooks cost so much.

But I wanted to give him that chance.

Which meant, in the end, I wouldn't take just the money. I'd take Max too . . . I knew the choice I'd make and it was him. It would be him every time, because the thing about Maxes in the wild? Once you catch one.

They stick forever.

Like a disease.

Like Hades.

And what woman in her right mind wouldn't want one all to herself? Max chose that moment to flash me a grin straight out of the movies. And not a B horror flick that goes straight to DVD. No, his grin was something out of a Channing Tatum movie. Just. Beautiful. Dark hair fell across his face, he brushed it away, licking his full, sculpted lips, and leaned his head against mine.

"You ready for the next surprise?"

"There's more?" I asked, elated. Never had a guy done anything as extravagant as claiming to bring me the moon and the stars. Heck, most guys thought they were doing an awesome job when they opened my door.

"With me"—Max pulled me into his arms—"there will always be more."

Grinning, I gripped his hand, my heart jumping up and down as we made our way back to the hut.

The excitement, however, was short-lived, as Max cursed under his breath and released my hand. "Show yourselves and live. Hide and die."

"What?"

Reid stepped out from behind the hut. "I'm here to supervise."

"Your own beheading?" Max nodded. "Very well, proceed. Just get down on your hands and knees and—"

"I wonder," came another male voice. "How many times he's said that in his lifetime? Hmm? Get down on your hands and knees and—"

A loud thump sounded and then a female voice chimed in. "Really, Jason, you should talk."

"Burn." Another male voice laughed.

And then the people belonging to the voices stepped out from behind the hut and waved.

"Really?" Max sighed and looked heavenward. "I go to synagogue."

"He does," Reid piped up. "You'd think he'd be given more grace or something."

"Max!" Milo put her hands on her hips. "It's our last night together. They're sending us home after the ceremony tomorrow."

"Ceremony?" we both said in unison.

"Yeah, for the final choice." Jason made quotations with his fingers.

"We have a full two days until the final vote." Max sighed. "Nice try, though."

"No." Reid scratched his head. "Actually it's tomorrow. A huge storm's coming in and they want to wrap up filming before the weather turns bad. If they wait it out, it will put us off schedule, cost a ton of money, and, well, piss Rex off, so we're going to move things forward."

"You can't just move a dating show forward!" Max shouted.

Reid paused and then looked at his watch. "Oh, look, they just did."

Max ground his teeth and wrapped his arm around my waist. "And the reason for you guys interrupting our awesome date?"

"What did he do?" Milo asked, her eyes full of curiosity. "Did he kiss you? Hold your hand? Make you jump off a cliff? I've heard he's super romantic. Never experienced it for myself and—"

Colt placed his hand over her mouth and sighed. "It worries me that she's so eager to hear about someone else's love life."

"Marriage." Max nodded. "Lose some romance, Milo? Pretty sure there are plenty of guys willing to help you out at the Sex Toys and More store. Really, give them a call. Mention my name, they may give you a discount." He held out a card.

Colt swore. "Take that card and I drown Max in the ocean."

"Weird, I was thinking of doing the same thing to Reid!" Max laughed. "Not anymore, though, we no longer have the element of surprise."

"Thank you?" Reid said it like he was wondering if he should be thankful.

"So." Jason clapped his hands together. "Last night together, mallows? Grahams? Chocolate?"

"Okay." Max released my hand. "I'm going to say this once."

"Oh, good." Jason nodded. "We hate when you're long-winded."

"Colt," Max seethed. "Slap Jason for me."

"I have enough bruises," Jason snorted. "It looks like I'm into BDSM, all right, bro? Just add another one to the list. I feel no pain."

At that moment Max bent down and threw a shell at Jason's stomach.

"Shit!" Jason bent over. "What'd you throw? Freaking conch shell?"

"I was just checking to see if you feel pain. Bonus points for being right." Max shrugged. "Now, if it's the last night, don't you think you should let Becca and me have some alone time?"

"No," they all said in unison. It was strange, watching them all communicate. Like they were bickering married couples.

"Fact." Reid held up his hand. "You like Becca, therefore she has to like us before she can join the group."

"So we're a group now?" Max sighed. "A club that only lets in cool people?"

"We have a motto." Milo winked. "*Star Wars* fans only."

The group fell into a hush. As if mentioning *Star Wars* were the equivalent of saying a prayer. So naturally I shrugged and said, "I'm only a fan of the older versions."

"Thank God," Colt whispered under his breath while Milo gave me a nod of approval and a thumbs-up.

"We're kind of like . . ." Jason went to the fire and sat on one of the pillows. "The family you marry into. You can't get Max without the rest of us."

"Thanks, guys." Max released my hand. "Run along, Becca, find someone who won't scare you shitless. It's okay, we'll always have the moon."

"We're not that bad!" Milo shouted. Colt winced while Jason said, "Could you muzzle her?"

"That's my wife!" Colt's pitch matched Milo's.

"You don't say," Reid said dryly. He patted the seat next to him and motioned for me to come over and sit. Reluctantly Max walked with me to the fire.

We sat in a circle.

"You guys start humming or throwing pieces of her clothing in the fire and chanting, I'm going to set Hades on you," Max pouted.

"Fine." Reid shrugged. "I'll just eat him."

"Good one." Max rolled his eyes. "You gonna eat my gecko too?"

"Dude, did you buy a farm?" Jason asked, looking confused.

"Yes, Jason." Max's eyes narrowed. "I came to a dating show in order to obtain a farm. It seems to win the fair lady's hand I need to produce enough livestock in order to appease her family."

"One goat and a gecko." Milo whistled. "Wayta aim high, Max."

"You should buy a cow." This from Jason.

"At least a golden retriever or something . . ." Colt added helpfully.

Max opened his mouth, his jaw clenching in irritation, but I interrupted instead. "Actually, I'd really like a cat."

Max paled.

Milo covered her mouth with her hand while Colt, Jason, and Reid started snickering.

"What?" I shrugged. "Max, you don't like cats?"

Was the guy sweating? He shifted next to me, scratching the back of his neck before clearing his throat. "I uh, I love cats, had one when I was little . . ."

"Really?" Reid asked smoothly. "What was this cat's name?"

"Er, Cat." Max gave me an apologetic glance. "I didn't have a very active imagination when I was young on account of Reid dropping me on my head."

"Imagine how much smarter he would be had I not purposefully dropped him off that balcony." Reid nodded seriously. "So Cat . . . what color was it?"

"He"—Max licked his lips—"was brown."

"A brown cat?" Milo piped up. "A boy cat or girl cat?"

"Boy." Max shifted again, pulling his legs out from underneath him and staring at the sand.

"Ah, and this boy cat—" Jason nodded. "He really furry? Lots and lots of . . . hair?"

"Yes." Max kept scratching.

Jason kept talking. "Did that hair get on you? Make you uncomfortable?"

Max didn't say anything, just kept staring at the sand.

"Did the cat rub itself all over you? Meow in front of your face? It's so cute how you walk around the corner and boom!" Jason clapped his hands. "There's the cat! Or how about when you're taking a shower and you yell, Cat, Cat, where are you, Cat? Only to find out he's been standing there. The. Whole. Time."

"Achoo!" Reid sneezed.

"Holy shit!" Max jumped to his feet and started running toward the ocean.

"Um, what's he doing?"

"Ailurophobia," Reid whispered. "Fear of cats."

"Do something!" I rose to my feet, getting ready to take off after him, but Milo pulled me back down onto the ground.

"He's fine," she whispered. "Just let him deal with it the way he knows how."

"By drowning himself?" I pointed to the shore as Max disappeared under the water.

"Any minute now," Reid said in a confident tone, checking his watch.

A minute passed.

"Any minute." Reid laughed and looked at his watch again. "Any . . . minute."

"Guys!" I yelled. We all rose to our feet and started running toward the shore.

The minute my toes touched the water Max burst out and pointed. "You lose, bitches!"

"Max!" I yelled. "You scared me to death!"

"You should know," Max heaved, inhaling and exhaling with force, "that nobody brings Max down."

"Bastard," Reid muttered. "I was getting ready to go all CPR on your ass."

"Really?" Max nodded. "On my ass? I think you're getting CPR confused with kissing my ass, both are, however, accepted."

"Fear of cats?" I crossed my arms.

"So we'll get another dog." Max nodded. "Besides, we already have a goat. I'm sorry, you're really cool and all, Becca. I love that sexy little mouth of yours and everything it makes me feel, but I have to draw the line somewhere. If you want a cat, you'll have to get your own twin bed at my house. We'll be like couples from the fifties where we each read at night, have our lampstand, and discuss politics. The cat will come between us, but if that's what you want . . . then I'll sacrifice, feel me?"

"How did we go from him having a fear of cats to them being married with a cat?" Jason asked, scratching his head.

"Oh!" Reid nodded and snapped his fingers. "She owns a cowboy hat and boots."

"So?" Colt snorted.

"And a rope," Reid added. "An actual rope."

"Ohhhh." The other two guys nodded at me in appreciation.

"Men," Milo grumbled. "Max, are you going to be okay?"

"Of course! I'm half fish!" Max stumbled toward us, then face-planted into the sand.

"Careful, merman, you tripped over your tail." I offered him my hand and helped him walk out of the water.

"Ha, she called me *merman*." Max's chest puffed out. "The last time Jason was called a name by a woman was when he was arrested for stalking. I believe she called him *asshole*. Was that it?"

"Clearing the air." Jason held up his hands. "Not arrested for stalking. I was arrested for looking like the dude that had been stalking her. She apologized."

"Still arrested." Colt coughed.

"So." Reid rubbed his hands together. "It's the last night. Therefore we're drinking wine, having marshmallows, and learning all about our new group member. That is—"

All eyes turned to me.

"If you want to be part of the group," he finished.

Throat suddenly dry, I nodded and then squawked out, "Sure, crazy likes crazy, right?"

"Right." Max kissed my temple. "Don't worry, they can't handle their liquor, once they're out we'll lock the hut."

"And let them get eaten by mosquitoes?"

"Fine, we'll let Milo and Colt in."

"Max—"

"And Jason! But I draw the line after Jason. Then again, if Hades shows up he can, like, stand in the corner or something, bless his goat heart, he probably wonders where his daddy is."

"And Reid?" I asked, stumbling next to Max as I tried to keep up with his pace.

"What about him?"

"He's blood."

Max grinned. "Right, but you also like his hair and he does the sex smile way too much around you. Reid stays outside. With the predators. Don't worry, though, I'll leave him a knife and enough water to last him twelve hours."

"How kind of you?"

"I have a huge heart," Max boasted, grabbing me by the hips and twirling me out in front of him. "Wanna touch it?"

"Your heart?"

"Or anything." Max bit down on his lower lip. "In fact, if you want to touch any part of me, don't even ask, just do what feels right. What feels good."

"There's something wrong with you."

"Probably because you aren't touching me, I get weird when I'm without you."

"Compliment or scary future reality?" I asked.

"Compliment," Max whispered against my mouth. "Touch me."

"No."

"Just my face."

"No."

"Just my hand."

"No." I was seriously fighting a smile; the man was ridiculous!

"Fine." Max tucked my hair behind my ears and whispered across my mouth, "Then just look at me every once in a while." He pulled back. "Yeah, just like that. That look right there would last me an eternity."

Okay, it was happening. I more than liked him. I leaned into his warm body and let out a happy sigh as we made our way back to the fire. He was dripping wet, but I didn't care.

He was also slightly crazy.

Again, didn't care.

I just wanted him—in any capacity he was willing to give me.

The night progressed, we laughed and teased one another, and I tried desperately to keep my eyes open, but I was exhausted. The last thing I remember is falling asleep in Max's arms, and for the first time in a long time, being excited about seeing a guy's handsome face in the morning.

CHAPTER FIFTY-FOUR

MAX

I'll deny it to my dying day . . . hell, I may even deny it now, but it needs to be said. The girl had the most beautiful nail beds I'd ever seen.

There. I said it.

Judge me all you want.

They were petite, white, clean . . . oh, hell, I was in deep. I was in so deep I didn't even want out. I watched her sleep, I watched her breathe, I watched her do everything while I continued running my hands up and down her arms.

I hated that our moment would soon be interrupted by cameras, almost as much as I hated that when we went back to the real world, I wouldn't be able to skinny-dip with her in the ocean, or feed goats.

Then again, I was rich enough to make both a reality, right?

But I wanted her to be proud of me.

Damn it! This is what women do to men! They give us sex and then there's this huge expectation to be awesome in every other area of our lives. And I really needed to be awesome in every area. Which was why, when I got home, I would call my dad. I would finally put on the big-boy pants I'd been hiding in the corner. Funny, how sometimes it takes someone else to make us realize that life's been passing us by.

I would have missed her.

And that thought terrified me. Had I not gone on the show, I would have missed the girl. I would have missed a future with those damn nail beds. I gripped her petite hands, and softly kissed each fingertip.

Missing those fingertips would have been such a crime.

Missing those lips? I shuddered at the thought.

I would never. Ever. Miss her, because she was going to be by my side forever.

"Rise and shine!" Reid pounded on the door. "Time to get ready for the ceremony!"

Becca stirred in her sleep. I got up and opened the door, contemplating punching my brother in the face. He sidestepped me, clearly knowing my reaction to his constant interruptions, and whistled low in his throat. "You ready for this?"

"Of course." I stretched my arms high above my head. "I've been ready for days. I just want it to be over with. Then I can take Becca on my white horse and ride off into the sunset."

"You don't own a white horse."

"We'll ride Hades."

"Hades isn't white."

"But he has white spots," I pointed out. "So it's . . . similar."

"Tell that to the damsel." Reid snickered and then his expression sobered. "Max, if this ends . . . I don't know . . . if it ends differently than you think? Don't freak out."

"The only way it could end differently is if Becca was a dude, and believe me, I know for a fact she's all woman."

"Right." Reid licked his lips nervously. "But what I'm trying to say is hypothetically . . . if the game were different and she chose the money and you and not just you. Would you be upset?"

I thought about it for a minute. "Not really. I mean, she was here for the money first, me second. It would make sense. Besides, she needs it for school, and even if I offered to pay for it, she wouldn't let me."

"Okay." Reid still looked nervous. He kept licking his lips and rocking back and forth on his heels, but I didn't have time to worry about it. The rest of the camera crew swept in. Soon Becca was gone and I was getting ready to reject a few women and accept the one I wanted.

Life couldn't be better. What could possibly go wrong?

• • •

Hours went by and finally it was time. The mood was set. Torches lit the walkway to the small hut where I was waiting. Each girl would walk down the aisle, wedding style, and offer me a bouquet. If I took the bouquet that meant she was the one. If I rejected the bouquet she was escorted off.

Each girl had left me a video to watch in which she pleaded her case to me.

And each video left me bored.

Until I reached Becca.

And saw a tear slide down her cheek as she said these past few weeks had been the best weeks of her life.

I couldn't wait to get off the damn island and spend more time with her.

One by one, the girls walked down the aisle.

Cat and Sammy came first; both of them looked beautiful. I had a brief moment where I was thankful I'd met them—but it was brief, short-lived.

As promised, I rejected each one. Sam laughed while Cat cried, and I was half-tempted to purr in her direction and see if she hissed back. I restrained myself, just barely.

The other two cursed me out.

The fourth one looked up at me with hate-filled eyes, then made a cutting motion across her throat and whispered the word *machete*. Pretty sure that was a death threat.

"Let's go." One of the producers pulled her aside. The girl wasn't willing to go without a fight. She kicked him in the shin, then lunged for me.

Reid went to help and got punched in the eye, but eventually, the last crazy was escorted away, leaving me with the one I really wanted.

Becca.

She slowly walked up the aisle. Her floor-length white dress shimmered in the moonlight, looking like a second skin. It draped across her body like the softest of silk, leaving a small train in the back. When she reached me, I placed my hand on the small of her back and felt nothing but skin. Backless. Thank God, I was going to make her twirl for hours in that damn thing.

"Max"—Becca grinned—"will you accept my bouquet?"

"You make it yourself?" I teased as cameras leaned in from all angles.

"Of course, I even put in a few weeds—I know how you love those."

"As long as you didn't hide Hades or a few cats in there I think we'll be good." I winked and kissed her softly on the mouth. "And yes, I'll accept the bouquet."

I expected music. I expected Rex to start clapping and say something like "That's a wrap." Instead nothing.

I looked up as Rex made his way toward us, dressed in a tux. Once he reached the front of the aisle he clasped his hands together. "Now that Becca is officially the last one standing, we'll take a brief moment to show the viewers the votes."

"Votes?" My eyes narrowed.

"Of course!" Rex laughed heartily. "Voting starts once we air the first episode, tonight. Viewers vote on who they think you'll end up with. It doesn't decide the show but it's a way to get our viewers involved. By the time this airs, we'll have live votes to report." He checked his watch as if to confirm the time and then looked back at the cameras.

"But how would they even know? Based off a few dates?" I scratched my head.

"That"—Rex nodded—"and the hidden cameras."

"Hidden . . ." I swallowed. "Cameras?"

Rex shrugged innocently. "It specifically says in both of your contracts that you refuse the right of privacy unless you're using the toilet. We had cameras in every hut, every post, every square inch of the property."

Becca paled and gripped my hand.

Rex kept talking. "Really, Max, you should have known, you initialed that part of the contract. Didn't you read it?"

My teeth ground together. "Clearly not well enough."

Becca's eyes welled with tears. Shit.

"So, most likely they'll vote for Becca. I mean, you were alone in that hut how many times? Don't worry, we censored most of it. This is a family show, after all."

I was going to kill Rex. I was going to wrap my hands around his neck and squeeze.

"Now"—Rex motioned to the cameras as one of the men started the countdown and called for *action*—"this season we're offering a different type of prize. The contestants have been told they can choose the money, the man, or both. But what they don't know is, there's a twist."

"Lovely," I whispered under my breath.

"After all"—Rex looked directly into the camera to my left—"how do we know the love is real? Is it love? Or is it lust mixed with greed? Becca—" Rex held out his hand. "Come here, my dear."

Becca released my hand and stepped in front of Rex. Her entire body was trembling.

"Your choice . . ." Rex pointed to me just as Reid came out from the hut with a giant check in Becca's name. "Do you choose Max? Or the money?"

A quarter of a million dollars or me? What sane person would choose *me*? Regardless of my money? Had I given her enough reasons to trust me? To trust me to take care of her?

"I—" Becca looked back and forth between me and the money. The more she hesitated the more my heart shattered. I tried to look at it in a logical way. I had money; I never had to worry about paying bills. Becca didn't, but she should trust me, right? I could take care of her, I wanted to.

"We need your answer, Becca." Rex held out his hands. "Will you choose love or money?"

Becca's eyes filled with tears as she looked my way. My gut twisted, and I reached for her, one final pitiful plea for her to choose me. It was getting hard to breathe. Becca looked at my hand and then into my eyes.

That look would haunt me for an eternity.

Rather than keep them trained on me, she closed the windows to her soul, and sold it all with one word. "Money," she whispered. "I choose the money."

CHAPTER FIFTY-FIVE

MAX

A week later . . .

"Don't do it!" I wailed, throwing popcorn at the TV. "Don't trust her! She's a monster!" I couldn't look away. I mean, I wanted to, but that's the thing about cartoons, the colors damn near suck you in because they're so pretty. "Stop! He's using you!"

"We're getting married!" the voice said on the screen.

"Stupid bitch." I threw another popcorn kernel. "Stupid Disney princess. Damn you, Walt!" The two main characters started singing. My eyes welled with tears. She really thought they were in love.

But it was a lie.

"Just wants your money and title, yo." I took another handful of popcorn with one hand, then opened my beer with the other. "Believe me, when things are all said and done, Elsa won't even want you, your own sister! And what does that leave you with? Hmm? A reindeer! And no man! A reindeer!"

Hades sighed next to me.

"You're different." I patted his head. "You're a goat, silly."

He started snacking on some popcorn from the same bowl and I didn't care. Everything had gone to hell anyway.

"Um, Max?" Milo called through the apartment. "You in here?"

"Max died!" I yelled back. "Hades ate me!"

Hades grunted.

"I taste good to all animals . . ." I took a long swig of beer. "But apparently my ass isn't made of money . . ." I sighed. "Actually it is, but not the point, is it, Hades? Hmm? Little guy." I tickled underneath his chin. When I looked up, Milo, Jason, Colt, and Reid were in my living room.

"'Sup?" I sniffed and took another drink of beer.

"'Sup?" Reid echoed and looked around the room. "Are you moving?"

"Nah." I pointed to the stack of clothes. "I've been unpacking, doing laundry and whatnot."

"For seven days?" Milo crossed her arms. "Max, when I left a few days ago you were in the same pants."

I looked down and frowned at the blue plaid pajama bottoms. "But these are my house pants!"

"They smell." Milo shook her head. "Take them off."

"Aw, baby, bored with little Colt so soon?" I teased. "And your wish is my command." I stood.

"No!" Colt held up his hands. "He drops his drawers and I'm not helping with this intervention."

"Wait." My hands paused at my waistband. "What intervention?"

"Max." Reid held up his hands. "You know I love you, Bro, but this . . ." He waved around the room. "It has to stop."

"I'm fine," I repeated. "I'm just . . . jet-lagged."

Jason took a look around. "Dude, look around you. You're living in your own filth!"

"I'M FINE!" I yelled just as the music crescendoed on the TV.

Reid sighed and pinched the bridge of his nose. "*Frozen*? You're drinking beer, in the dark, with a damn goat acting like a trained dog, and you're watching a Disney freaking musical about princesses?" His voice rose at the end. "And you see NOTHING wrong with this picture? Nothing at all?"

I looked around the room. "Well, you're kind of blocking my view, and Olaf's set to make his big entrance in a few, but other than that . . . no. I'm straight."

"You're SAD!" Milo shouted. "Just admit it!"

"I'm HAPPY AS A DAMN CLAM!" I shouted back at her. "I've got my goat! I've got a nice apartment. The nice lady next door said I could adopt her turtle! Things are looking up!"

And silence.

I shifted on my feet, uncomfortable that no one was saying anything. A long stretch of silence never boded well for a person with my personality type. It made me want to poke myself in the eye with a sharp pencil.

"Becca's sorry," Milo blurted.

Jason and Colt restrained her as she tried to run toward me.

Reid sighed heavily. "It's true, she told me."

"Me too," Jason agreed.

"What?" I threw my empty beer can onto the ground. "You guys all BFFs now? What, do you freaking watch *Star Wars* together and have naked pool parties? Some friends you are!"

Milo's eyes filled with tears. "But—"

"Get out!" I yelled. "Get out of my apartment!"

"I didn't want to have to do this," Reid said in a calm voice. "But you've left me no choice."

I rolled my eyes.

To be fair, I didn't even see the punch coming until I was falling backward onto Hades. The last thing I remember before my eyes fluttered closed is the smell of popcorn on Hades's breath and the sad realization that it might be the last thing I remember, before I went to sleep.

CHAPTER FIFTY-SIX
BECCA

I regretted it the minute the word left my mouth. It wasn't so much the fact that I'd chosen money over Max. It was the fact that I'd turned away from him. He'd reached out to me, offered me his hand, and I'd ignored him. Unwilling to trust him just a little bit. The crappy part? Now I had no idea what would have happened, because that one little decision changed everything.

How bad did I suck?

Really bad.

But what if Max and I wouldn't have worked out? It was a fear-driven choice. I needed the money. I needed to finish school. The thought of going back to Starbucks and working there for the rest of my life made me sick to my stomach.

Everything had been going fine that day. I'd decided to choose Max, and then the stupid confessional had happened and I, like the rest of the girls, got to see the edited clips of what was going to be airing on TV.

Max looked happy—with every girl.

He was polite, sweet, sexy.

What did I have that was any different from what those girls had? I mean, yeah, I giggled less, but in the long run I had nothing, no words from him proving that what we shared was more than a fling, or that it was more than the show. He said I was different—I'd needed more words, more reassurance. I should have asked him, but instead I'd chickened out and chosen money, the great dollar over the chance at happiness.

Eventually I just went to Milo's house, you know, after stalking the entire family on Facebook, and begged for his contact info. And when begging didn't work, I burst into tears.

Two episodes had aired on national television.

I spent both evenings glued to the TV watching Max's smiles. His confessionals had me laughing my ass off, but the thing that had me ready to swim in a tub of ice cream? He liked me. Really liked me. You could see it in the way he talked about me, the way he talked to me. I'd let the man of my dreams go, and it was all my fault.

The gang, as I now referred to them, said that Max wasn't ready to see me. I'd gotten a text earlier that afternoon from Milo saying they were going to fix everything. I wasn't sure how confident that made me. When that group got together it seemed like more of them ended up in the hospital than actually hanging out.

I drummed my fingertips against the table. Milo had said they all wanted to meet at a local bar. The music was hell on my ears. It was open mic night so I'd had the misfortune of hearing Taylor Swift cover songs for the past hour while people drank and clapped around me.

I checked my phone again just as someone plopped into the seat across from me.

I looked up. "Reid?"

"What up, gorgeous?"

"My weight," I answered truthfully.

He sighed and reached across the table. "What was it this time?"

"Rocky road." I sighed. "I promised myself only one scoop, but it turned into three, then four, then . . ." My voice cracked.

"It always turns into more." Reid squeezed my hand. "Would it make you feel better to know that Max has been wearing the same pair of ugly pajama pants for the past week?"

"I'd feel better if he was happy." I slouched in my chair.

"Yeah?" Reid leaned back, releasing my hand. "So, say you got a do-over? What would your answer be?"

I grinned sadly and shook my head. "Max. Every. Time. It would be Max."

"Thought so." His smile matched mine.

"But"—I held my hand up—"he hates me."

"Does he?" A deep voice said from behind my chair. I froze, unable to move. I felt the air shift as the person moved from behind me to right across from me, taking Reid's seat.

"Max?" I breathed.

"Damn, you were expecting Hades, weren't you? I'll bring him later, swear on my life. But he's been puking up popcorn all night, so yeah . . ."

"Popcorn?"

"Sensitive stomach for a goat." Max shrugged. "Who knew?"

He looked good. Too good. I didn't deserve him. I'd shattered whatever trust we both had in each other the minute I chose the money.

"I like you fatter." Max eyed me up and down.

"Excuse me?"

"Ice cream, just like milk, does the body good."

"What?"

"Sorry." Max sighed. "They gave me half a pill on account I refused to calm down after Reid punched me in the jaw."

"Oh, my word!" I covered my mouth with my hands. "Are you okay?"

"Well, it's no picnic but I'm pretty sure I'd rather get punched in the face than have the girl I like stomp all over my still-beating heart, throw sand on it, stomp again, then spit in my face and walk away." His face fell. "Not that that's happened a lot in my lifetime. Once, only once."

"What if the girl"—my voice quivered as tears welled in my eyes—"was really sorry? And has spent the last seven days hating herself, and missing the guy, and the goat, and the stupid gecko, and even did a zombie marathon to prove her affection?"

"Then"—Max leaned forward—"the guy may be listening."

"What if"—my heart hammered against my chest—"the girl misses the biting, the teasing, even the orgasmic climbing? What if she just wants life to be an adventure with this guy, what if she was given a second chance to say yes to Max?"

"Would she?" Max tilted his head. "Or would she still say no? Maybe I didn't judge her fairly, after all, an education . . ." His smile was soft. "It's important. Of course this is coming from a poli-sci major who's supposed to be taking over his father's hotel empire, so what do I know? Right?"

I looked down at the table, my cheeks heating in shame. "The girl should have found another way . . . she should have trusted her heart rather than her head."

"Overthinking is a total menace to society." Max nodded emphatically. "I recommend doing no thinking. Say right now . . . I'm thinking"—he leaned in farther, his face an inch from mine—"that it's a stupid idea to put myself out there again. I mean what type of guy puts himself on the spot only to get rejected twice? But . . ." His gaze lowered to my lips. "I'm going to choose to listen to my heart . . . meaning I can't be held responsible for what I'm about to do next."

Instead of kissing me, like I'd assumed he would, Max left the table, and walked onstage with Reid.

"Um?"

"A poem." Max cleared his throat into the microphone. "Reid, will you?"

Reid nodded and began strumming some chords on the guitar he pulled from the stage as Max spoke into the microphone again. "Her eyes are brown, her face is young. When I first met her my heart said she was the one."

And tear number one just fell down my face.

"But the things about numbers, sometimes they get confusing, meaning a man may not be of her choosing." Max winked. "After all is said and done, after the cameras and the fun. It's only fair to give said lady a second chance. So I rip open my heart, shed a bit of my soul, and stand in front of complete strangers wanting to know . . ." Max paused as the spotlight fell onto my table. "Will you? Will we? Can it possibly be . . . that in that heart of yours you'd find space for two? A space for me? The ending is yours. The story just beginning. I only ask for a continuation into what started as me and you, and ended in a complete bust. Change the ending. To a story of us."

It was impossible to see the stage. Tears continued plowing down my face like I was having an allergic reaction to the smoke, when really . . . it was Max. All Max.

I should have been the one on the stage. Heck, I should have been on my hands and knees, which just proved again how amazing Max really was. He didn't care what others thought. I think he proved over and over again that when he wanted something, he simply went after it.

And he wanted me.

Even though I didn't deserve a second chance.

"Us," I said loudly. "I really like the sound of that."

"Ooh, good," Max said into the microphone. "Does that mean the guy gets to kiss the girl now? He's been waiting for seven whole days, and Disney encourages kissing . . ."

Disney? What? I made a mental note to ask later as Max made his way off the stage and stalked toward me.

He didn't gently kiss me.

His hands wrapped around my hips, lifting me into the air, forcing me to wrap my legs around his lean body. And he attacked.

His kiss forceful, warm, welcoming. Perfect.

"Now that," a woman said from a nearby table, "was a kiss."

"Damn straight," I whispered across his mouth.

"I'm thinking . . ." Max's teeth tugged my lower lip. "Rope, hat, boots, what say you?"

"You want me to tie you up?"

His eyes darkened. "Aw, sweetie, the rope's for you. The cowboy boots? You. The hat? You . . . imagine all the trouble I can get into with just a few props."

My entire body pulsed with excitement.

"Feel me?" he whispered, across my lips.

"Hard not to." I sighed as he lowered me slowly down his body.

"Cute." He gripped my hand in his and dragged me out of the bar. I almost stumbled into him as we made it to his waiting car.

"Oh, and by the way." Max opened the door for me. "You're not giving the money back. That's stupid. I'm investing it for you."

"You know how to invest money? And what banks are for?"

"Hilarious." He rolled his eyes, "I'm actually good at it . . . after getting punched in the jaw I even had a fleeting thought that I should do something like that . . . with investments."

"I think . . ." I pressed my palm against his cheek, "That you'll be extraordinary at whatever you put your mind to."

"Good." He cleared his throat. "Because right now my sole focus is on multiple orgasms—you know, just to prove they can happen outside of the Island. All in favor, raise your hand?"

I threw my head back and laughed.

"Oh." He snapped his fingers. "And you're going back to school and you're going to be awesome and I'm going to cheer for you when you graduate and we're marrying at midnight."

"Tonight?" I gasped.

"Near future. I just got carried away with my dominant voice. It's so hot I almost turned myself on." He winked.

"Sadly, probably true."

"Hey, I can't help that I have a normal and healthy obsession with my own voice." He buckled my seat belt, his hands slowly moving from the buckle up to my face. "I like you like this."

"Unable to escape?"

"Yeah." His eyes drank me in. "Unable to do anything except sit, while I memorize every part of your face. You know, just in case you try to leave me again, no worries. I'll just put up lost posters everywhere and offer a giant-ass reward. No escaping me now, woman. Once a Max settles down, it's forever."

"Oh, good." I laughed. "That's . . . really, really good."

"Now . . ." Max pulled back and sighed. "Let's go get those boots!"

"Cowboy up, partner." I winked.

"God, I love you."

I froze.

Max froze.

The earth stopped moving.

And then we both burst out laughing.

"Yeah . . ." I leaned in and kissed his mouth softly. "I kind of love you too, but only if you kill all the zombies."

"Dude." Max placed a hand over his heart. "Always. I will always kill the monsters as long as when you run from them you're naked and screaming. Now that's a visual."

"You'll never grow up, will you?" I laughed again.

"God, I hope not." Max shut the door and walked around to the other side; when he opened it he started the car, turned, and asked, "You a fan of fro-yo?"

Life with Max would never be normal.

Ever.

EPILOGUE

MAX

Three months later . . .

"I think your lizard's dead." Colt pointed at Little G, who was chilling on his usual pillow on the coffee table.

I rolled my eyes. "He has a name: Little G. Use it or you aren't welcome in my home. And he's not dead, he's resting his eyes."

"Dude." Colt shook his head. "Please don't turn into that crazy couple who refuses to have kids and only adopts animals, then end up wearing matching shirts."

Just then Jason walked in. His T-shirt had a picture of Hades on it with the saying, "I'm adopted."

After the show we'd started a nonprofit for wild animals where kids could pick a pet, adopt it online, and then feed it and take care of it like it was really theirs. It was all virtual, but people loved it.

Including Jason.

Thus the shirt.

"What?" Popcorn fell out of his mouth.

Colt rubbed his face with his hands. "Nothing."

"Who's the next Bachelor?" Becca ran into the room, nearly colliding with Jason, and jumped onto my lap, her arms twisting around my neck exactly where I wanted them to be. Milo followed and sat next to Colton, a knowing grin on her face. She'd helped me plan what was about to happen—meaning I'd renominated her to be on my zombie apocalypse team and told her we could still be friends.

"You're cute." I nodded. "I think I'll keep you."

She rolled her eyes, "Max, focus, who's the next Bachelor?" Her eyes greedily scanned the TV screen.

"Jason." I nodded confidently.

Jason started choking on popcorn.

Colt burst out laughing and didn't stop until Milo playfully swatted him. "He's kidding, man."

"Ha-ha." Jason said in a hoarse voice.

"Please." I rolled my eyes. "Like you could handle it."

Reid strolled into the room and smirked. "Because you handled it so well, little brother?"

"Where's Hades?"

"Sleeping." Reid looked heavenward. "Can't I be without that damn goat for one minute?"

"No," we all said in unison. Since bringing Hades home, Reid had moved into the area, and the two had become inseparable. Reid actually ignored us to hang with the goat whenever he visited.

"Why didn't they announce anything?" Becca asked, crossing her arms.

I pulled her tight against my chest. "I think you have an unhealthy obsession with this show . . . we should turn it off."

"No!" She reached for the remote. I wasn't actually going to turn it off, plus I had a surprise, or Oompa Loompa did.

"Do you ever wonder," Rex said from his spot on the beach on TV, "what happens to our couples afterwards? Well, I have it on good authority that our last Bachelor's getting hitched! Congrats from all of us to Max and Becca!"

Becca stilled on my lap.

I grinned and waited for her to yell or say something.

"Um?" Becca turned and glared. "Is that how you're proposing?"

"No." I shook my head. "That was me preparing you for the most epic of proposals ever in the history of the universe. I figure it's only fair."

Milo rolled her eyes in my direction.

"What?" Becca asked.

"Fair," I repeated. "I didn't want you to have a heart attack or blame me because your makeup starts watering all over the place from the tears."

"Tears?" She squinted. "Do you see tears?"

"Oh." I nodded. "There will be tears, lots and lots of tears."

"I'm waiting."

"Impatient . . ." I sighed. "When will she learn, guys? Max's way is the best way, the only way, the—"

Becca clapped her hand over my mouth. "Are you seriously going to ruin the proposal before it even starts?"

I shrugged.

And that's when the music started . . . the commercial break had taken longer than I'd thought.

The music was soft—classical—and on the TV screen were pictures and images of Becca and me on the show together. Each image brought up a different memory . . . I wanted to remind her how we'd fallen in love.

When the screen went to black words popped up that said, "Will you marry me, Becca?"

"So here's the thing." I gently pushed her from my lap, set her on the couch, and got down on both knees. "It's important that we always revisit our past . . . revisit how we fell in love, why we fell in love . . . so that when we're looking towards our future, we realize what we have is based on something solid, something real, not just a TV show, but lots of amazing moments that, well, most of the known world witnessed." I smiled as a few tears streamed down Becca's cheeks. "I love you, I want to make you my wife. I want to have children with you, spend eternity with you, possibly start a goat farm if you're cool with it, and totally get a girl gecko for G . . ."

Becca burst out laughing, then covered her mouth with her hands.

"But most of all?" I pulled the three-karat princess-cut engagement ring from my pocket. "I just want you. Every day. Every night. Every moment. I want you."

Her breath hitched as I held the ring out in front of me.

"I was going to put it on the goat but we were afraid he'd eat it." I sighed.

Becca grabbed the ring and shoved it on her finger, then jumped off the couch and tackled me to the ground, nearly taking Little G with us. "Yes! Yes! I'll marry you!"

"Good." I sighed against her mouth. "Because you would have broken Little G's heart had you said no."

She raised her eyebrows. "*His* heart?"

"And mine," I admitted. "I love you . . ."

"I love you too."

"Can someone thank me now?" Jason interrupted.

Becca moved away from me and held out her hand, helping me up. "What?"

"For putting Max on the show." Jason puffed out his chest. "That was all my idea."

"Oh, I'll be thanking you . . ." I smirked. "But not until after I'm done thanking my brother . . . my dear sweet brother."

Reid's eyes narrowed. "I don't like the sound of your voice."

"I'd be afraid, man," Colt said from his spot on the couch. "Revenge is a bitch."

"Please," Reid snorted. "I hardly think I'm in danger of being Max's next target."

The room fell silent.

Reid shifted in his seat.

"Thank you." Becca broke the silence. "For forcing Max on the show . . ." She turned in my arms and kissed my mouth. "And thanks for not jumping out of the plane."

"Shark-infested waters," I said honestly. "I would have died."

"Aren't you so glad you didn't?"

"Very." I growled against her mouth, "Wanna see how much?"

"I think we can all . . . see." Colt choked while Milo giggled next to him.

"Stay out of this," I barked. "Open the champagne, turn the TV on as loud as possible, and we'll possibly be back in two hours."

"Two hours?" Jason laughed. "Please . . ."

"Last night it was three." Becca winked.

More popcorn fell out of Jason's mouth.

"She's lying." Reid rolled his eyes, "No way can a man—"

"He can." She whispered into my ear, "He does."

"Damn straight." I picked her up into my arms and charged down the hall. I was going to spend the next two hours showing her just how much I loved her . . . and how thankful I was that Jason had decided to give me the push I needed.

Even if it did make me want to kill him.

I'd get him back.

But first . . . I was going to make love to my woman.

Later . . . I'd get even with both Jason and Reid.

They wouldn't see it coming.

ABOUT THE AUTHOR

Photo © 2014 Lauren Murray

Rachel Van Dyken is a *New York Times, Wall Street Journal,* and *USA Today* bestselling author of Regency and contemporary romances. When she's not writing, you can find her drinking coffee at Starbucks and plotting her next book while watching *The Bachelor.*

She keeps her home in Idaho with her husband and their snoring boxer, Sir Winston Churchill. She loves to hear from readers! You can follow her writing journey at www.rachelvandykenauthor.com.

Made in the USA
Middletown, DE
12 July 2017